P9-DFE-736

INSPECTOR WITHERSPOON ON THE SCENE . . .

"When you went into the study, did you touch anything? Did you move your husband?"

"No, I could tell that he was dead," she replied. "There was so much blood and he lay there so quietly."

"And that's when you sent for the police, correct?"

"No, actually, one of our guests sent for them. He'd heard the commotion and walked into the room right behind me. He was the one that ran and got the constable on the corner. The next think I knew, the house was swarming with policemen."

The inspector frowned. "Who was this guest, Mrs. Mc-Court?"

MRS. JEFFRIES
and the
Mistletoe Mix-Up

Emily Brightwell

BERKLEY PRIME CRIME, NEW YORK

THE BERKLEY PUBLISHING GROUP
Published by the Penguin Group
Penguin Group (USA) Inc.
375 Hudson Street, New York, New York 10014, USA

Penguin Group (Canada), 90 Eglinton Avenue East, Suite 700, Toronto, Ontario M4P 2Y3, Canada
(a division of Pearson Penguin Canada Inc.) • Penguin Books Ltd., 80 Strand, London WC2R 0RL,
England • Penguin Group Ireland, 25 St. Stephen's Green, Dublin 2, Ireland (a division of Penguin
Books Ltd.) • Penguin Group (Australia), 250 Camberwell Road, Camberwell, Victoria 3124, Australia
(a division of Pearson Australia Group Pty. Ltd.) • Penguin Books India Pvt. Ltd., 11 Community
Centre, Panchsheel Park, New Delhi—110 017, India • Penguin Group (NZ), 67 Apollo Drive,
Rosedale, Auckland 0632, New Zealand (a division of Pearson New Zealand Ltd.) • Penguin Books
(South Africa) (Pty.) Ltd., 24 Sturdee Avenue, Rosebank, Johannesburg 2196, South Africa

Penguin Books Ltd., Registered Offices: 80 Strand, London WC2R 0RL, England

This is a work of fiction. Names, characters, places, and incidents either are the product of the author's
imagination or are used fictitiously, and any resemblance to actual persons, living or dead, business
establishments, events, or locales is entirely coincidental. The publisher does not have any control over
and does not assume any responsibility for author or third-party websites or their content.

MRS. JEFFRIES AND THE MISTLETOE MIX-UP

A Berkley Prime Crime Book / published by arrangement with the author

PUBLISHING HISTORY
Berkley Prime Crime hardcover edition / November 2011
Berkley Prime Crime mass-market edition / November 2012

Copyright © 2011 by Cheryl Arguile.
Cover illustration by Jeff Walker.
Cover design by Annette Fiore Defex.

ISBN: 978-0-425-25170-6

BERKLEY® PRIME CRIME
Berkley Prime Crime Books are published by The Berkley Publishing Group,
a division of Penguin Group (USA) Inc.,
375 Hudson Street, New York, New York 10014.
BERKLEY® PRIME CRIME and the PRIME CRIME logo are trademarks of
Penguin Group (USA) Inc.

PRINTED IN THE UNITED STATES OF AMERICA

10 9 8 7 6 5 4 3 2 1

To Charles and Pat Richards—
good people and good friends,
thanks for the wonderful lunches we've shared.

CHAPTER 1

Elena McCourt crossed her arms over her chest and glared at her husband. "You can scream and shout all you like, Daniel," she cried, "but I'm not throwing the girl out into the street, especially in weather like this."

Daniel McCourt frowned at his wife, hoping to intimidate her into submission. He wasn't used to her standing up to him, and he was desperate to reestablish his authority. "You'll do as I say." He shoved back in his chair and noted with satisfaction that she flinched. "I'm the master here, and I'll thank you, madam, to get ready to play hostess to your guests."

She swallowed nervously but held her ground. "They're your guests, not mine, and if you'll remember correctly, I'm the legal owner of this house, and it's my money that pays for the upkeep and the servants. Annie stays." She jerked her head toward a row of exquisite Chinese ceramic plates artis-

1

tically displayed on the shelf next to the door. "I don't really care if she cracked one of those heathen plates or not. She stays."

He gasped, shocked to his core that she'd defy him while they had company arriving. He'd never thought her capable of making any sort of scene. But he couldn't let her see how her behavior worried him. He couldn't show weakness. That would be fatal, especially now. "Those heathen plates, as you call them, are from the Ming dynasty and are worth a fortune." He pointed to an intricate green-and-gold-patterned dish at the end of the row. "And that stupid girl cracked the rim on that one. It's worthless now."

Elena brushed nervously at a lock of wispy blonde hair that had slipped out of her elaborate coiffure. She opened her mouth, but before she could get the words out, there was a knock on the door.

"Come in," Daniel yelled.

Haines, the butler, stepped into the room. "Mr. and Mrs. Brunel have arrived. I escorted them into the morning room with the other guests."

Daniel glanced at the ornate gold and white carriage clock on his desk. "They're ten minutes late. That's not like Leon."

"Begging your pardon, sir," Haines said. "But they were right on time."

"Why didn't you announce them?" he demanded.

"I would have, sir, but I was delayed by Mr. Raleigh. He needed a glass of water to take a headache powder, and as all the other staff were busy, I had to go to the kitchen to get it for him myself."

"Oh, what difference does it make when they arrived," Elena said soothingly. "They're here now."

"Humph," Daniel grunted. He was glad to hear the mollifying tone in his wife's voice. "Well, see that in the future, you announce the guests right away, Haines. Tell the housekeeper we'll have tea served now."

"Not yet." Elena countermanded the order. "We'll wait for ten minutes. Cook was having trouble with the oven. It's overheating, and the kitchen is ridiculously hot."

"For goodness' sake, it's the middle of winter," Daniel snapped. "Have them open the side doors if it gets too hot. I'm hungry, and I want my tea."

Haines looked with an uncertain expression from his master to his mistress. All the servants knew that it was Mrs. McCourt who owned the house, but until recently, Haines had never heard her contradict one of her husband's orders.

"Oh, alright," Daniel muttered churlishly. "Serve tea in ten minutes." Like any good general, he'd decided to pick his battles carefully. Besides, as much as he hated her current behavior, right now he needed to stay in her good graces.

Elena McCourt smiled wanly at the butler and nodded her agreement. "Open the connecting door, Haines, and then bring the guests into the drawing room before you go downstairs."

"Very well, madam." Haines cut across to the double doors on the far side of Mr. McCourt's desk. He opened them wide, revealing the main drawing room.

A cheerful fire blazed in the hearth. Garlands of greenery had been strung across the mantelpiece and an evergreen tree, its branches festooned with unlighted candles, ceramic ornaments, and chains of boldly colored paper stood in the corner. "When should we light the candles, madam?" he asked.

"It's not quite dark as yet, so we'll wait until after tea is finished," she declared. "There's no point in Duncan having to stand there with a bucket of wet sand while we eat."

"He'll stand there as long as we want," Daniel said crossly, annoyed that she'd taken over the decision making from him. "That's what footmen are paid to do."

Haines nodded to her and hurried out. He was relieved he wouldn't have to explain that the footman wasn't back yet.

Elena walked to the door leading to the hall, and her hand had just reached for the knob when her husband's voice stopped her.

"As soon as the guests have gone, you and I are going to have a nice sit-down and discuss a few matters," he said in a low voice.

"Actually, I was going to suggest that myself," she replied without turning to look at him. "I've a number of matters to discuss with you." She heard his quickly indrawn breath of surprise, and she smiled as she continued on into the hall, closing the door quietly behind her. She started in surprise. "I thought Haines took you and Mrs. Brunel into the morning room."

Leon Brunel, a tall man with wispy light brown hair, thin lips, and deep-set blue eyes, stood in the foyer, his attention focused on a tall blue and white ceramic vase that sat in the middle of the ornate claw-footed entry table. Brunel gave her an embarrassed smile. "Do forgive me, Elena, but when I saw this beauty here"—he pointed to the vase—"I had to have a closer look. When did Daniel acquire this? And from whom?"

"It's not new," she replied. "I'm sure it was sitting there when you and Glenda came to dinner last month. But he acquired it from the Saxon collection." She wondered whether he'd overheard any of their argument. It would be very much like Leon to eavesdrop. "As a matter of fact,

Nicholas Saxon is here now. Daniel invited him to tea. Perhaps you can talk him into selling to you, instead of Daniel, the next time."

Less than a mile away, at the home of Inspector Gerald Witherspoon, the servants were just finishing their afternoon tea.

"What time is dinner tonight?" Phyllis asked. The housemaid was a plump, round-faced girl with dark blonde hair tucked up in a tight bun under her maid's cap.

"It's going to be late," Mrs. Jeffries, the auburn-haired, older middle-aged housekeeper, replied. "The inspector said he was going to stop and do a bit of shopping on Oxford Street before coming home tonight. I think he's buying a doll for his new godchild."

"That baby is goin' to be spoiled," Mrs. Goodge, the cook, warned. She was a portly, white-haired woman with wire-framed spectacles.

Mrs. Jeffries glanced at Wiggins, the brown-haired, apple-cheeked footman, who had ducked his head to hide a smile. He was too polite to say what they were both thinking.

But Phyllis, having joined the household more recently than the others, blurted it out: "But you spoil her worse than anyone." She giggled. "She can't so much as whimper before you're swoopin' in to pick her up and rock her. She'd barely been born when you gave her that silver spoon with her initials engraved on it."

"And fine initials they are, too," the cook replied.

The baby in question was the infant daughter of Smythe, the household coachman, and Betsy, the maid. Smythe had joined them for tea and had left only moments earlier, but Betsy was at their flat with their two-month-old daughter.

"Of course they are. They're yours and Luty Belle's," Mrs.

Jeffries declared. The household of Upper Edmonton Gardens had been delighted when Betsy announced she was naming her baby daughter after Mrs. Goodge and the household's dear friend, Luty Belle Crookshank. The two women, along with Inspector Witherspoon, were the baby's godparents.

Betsy had privately pulled Mrs. Jeffries, Wiggins, and Hatchet, Luty Belle's butler, to one side and told them her plans. She'd explained that as both of the women were elderly, she wanted to honor them while she could. She'd also promised that if she and Smythe were blessed with another child, the three of them would be asked to be godparents. They had understood Betsy's reasons and applauded her decision.

Hatchet was especially pleased. He'd clasped Betsy's hand and said, "Madam is utterly delighted about this. Little Amanda Belle has given her so much joy and made her so very, very happy. You've no idea how much this means to her."

"Luty means a lot to me and Smythe," Betsy had replied. "As does Mrs. Goodge and I'm so glad that her name, Amanda, goes so well with Luty Belle's." She'd turned to Mrs. Jeffries. "And if I have another girl, she's going to be named after you."

"Oh my goodness, please don't do that," Mrs. Jeffries had protested. "My name is old-fashioned and difficult to spell. No one should have to go through life being addressed as 'Hepzibah.'"

"You can name 'er after me," Wiggins had offered. "If it's a girl, she can be Alberta, and if it's a boy, you can call 'im Albert." Hatchet had merely laughed and said he hoped he'd get a chance to be a godfather to any child of Betsy and Smythe.

"Luty spoils the baby more than I do," Mrs. Goodge declared. "And so do you and the inspector. The baby so much as puckers her brow and one of the two of you is pickin' her up."

"And why shouldn't we spoil her?" Mrs. Jeffries said defensively. "She's the only baby we've got."

Hepzibah Jeffries was the widow of a Yorkshire policeman, and they'd not been blessed with children. Mrs. Goodge had never married, and as was the custom in most wealthy households, the use of the "Mrs." in front of her name was a courtesy title. Luty Belle was a rich American widow who'd been married to an Englishman, and they'd never had children, either.

The inspector's household was now spread across two separate domiciles. Smythe, Betsy, and Amanda lived in a lovely flat nearby, while the rest of them stayed here in the inspector's house.

"Amanda's a sweet little one," Wiggins added. He eyed the last slice of brown buttered bread left on the platter. Mrs. Goodge shoved the plate toward him. "But I get a bit nervous when I 'old 'er. I'm scared of droppin' the wee one."

"You'll not drop her," the cook said. "But what concerns me is us gettin' another murder. Betsy won't take kindly to havin' to stay home with the baby while we're out and about."

Mrs. Goodge was referring to the fact that Inspector Gerald Witherspoon had solved more homicide cases than any policeman in the history of the Metropolitan Police Department. He'd been in charge of the Records Room at Scotland Yard when he'd inherited this house and a fortune from his aunt Euphemia Witherspoon. He'd hired Mrs. Jeffries, who'd come to London after the death of her husband, to run the household. During those horrible Kensington High

Street murders, Mrs. Jeffries had encouraged the inspector to ask a few questions here and there about the case while she also secretly tasked the rest of the household with learning what they could about the victims and suspects. At the time, none of them had realized that they were helping gather vital clues and that their machinations had ensured the inspector solved the murder. By the time the inspector got his second case, the household had understood what was going on, and they'd made a pact to keep their activities secret from Inspector Witherspoon. They now had several friends who insisted on helping.

"But I don't go out and about much!" Phyllis exclaimed.

"You've only 'ad one case," Wiggins argued. "And ya didn't come into it until the very end. Just wait and see. You'll soon be itchin' to get out and snoop about like the rest of us. Mrs. Goodge is right. What'll we do if we get another case? We can't let Betsy leave the baby."

"Let's hope we don't get another case for a good while," Mrs. Jeffries commented. "Perhaps this year, we'll be able to enjoy Christmas without all of us running about trying to solve a murder."

Mrs. Goodge chuckled. "You're not foolin' anyone, Mrs. Jeffries. Admit it—you're just like the rest of us. You're bored stiff and would like nothin' better than a good puzzle to sort out."

Daniel McCourt stalked into his study. He couldn't believe it. He was furious. What should have been a wonderful moment of triumph for him was ruined, absolutely ruined. He stormed around his massive rosewood desk and kicked his chair back, wincing as it banged into the wall hard enough to rattle his display of Oriental swords. Someone was going to pay for this. Someone was going to get the sack. He wasn't going to be humiliated this way in front of his guests. As soon as he could track down which servant it was who had been careless with the paraffin, he was going to show that person the ruddy door, and woe to his wife if she tried to stop him.

From outside, he could hear the sounds of windows and doors being opened. Fat lot of good it would do to air the place out now; the damage was done. Someone had gotten careless, and a small, ridiculously smelly fire broke out downstairs in the servants' hall. The fire was quickly doused, but the appalling odor spread through the house until it was unbearable. He shook his head, angered and amazed by how rapidly paraffin could stink up a place this size.

Another wave of sick rage swept him, and he smacked his fist against the desktop. He'd wanted to see the look on all their faces when he produced his treasure. But his stupid wife had insisted the odor was so bad that everyone had to go, and though they'd been polite, the guests had fled the premises faster than rats deserting a sinking ship.

Someone was going to pay for spoiling his big moment. God almighty, he'd only invited them for tea so he could flaunt it. He grimaced and balled his hands into fists. Elena was going to pay as well. This was all her fault. If she and Leon had kept their mouths shut and pretended not to notice the odor, he'd be reveling in his triumph right now.

He glanced up at the swords mounted over the top of the double doors. Good gracious, the bottom one was gone. Alarmed, he shot out from behind the desk and stared at the display. He concentrated on the order of the swords, trying to recall exactly which one had been in that spot.

The Katana was still there with the Chinese Won dynasty sword just below it and the Mongolian . . . Oh my Lord, the Hwando was gone.

"I see that you've noticed I've borrowed one of your swords," a quiet voice said from behind him.

McCourt whirled about, his eyes widening in disbelief just as the blade of his missing sword slashed into his neck. He grabbed at his wound as blood spurted from the severed artery on his left side. The blade came down again, this time on his right. He couldn't understand what was happening to him. He tried to speak, but his voice came out as a weak croak. The room began to go dim, and he sank to his knees.

"Don't bother shouting for help. Everyone is outside," the voice continued. "But it'll be over soon, and you won't suffer unduly. I'm not a monster, you know."

McCourt blinked hard, trying to keep the face of his killer in focus, but it was impossible. His eyelids closed, and he slumped to the floor.

It didn't take Daniel McCourt's killer very long to finish what had to be done. Then he dropped the bloody sword beside McCourt's dead body and calmly strolled out of the house.

The middle-aged couple stood in front of the toy store on Oxford Street and stared at the display of dolls in the window. The woman was an attractive blonde of medium height with a slim figure, blue eyes, and a sweet smile. She wore an elegant double-breasted winter cloak in dark green with a rolled fur collar. The man wore a black overcoat and bowler. He had wispy brown hair, a mustache, pale skin, and deep-set eyes. A pair of spectacles had slipped down his rather long nose.

Lady Ruth Cannonberry looked at Inspector Gerald Witherspoon and said, "Don't you think she might be a bit young for a doll? She's not even three months old."

The inspector frowned as he shoved his spectacles back

up to their proper position. "But she's very advanced for her age; she already recognizes me. She smiles and makes the most wonderful little cooing noises every time I take her upon my lap. Besides, it's such a pretty doll. I do want her to have it."

Lady Cannonberry, or Ruth as she was known to the Witherspoon household, didn't want to spoil his delight in buying a present for his godchild. "You're right, Gerald. It is a lovely doll, and she should have it."

Witherspoon glanced at her. "You don't think I'm being silly, do you?" he asked. Ruth Cannonberry was his neighbor and his very good friend. Her opinion of him mattered greatly, and he didn't wish to appear ridiculous in her eyes.

"Of course not!" she exclaimed. She reached out a gloved hand and patted his arm. "Amanda is your godchild, and it is only natural that you'd want to get her something wonderful for her first Christmas."

Relieved, he smiled. "Good. I wouldn't like you to think I was being foolish. Let's go inside and get it." He took Ruth's elbow and they turned toward the shop door just as a constable came racing around the corner on the opposite side of the road. Witherspoon stopped in his tracks, his attention on the policeman. "That's Constable Griffiths. I saw him this afternoon at the station. What's he doing in this district?"

"I expect he's looking for you," she replied. She watched the constable scan the faces along Oxford Street until he spotted them. Ignoring the heavy traffic, he dashed into the road and weaved his way through coopers' vans, hansom cabs, and private carriages. "He's seen us now."

Griffiths made it across the road safely. "Sorry to bother you, sir, but there's been a murder," he said as he halted in front of them.

Witherspoon sighed inwardly. Of course there was a murder; there always was at Christmas. "Where?"

"Victoria Gardens, sir." He caught his breath. "Number twelve. The victim is a man named Daniel McCourt."

"Isn't Inspector Craddock on duty tonight?" Witherspoon wasn't trying to ignore his obligation; he didn't want to step on Craddock's toes. Promotions in the Metropolitan Police Force often came because an officer successfully concluded a murder investigation, so moving onto another policeman's patch could result in a lot of bad feelings.

"Yes, sir, he is. But we've already had a message from the Yard, and Chief Inspector Barrows wants you to take the case. But not to worry, sir. Inspector Craddock won't get annoyed. He doesn't like murders."

Neither did Witherspoon. "Right, then. I'll escort Lady Cannonberry home and get over to Victoria Gardens. Has someone sent a message to Constable Barnes?"

"Constable Coleman went to fetch Constable Barnes, sir," Griffiths replied.

"Gerald, there's no need to see me home," Ruth interjected. "Just flag down a hansom and I'll go straight to your house. I can let your household know you won't be home for dinner until very late. Wiggins can escort me across the garden."

Witherspoon hesitated. He was torn between doing his duty as a policeman and as a gentleman. "Are you certain you'll be alright?"

"I'll be fine." She turned her attention to the crowded road, scanning the traffic for a cab. "If I'm going to fight for equality for women, I must be prepared to have the courage of my convictions, and that certainly means being competent to see myself home." She spotted a hansom dropping off a fare fifty yards up the street and raised her arm, waving at the driver. As soon as she was sure he'd seen her, she turned and gave the inspector a brilliant smile. "Don't be concerned, Gerald. I'm a grown woman, and I'll be fine."

The cab pulled up, and Witherspoon helped her into the seat. "I know you value your independence, but promise me you'll have Wiggins escort you home tonight. Yes, the communal gardens are always locked, but it's still not a good idea for you to walk there alone."

She patted his hand. "I promise. Don't worry about me. You've a murderer to catch."

Constable Barnes saw the cab come around the corner onto Victoria Gardens, so he stopped and waited, hoping it was the inspector. He'd already put in a whole shift today, and he was tired. But this was murder, and he worked with the inspector, so he'd not complain. His back was still ramrod straight, and he could move quickly if he had to, but he wasn't a young man anymore. Under his policeman's helmet his curly hair was now completely gray, and his eyes weren't as sharp as they used to be.

The hansom halted across the road, and Witherspoon got out. The inspector paid the driver and hurried over to Barnes. "I'm so sorry you had to get called out, Constable," he began.

Barnes raised his hand. "Not to worry, sir. If you get called out, then I need to be called as well. I've only just arrived, myself. Too bad it's so dark. We can't see too many details of the house. But this is a posh neighborhood. These are full-sized houses, sir, not town houses."

"Yes, and I imagine we've been sent for because the victim is a very rich man," the inspector muttered. The two men started toward the walkway leading to number 12. Two uniformed policemen stood at the door. They recognized the inspector and stood just that bit straighter as he approached.

To the rank and file of the Metropolitan Police Force, Gerald Witherspoon was a legend. Not only had he solved more cases than anyone, but he was known to always mention the good work of subordinates in his reports. He gave credit where credit was due and frequently defended his men against unfair criticism and pressure from above. Witherspoon, of course, didn't notice the two policemen seemed to have grown an inch or two, but Barnes did, and he smiled to himself.

"Good evening, officers," Witherspoon said. "I'm—"

"We know who you are, sir," one of them interrupted. "And the police surgeon is already inside waiting for you. He's sent for the mortuary van." He opened the front door and stepped aside so they could enter.

The foyer was patterned in black-and-white tiles with a wide staircase on the far left of the space. Directly in front of the two policemen was an enormous round table with an intricately carved claw-foot on top of which stood a tall blue and white ceramic vase. The walls along the sweep of the staircase were covered with paintings of pastoral scenes, old-fashioned portraits, and, oddly enough, one large wall hanging in a bright red fabric covered with white Oriental lettering. Another table, this one with carvings over every surface except the top, stood in the crook of the stairs. A long hallway with a red-and-gold-patterned carpet led off to the rooms on the far side of the stairs. Overhead was a crystal chandelier.

"You're right, sir," Barnes muttered as a door along the hall opened and a policeman stepped out into the hall. "These people are rich."

"Inspector Witherspoon, the body is in here, sir," the constable called.

Barnes took the lead. He knew the inspector was rather squeamish about bodies.

"Gracious, that smells like paraffin," Witherspoon muttered to no one in particular as he followed the constable.

"It is, sir." The constable held the door open for them. "They had a small fire here earlier today, and it's stunk up the whole house."

They stepped inside, and then both of them stopped and simply stared. It was a man's study, but it contained such colorful objects that it could easily have been a display at the British Museum. Ceramic plates and vases, all in brilliant hues and of different sizes, were arranged along the bottom shelf. On the shelf directly above stood a long line of carved figurines in muted shades of green, amber, and lavender, two bronze or brass statues of a seated Buddha, and a row of boxes of various sizes. In the corner was a huge brass gong housed in a six-foot black, wooden case. A tall rosewood armoire with long, narrow drawers and gold handles was on the far side of the open double doors. A set of five-foot-tall ceramic vases in green and gold flanked the now open doors. Above the doors, a series of swords were arranged in an artful display. There was a set of empty hooks at the bottom, and hanging from one of the hooks was a bundle of mistletoe.

The study opened onto a drawing room, and the body was lying half in the study and half in the drawing room. The inspector steeled himself and walked toward the corpse. He swallowed heavily when he saw the body was drenched in blood.

Barnes brushed past him and blocked his view. "How long has the man been dead?" he asked the constable at the door.

"Not more than three hours, sir," the constable replied. "Mr. McCourt had guests for tea at half past four, and it's only now half past seven." He looked at Witherspoon. "We've not moved the body, sir. Even the police surgeon didn't move him."

"There was no need to," a voice said from the drawing room. A tall, thin man with black hair and a clean-shaven face came into the study. "It was obvious what killed the poor fellow. He bled to death when both his arteries were severed by that." He pointed to a sword lying on the floor beside the body. "I'm Dr. Benton, the police surgeon. You must be Inspector Witherspoon and Constable Barnes."

"We are," Witherspoon replied. He took a deep breath and forced himself to move closer to the victim. Barnes, to his credit, had already knelt down by the corpse. He reached for the sword. It was sharp, curved, and lethal looking with a carved metal scabbard. "We'll need to take this into evidence," Barnes said as he got to his feet. He offered the weapon to the inspector. "Did you want to have a look at it, sir?"

Witherspoon didn't, but he took it anyway. "My gracious, what is this thing? I mean, I can see that it's a sword, but I've never seen one quite like this."

"It's an Oriental weapon of some sort," the doctor replied. "I believe I heard the butler refer to it as a long Hwango or Hwando or some such thing, but it's most definitely your murder weapon. It's quite sharp, so you might want to instruct your men to handle it very carefully."

The inspector nodded and waved the constable over. "See if you can find something to wrap this thing in without disturbing the bloodstains." Holding the sword by the scabbard, he put the tip on the ground and eased the hilt toward the constable, who took it and left the room.

Witherspoon turned his attention back to the dead man. In life, he'd been short, rather stout, and fair-haired, with a bushy handlebar mustache. The inspector made himself kneel down and examine the fatal wounds. It was difficult to see, because of the blood, so he reached toward the victim's shirt and pushed the fabric to one side. He swallowed convulsively as bile rose in his throat. "Ye gods, the poor man has been stabbed on both sides of his throat."

"They were more like slashes than stabs," the doctor replied. "Once the arteries were severed, he bled to death in minutes."

"Why didn't he call for help? Was he alone here?" Witherspoon asked.

"I'm afraid I can't answer that," Dr. Benton said as he headed toward the hall door. "May I take the body now? I think I just heard the mortuary van, and I'd like to get him back to the morgue for the postmortem."

Surprised, Barnes said, "You'll be doing the postmortem tonight?"

Benton stopped in the doorway. "Yes, I'll send you my report tomorrow morning." He disappeared.

"Have you seen enough, sir?" Barnes got to his feet.

"Yes, most definitely."

Ruth normally would have gone round to the back entrance of the inspector's house, but as she was in a hurry, she paid the driver and dashed up the front steps. She banged the knocker hard and waited impatiently. After what seemed ages but was in reality only a few moments, the door opened. "Why, hello," Mrs. Jeffries said, her expression surprised. "I thought you were shopping with the inspector?"

"We were, but there's been a murder and we've no time to lose!" Ruth exclaimed. She charged past the housekeeper into the house. She had no doubt whatsoever about her welcome. As one of the select few who "helped" the household with the inspector's cases, she knew precisely what to do. Holding her heavy skirt, she raced down the hallway toward the back steps. "Is everyone in the kitchen?"

"For the most part," Mrs. Jeffries said as she hurried after her. "Smythe has gone home for the day, but we can easily fetch him back." She was suddenly very excited, and as a good, decent woman, she knew she shouldn't be. A murder meant that some poor soul had lost his or her life.

They flew down the steps, uncaring of the racket they made on the thinly carpeted staircase.

Mrs. Goodge, who'd just sat down to give her feet a rest, looked up as the two women rushed into the kitchen. "Goodness me, what's wrong? Is there a fire?"

Phyllis, who'd been putting the last of the teacups into the cupboard, froze in place, while Wiggins, who was still at the table, leapt up.

"We've got a murder," Ruth blurted out. She glanced at the housekeeper. "Oh dear, I don't mean to take over. I should have let you tell them." Though she was the widow of a lord, Ruth Cannonberry had been raised in very modest circumstances. She was the daughter of a country vicar who took the biblical instruction to "love one's neighbor as one-self" very seriously. Consequently, she believed in working for social justice by helping the poor and oppressed and reforming the English class system, riddled as it was with inequality. When she was with the Witherspoon household, she insisted they call her by her first name, but she understood that in front of outsiders or the inspector, they'd be uncomfortable with such an arrangement and would then address her as "Lady Cannonberry." She was very fond of Inspector Witherspoon and only restrained herself from some of the more radical actions of her women's suffrage group because she didn't wish to embarrass him. She loved to help on his cases and was happy to use her upper-class connections to ferret out information.

Mrs. Jeffries waved her hand impatiently. "Don't worry about that. Sit down and tell us what happened." She pulled out her chair at the head of the table.

Ruth took her spot next to Wiggins. "Gerald and I were shopping on Oxford Street when all of a sudden Constable Griffiths appeared and announced that a man by the name of Daniel McCourt had been murdered."

"'Ow did Griffiths know where to find ya?" Wiggins asked curiously.

Ruth thought for a moment. "I don't really know. I suppose Gerald must have mentioned we were going to shop on Oxford Street."

"What does it matter how the constable found them?" Mrs. Goodge complained. "Let her get on with it. We've a murder to solve!"

"Of course I don't have much in the way of information," Ruth said quickly. "But here's what I do know. Constable Griffiths spoke quite freely in front of me, so I've got the address of the murder victim. He lived at number twelve Victoria Gardens in Kensington. That's close by."

Wiggins got up again and started for the coat tree. "Should I nip over and get Smythe on my way there?"

Mrs. Jeffries winced inwardly. She hadn't decided what they'd do about Betsy if they got a murder. What if she did want to be actively involved right from the start? Mrs. Jeffries pushed that thought from her mind and decided they'd cross that bridge when they came to it. Right now they had to get down to business. "Absolutely."

"What about Luty and Hatchet?" Ruth asked. "They both get quite annoyed if they're not informed immediately."

"They won't be home," the cook said quickly. "They're at Lady Darren's Christmas Ball."

"We'll tell them about it tomorrow morning." Mrs. Jeffries looked at the footman. Wiggins had put on his coat and was winding a long scarf around his neck. "When you get to Victoria Gardens, see if you can find out what time the murder took place. That'll give us a starting point."

"We'll see what we can suss out," Wiggins promised as he put on his gloves. He started for the back door, and Fred, the household's brown and black mongrel dog, jumped up from his spot by the cooker and trotted after him. Fred wagged his tail hopefully. The footman paused and patted the dog's head. "Sorry, Fred old boy, but walkies will 'ave to wait until I get back. You stay 'ere and guard the ladies."

He left Fred staring mournfully after him as he disappeared down the hall to the back door. After a second or two, the dog went back to his spot by the cooker and lay down.

"Did you learn anything else?" Mrs. Jeffries asked Ruth.

She shook her head. "Not really, though now that I think of it, the victim's name sounds very familiar. But I can't remember in what context."

"McCourt, McCourt," the cook muttered. "I've heard that name, too. Oh, now I remember. He married Elena Herron. I was workin' at Lord Rotherhide's country house in Sussex. It was years ago, but I remember that everyone in the Rotherhide family was stunned by the match."

"Why?" Phyllis asked. "Were they unsuited to each other? Was she from a poor family?"

"Goodness no." The cook laughed. "The Herrons were rich as sin. They weren't old landed gentry or aristocracy. They made their money by workin' for it. But their pedigree or lack thereof wasn't what set the tongues to waggin'. They were Catholics, and Elena Herron had wanted to become a nun. Instead of enterin' the convent, it was suddenly announced she was marryin' this man, and no one had ever heard anythin' about the fellow. Lady Rotherhide was furious, as she had a son close to Elena Herron's age, and I remember overhearin' her tell her husband that if they'd known the girl wasn't goin' to become a nun, they'd have encouraged their son to court her."

"Were the Rotherhides Catholic?" Phyllis asked.

"No, they were just out of money, and the Herrons had plenty of that." The cook laughed again.

No one questioned Mrs. Goodge's recollection. Not only did she have a very good memory, but she'd spent a lifetime working in the most aristocratic houses in all of England. She also had a vast network of old friends and colleagues she could call upon for information. She generally did her share in their investigations without ever having to leave the kitchen. If one of her old coworkers couldn't be found to help her learn what she needed to know, she had an army of tradesmen, delivery boys, rag and bone men, and fruit vendors whom she plied with tea and treats. She'd sit them down and go over every single name connected with a case, and oddly enough, she always managed to learn something useful.

Mrs. Goodge was very proud of what she'd accomplished in the twilight of her life, but more importantly, she was proud of herself and her ability to change.

She'd come to the Witherspoon household after being sacked at her last place of employment for being "too old." At that time, she'd considered working for a policeman—even a rich policeman with a big house—a bit of comedown in the world, but she'd needed a roof over her head and a salary, so she'd swallowed her pride and taken the position. That had been the best thing she'd ever done in her life.

She'd discovered that working for justice changed every-thing. No longer did she think that people had to stay in their place and doff their caps to their "betters." She'd seen too many of those "betters" commit unspeakable acts of murder. She'd learned that the poorest of people could have the most honor and the richest be so steeped in wickedness that even the devil wouldn't want them. But the very best result of coming to work for Gerald Witherspoon had been that in her old age, she'd finally found a family.

"Excellent, Mrs. Goodge. We've only just learned of the murder, and thanks to you, we already know something use-ful. Do you remember anything else?"

"Not off the top of my head, but I'll put some feelers out and see if I can make contact with some of the other people who served in that household," she replied.

"Wiggins will probably be out very late tonight," Ruth murmured, her expression thoughtful. "Why don't I send one of my footmen to Luty's home first thing tomorrow morning with a message. That way poor Wiggins can sleep in and get a bit more rest."

"What a good idea," Mrs. Jeffries agreed. "Then they can be here bright and early tomorrow."

Smythe and Betsy lived on the first floor of a three-story brown brick house less than a quarter mile from Upper Ed-monton Gardens. Wiggins knocked softly on the front door of the flat so as not to wake the baby. A moment later, the door opened and Smythe stuck his head out.

"We've got a murder," Wiggins said softly. "We need to get to Victoria Gardens straightaway."

Smythe stepped back and waved him inside. He was a tall, heavily muscled man with strong, hard features. He had black hair streaked with a few strands of gray at the temples, dark brown eyes, and a kind smile that softened his harsh face. "I'll just nip in and let Betsy know. She's already gone to bed. This bein' a new mum is 'ard on the lass."

"Do ya think she'll get upset?" Wiggins frowned anxiously as Smythe turned toward the hallway. "She 'ates bein' left out of things."

"I don't think she'll mind this time," he whispered. "These days all she wants to do is get a bit of sleep. Amanda will be up and wantin' to nurse in an hour or two."

While he waited, Wiggins glanced around the flat. He'd been there a number of times, but he noticed that there was now a new mirror with a gilt frame over the fireplace, and there were two nice blue pillows on the settee. Not for the first time, he wondered how Smythe and Betsy could afford the place. It was quite a large flat, with a proper dining room, a kitchen, a parlor, and two bedrooms. But he shrugged as he heard the click of a door being closed down the hallway. Smythe was older than Betsy, and Wiggins thought the poor bloke must have saved long and hard to be able to afford a place like this.

"Would you like for us to call someone for you, ma'am?" Witherspoon asked the petite, blonde-haired woman sitting on the sofa. "This has obviously been a terrible shock to you."

"No, I'm alright, Inspector," Elena McCourt murmured. "But I've no idea what I can tell you. My husband was perfectly fine during tea." Her blue eyes flooded with tears. "I don't understand what could have happened. One moment he was here, and the next, he's lying there dead in a pool of blood."

"Who found the body, ma'am?" Witherspoon asked. He hated this part of his job, but he knew his duty. No matter how difficult it might be, the sooner one started taking statements, the faster one could solve the case. Constable Barnes had gone off to begin questioning the servants.

"Haines, our butler." She brushed at her cheeks. "I was upstairs when I heard him call for me to come down immediately. It was shocking. Haines never raises his voice, so I knew right away that something was terribly wrong."

Witherspoon nodded. "When you went into the study, did you touch anything? Did you move your husband?"

"No, I could tell that he was dead," she replied. "There was so much blood, and he lay there so quietly."

"And that's when you sent for the police, correct?"

"No, actually, one of our guests sent for them. He'd heard the commotion and walked into the room right behind me. He was the one that ran and got the constable on the corner. The next thing I knew, the house was swarming with policemen."

The inspector frowned. "Who was this guest, Mrs. Mc-Court?"

"My husband's cousin, Arthur Brunel." She looked confused. "I was surprised to see him here this afternoon, but Daniel had invited him for tea."

"Why were you surprised, ma'am?"

"Because he loathed my husband, Inspector. He accused him of cheating him out of his rightful share of his father's estate."

CHAPTER 2

"This has all been quite shocking, Constable," the butler murmured as he took a spot on the bench across the table from Barnes.

They were in the servants' dining hall on the bottom floor of the house. The table was rickety and pitted with nicks and scars. There were racks of dishes along one wall, and on the opposite side, storage shelves containing chipped crockery jars, mismatched glassware, and an old coffee grinder with a rusted handle. At the far end of the room, a set of gray and green checked curtains hung limply at the single, narrow window. Barnes wondered why the rich always condemned their servants to eat in the most dreary and cheerless rooms.

He wished he could hold his breath, as the smell was still bad, but instead, he nodded sympathetically at the butler. The poor man really did look shaken; his face was pale, his hands trembled slightly, and around his mouth was a thin white line. "I'm sure this is upsetting for all of you," Barnes began. "But if we're to sort out what happened, you and the other staff members of the household must be very honest."

"I wouldn't think of lying to the police," Haines replied. "I know my duty."

"You'd be surprised at how often people do lie to us," Barnes replied with a smile. "Servants sometimes think they're protecting either one of their own or their masters by not telling us what they know or what they've seen."

"That won't be the situation here, I assure you." He sniffed disapprovingly. "No one in this house would protect either of the McCourts."

"They weren't liked by the staff?" Barnes pulled out his little brown notebook and his pencil.

Haines closed his eyes for a moment. "I didn't mean that, Constable. I just meant that Mr. and Mrs. McCourt run a very formal household, that's all. They weren't given to encouraging familiarity from the staff."

"I understand. It's the sort of place where a servant could live and work but the master and mistress made sure everyone was kept in their place, right?"

"That's correct. I don't mean to imply there was any cruelty on their part, but it isn't the kind of household that creates loyalty from the servants. Though recently, Mrs. McCourt did take a stand against Mr. McCourt sacking one of the housemaids. The girl had accidentally chipped one of the plates in his Oriental collection."

Barnes made a mental note to follow up on that comment, but right now he wanted the man's statement while the memory was still fresh in his mind. "Can you tell me what happened here today?"

"You mean, when I found the body?" Haines swallowed convulsively.

"You can start there."

"When I went into the study, I didn't even see Mr. Mc-Court lying there on the floor. For some odd reason, the first thing I noticed was the bundle of mistletoe hanging down from the middle of the doorframe." He broke off with a harsh laugh. "I was afraid one of the maids might have put it up, and I knew that Mr. McCourt would be angry. Then I looked down and saw him lying on the floor. I thought he'd had a heart attack or a stroke, but as I got closer, I saw all the blood."

"Do you recall what time it was when you found him?"

"All of the staff had been out in the garden until the hour, so it must have been a few minutes past five o'clock. That's when we all came back inside. Bad smell or not, it was too cold to stay out, and it was getting darker by then."

"Where was Mrs. McCourt when you found the body?"

"Mrs. McCourt had gone upstairs. The maid hadn't opened the balcony door off the master bedroom, so she went up to do it herself."

"I thought you just said they ran a formal household." Barnes stared at him curiously. "So why did she go up? Why not send up the housemaid?"

"It is a formal household." He clasped his hands together on the tabletop. "I'm sorry, I know I'm babbling and not making any sense. But it isn't every day that one's master gets his head almost chopped off by a madman—"

"I know," Barnes interrupted him. "Please, take a deep breath and concentrate on everything you heard and saw this afternoon. Take your time and tell me in your own words. What happened here? Why were the servants out in the garden on a cold winter day?"

Haines closed his eyes briefly, unclasped his hands, and stretched out his fingers. "There had been a bit of a fracas earlier during tea."

"A fracas," Barnes repeated.

"Mr. McCourt had invited a number of guests for tea," Haines explained. "And just before the tea was to be served, a fire started in the servants' hall. The flames were put out straightaway, but unfortunately, there was the most ghastly odor, and it soon became obvious that the guests were uncomfortable, so Mrs. McCourt asked them to leave. When they were gone, she ordered all the windows and doors to be opened to get the smell out of the house and told us to go out into the garden for ten or fifteen minutes to get past the worst of it."

"Did both the McCourts go outside with the staff?" Barnes jotted down the facts as quickly as he could.

Haines shifted uncomfortably. "No. Mr. McCourt went into his study, and Mrs. McCourt went upstairs to open the balcony door off the master bedroom. She said she'd stay out on the balcony instead of coming back downstairs. I'll admit it was odd that she didn't ask the maid to do it, but I expect she had her reasons."

"If the smell was that bad, why didn't Mr. McCourt go outside as well?" He stopped writing and looked up at the butler.

"Mr. McCourt didn't share with me personally his reason for staying inside, but I did overhear him tell Mrs. McCourt the odor wasn't that bad and just to prove it, he'd stay inside."

"Were all the windows and doors still open when you found Mr. McCourt's body?"

"Yes, Mrs. McCourt instructed me to leave them open until it got full dark."

"Did she give you any other instructions before she went upstairs?"

"She asked me to get everyone together in the kitchen at five fifteen. She wanted to find out who was responsible for the fire."

Barnes had no idea where his questions might be leading, but over the years he'd learned to trust himself. "She was going to sack the person responsible?"

Haines pursed his lips in thought. "I don't think so," he said slowly. "I think she wanted to be sure the fire was an accident, and if that was the truth, I've a feeling she intended to protect the person. It would have been Mr. McCourt, not her, who'd have given someone the boot."

"Was the fire an accident?"

"That's just it; no one would own up to knowing anything about it." He sighed. "When we were out in the garden, the housekeeper and I questioned everyone. We've three maids, a scullery, a footman, the cook, and a housekeeper, and none of them so much as touched a lamp today. As a matter of fact, except for the footman who'd been sent out to get the wet sand, every single servant was in the kitchen when the fire started."

Elena McCourt smiled sadly. "Forgive me, Inspector. I'm not explaining this very well. Let me start at the beginning. We had guests today, and my husband was the one who sent out the invitations. I didn't even know until a couple of days ago that a formal tea had been arranged."

The inspector was no expert about such matters, but it had always seemed to him that it was the lady of the house who managed social affairs. His surprise must have shown on his face, because she quickly said, "I know it sounds odd, as I'm the one in charge of our social calendar, but occasionally, Daniel took it upon himself to arrange something. But that is beside the point."

Witherspoon wasn't so sure of that. But he didn't want to interrupt her, so he merely nodded.

She continued. "The guests were Mr. and Mrs. Leon Brunel, Mr. Saxon, Mr. Raleigh, Mr. Cochran, and, of course, as I've already mentioned, Mr. Arthur Brunel."

"You said that Arthur Brunel was your husband's cousin—"

"And you're wondering if the other Brunel is related as well," she interrupted. "Arthur is a half brother to Leon Brunel, so yes, both men were Daniel's cousins."

"And Mr. Arthur Brunel and your husband weren't on good terms; is that correct?" he pressed.

"Daniel was the executor for Elias Brunel; he was Leon and Arthur's father. They had different mothers. Leon is the elder. When the estate was settled three years ago, Arthur accused my husband of conspiring with Leon to cheat him out of his full share," she explained. "That's why I was so surprised when he arrived today. He's not spoken to Daniel in three years."

The inspector wanted to understand the basics of the situation before he delved further into the relationships between the victim and those who might be the suspects. Sometimes if he heard too much information in one sitting, he got a bit confused. "I see. Before we get any further into Mr. McCourt's differences with his cousin, could you tell me what happened today?"

She looked surprised but nodded assent. "If you like. When the guests arrived, they were shown to the morning room. Usually, they'd have been put in the drawing room, but for reasons of his own, my husband instructed our butler to take them all to the morning room."

"May I have the full names of all the guests, please?" he asked.

"Yes, of course. Leon and Glenda Brunel, Nicholas Saxon, Jerome Raleigh, Charles Cochran, and Arthur Brunel."

"And those who are not cousins are friends of the family?" he inquired.

"No. Mr. Saxon is a business acquaintance only. He had a rather extensive Oriental antique collection, and he's sold my husband a number of pieces," she explained. "Mr. Raleigh is one of the experts Daniel uses to authenticate and evaluate pieces he's thinking of buying. Charles Cochran is a solicitor who worked with my husband years ago. He's also interested in Oriental antiquities. I suspect they were all invited today so that Daniel could show off his latest acquisition."

"What kind of acquisition?"

She shrugged. "I don't know. He didn't tell me he'd bought anything recently, but he must have, as that would be the only reason he'd have those particular people over for tea. But you want the sequence of events, don't you?" She sighed heavily. "Oh dear, this is awkward, but I don't suppose I've much choice. Better you should hear it from me than from anyone else. While our guests were sitting in the morning room, I was having a horrible row with my husband. We were in his study."

"What did you argue about?"

"He wanted to sack a housemaid for chipping one of the plates in his collection. I refused to let him do it, and he was utterly furious at me. I'm sure that Leon Brunel will mention it when you talk to him. He was right outside the door when we were shouting at each other."

"Mr. Brunel was eavesdropping?"

She laughed. "That's what I suspect, Inspector. Like my

husband, Leon's a collector. He claimed he was admiring the Chinese vase on the entry table, but I didn't believe him. That vase has been sitting there for two months, and I know he's seen it on previous occasions, but I could hardly call him a liar to his face."

"Did you and Mr. McCourt quarrel often?" the inspector asked softly. As all policemen knew, the most likely person to have murdered a husband was his wife.

She thought for a moment. "No, for most of my marriage I never questioned Daniel's decisions. But recently, his passion for his collecting was overtaking every other consideration in our lives."

"He collects Oriental art and antiquities," Witherspoon commented.

"That's right, and I simply couldn't let some poor housemaid get tossed into the street for chipping a plate, even if it was from the Ming dynasty."

Witherspoon nodded and asked, "What happened then?"

"The guests were shown into the drawing room, and we went in to tea. But before anything could be served, there was a terrible ruckus from downstairs. Someone had knocked over a paraffin lamp, and the rug had caught fire. Thank goodness it was put out before it spread, but the result was the whole house smelled dreadful." She made a face. "We all sat there chatting and pretending the odor wasn't disgusting, then Leon commented that it looked as if his wife were about to faint, so I knew we couldn't go on. I asked everyone to leave. Daniel was furious about that as well, but he could hardly insist people stay."

"Did all the guests leave at once?"

"I thought they had, but I might have been mistaken." She frowned. "Frankly, at that point, I was so busy giving instructions that it never occurred to me anyone would have stayed in the house. I told the servants to open up all the doors and windows and then to go out into the garden and stay there for at least ten or fifteen minutes. I wanted them to get past the worst of the smell."

"Did you go outside with them?"

She shook her head. "No. I started to, and then as we were leaving, I asked the upstairs maid if she'd remembered to open the balcony door off the master bedroom. She said she hadn't and started to go upstairs, but I stopped her and said I'd do it. The access to that door is behind an ornate Chinese table from the Qing dynasty, and I suspect the reason she'd not opened it was because the poor girl was terrified of scratching the wretched thing."

"Was she the one who'd chipped Mr. McCourt's plate?" Witherspoon guessed.

"No, but because of the way Daniel had reacted when that had happened, the girl and every other servant in the household were now terrified of going near his collection. So I went up and opened the door. I stayed out there for ten minutes and came back in when I heard the butler shouting for me. I'd told Haines to gather everyone in the kitchen at a quarter past five so we could sort out what had happened. I didn't want Daniel browbeating people because his great moment had been ruined."

Witherspoon watched her carefully. He had a feeling she hadn't liked her late husband all that much. "Why did Mr. McCourt not go outside with everyone? Wasn't he bothered by the odor?"

"Two reasons." She smiled cynically. "One, he wanted to prove a point that we were all overreacting and that the smell wasn't as awful as I claimed; and two, he'd never leave his precious collection unattended with all the doors and windows unlocked."

"I see," he said. "During the time when you were all in the drawing room before the fire started, were your husband and Arthur Brunel friendly to each other?"

She thought for a few seconds before she replied. "They were civil, but there was no genuine warmth between them."

"Was Arthur Brunel interested in Oriental art and antiquities?"

"Absolutely not. Leon's been collecting for years—that's one of the reasons Daniel became interested. But Arthur never cared for any kind of antiquity. He said it was just a bunch of old junk that cluttered up people's lives and homes. I can't imagine why Daniel invited him, and more importantly, I can't imagine why he accepted the invitation."

"Cor blimey, we'd best be careful," Wiggins muttered. They were on the corner of Victoria Gardens with a good view of the front of number 12.

"Maybe we ought to duck back a little farther," Smythe suggested. "There's constables everywhere, and most of them know us by sight. I don't want anyone mentionin' to the inspector that they spotted us 'angin' about the murder house."

Over the years, everyone in the inspector's household had had plenty of contact with the constables from Witherspoon's station at Ladbroke Road. This murder was in the inspector's district, so the policemen doing the house to house and the general search of the neighborhood would easily recognize them.

"We passed a pub just round the corner back there." Wiggins pointed the way they'd just come. "Let's go see if we can 'ear anythin'. Bad news always travels fast."

"That'll be better than standin' out 'ere in the cold," Smythe agreed.

"Smythe, do ya mind if I ask ya somethin'?" Wiggins wound his scarf tighter around his neck as the two of them began walking.

" 'Course not."

"Every time I come to your and Betsy's house, I notice you've got more new things, you know, like that gilded mirror. I know you've saved your wages for years, but surely furnishin' your flat is costin' you an arm and leg."

Smythe cringed inwardly. For ages he'd meant to tell the lad the truth: He'd come back from Australia a rich man and had only kept up being a coachman because he wanted to make sure the servants at Upper Edmonton Gardens weren't going to take advantage of Inspector Witherspoon the way former ones had taken advantage of the inspector's late aunt. Time had slipped by, and before he knew it, they'd been solving murders and he'd fallen in love with Betsy. At that point, he'd not wanted to leave. He'd told Betsy the truth, of course—no man should have secrets from his wife—and Mrs. Jeffries had guessed that he wasn't poor, but he'd never found just the right moment to tell Mrs. Goodge and Wiggins. Now he was in a right old pickle. If he told them how rich he was, he was afraid they'd feel like he'd deliberately played them for fools, and that wasn't the way it happened. He intended to tell them both the truth. But not right now. He had to wait for just the right moment. "I 'ad a bit more money than just my wages," he muttered as they came to the pub. "When I was out in Australia, I did a bit of prospectin' and 'ad a bit of luck a time or two," he explained.

"Cor blimey." Wiggins laughed. "Maybe I ought to go to Australia. Maybe I should try my 'and at prospectin'. I'm glad you're takin' care of our Betsy. She's not 'ad an easy life, and I'll bet she's right proud of all 'er nice things."

"She seems to be 'appy," he said as they reached the pub.

He yanked the door open, and they stepped inside. People were crowded up against the bar, there was sawdust on the floor, and every table was occupied. The wooden benches along the side walls were full as well. Just then, two men in railway uniforms put their hats on and left the bar. Smythe and Wiggins hurried to the empty spot and wedged themselves between a postman and two older women drinking gin.

"What'll you 'ave, gents?" the barmaid asked.

"Two pints, please," Smythe replied. He glanced at Wiggins and saw that the lad had already cocked his ear toward the two women. He glanced at the postman. "Nice evenin'."

The postman shrugged. "Guess so. Seems cold to me."

"Saw there was a load of police just up the road. I wonder what 'appened."

"Don't know." He turned his attention straight ahead and stared at the rows of bottles on the shelves behind the bar.

Smythe sighed inwardly. Just his luck to be stuck next to someone who wasn't interested in chatting. The barmaid slid their pints on the counter and grinned at Smythe. "That'll be eight pence for the two of 'em."

He gave her a shilling. "Keep the change, luv," he replied. Maybe he'd have better luck with her. "I saw there was police just round the corner. Wonder what 'appened."

"Thank you, sir." She turned, made change from the till, and pocketed the four pence tip he'd given her. "Murder was done in that house." She swiveled back to the bar. "Fellow 'ad his head chopped off."

"His 'ead weren't completely cut off," a grizzled old man on the other side of the taciturn postman interjected. "I 'eard his throat was just slit."

"How would you know?" The barmaid sneered. "My Janet works over on Victoria Gardens and she got 'er information directly from one of the housemaids."

"News travels quick round 'ere," Smythe said conversationally. He wasn't surprised the people in the pub already knew about the murder. "Who was the poor sod that got done in?" He took a sip of his beer.

"Feller named Daniel McCourt," the barmaid said quickly.

"Do they know who killed 'im?" Wiggins asked.

"'Course not," the woman standing next to Wiggins answered. "'E was only murdered at teatime."

"Mind you, it's his wife I feel sorry for," her companion, a slight woman with thinning red hair, said. "Mrs. McCourt's just come back this week from her aunt's funeral, and now she's lost her husband."

The postman put his empty glass on the counter and left.

"I don't think she'll mind losin' 'im all that much," the barmaid said as she snatched up a dirty glass and put it under the counter. She pulled out a damp tea towel and wiped the wet ring off the wood. "From what I 'ear, she weren't all that fond of 'im."

"'Ow do you know that?" The red-haired woman glared at her.

"Because Janet and one of the McCourt maids 'ave their afternoon out together. Just the other day Janet said the only thing Annie wanted to talk about was how badly Mr. McCourt treated his wife."

"And what did your Janet want to talk about, her new fellow?" The red-haired woman cackled. "Are they goin' to be gettin' married soon?"

"Sounds like you two know a lot about what goes on round 'ere," Wiggins interrupted quickly. He gestured at the empty gin glasses in front of the women. "May I buy ya both another?"

"Why would ya want to do that?" The one closest to him eyed him suspiciously.

Wiggins had his story all worked out. He leaned closer to her. "Well, don't tell anyone, but I work for a newspaper, and they sent me round 'ere to see if I could find out what was goin' on with the McCourt murder. But the police won't tell me anythin'. You ladies sound as if ya know what's what."

The red-haired woman jerked her thumb toward Smythe. "And what does the big fellow do? Work for a newspaper as well?"

"Nah, 'e just comes along as a bit of insurance when I'm out and about at night. Sometimes you can run into a rough type, if ya know what I mean."

The woman surveyed Smythe up and down then broke into a broad, toothy grin. "That's right clever of ya; this one looks mean enough to scare off the devil himself if he got in yer way."

The plump, gray-haired woman in a black bombazine dress sat down in the spot just vacated by the butler.

Barnes smiled at her. "You are Mrs. Williams, the house-keeper."

"I am," she replied with a strained smile.

"Can you tell me what happened here this afternoon?" He flipped to a clean page in his notebook.

"I'm not sure where to begin." She frowned in confusion. "I didn't see who killed Mr. McCourt, so I don't really know what you're wanting me to say."

"I understand that. What I want you to do is tell me what you did this afternoon, what you saw, and if you noticed anything unusual. Just start where you want and use your own words," Barnes instructed.

"Alright then. I'll do my best." She took a deep, calming breath. "After luncheon was served, everyone in the household went about their usual routine."

"You mean they did their normal chores?"

She nodded. "That's right. The girls cleared up the luncheon things, and then everyone went about their business. I went to the linen cupboard and inspected the serviettes and runners that were going to be used for the afternoon tea."

"Where's the linen cupboard?"

She pointed toward the hallway. "It's the door directly across from here. I saw that everything was in order, and then I went to the kitchen and had a word with Cook. She assured me everything was ready for tea."

"What time was this?"

She thought for a moment. "About half past two. Luncheon ran very late today. Mrs. McCourt didn't get home from her shopping until a quarter past one."

"When you were down here, did you notice anything unusual?"

"No, there was nothing out of place at all." She sighed. "And the outside door was closed, so no one could have gotten into the house."

He looked up from his notebook. "How many doors are there down here?"

"Three." She pointed to the hall again. "There's the back door at the end of the hall. That leads out into the garden." She pointed in the opposite direction. "Then there's the door off the kitchen and there's the servants' entrance along the side."

He'd already seen the back door and the servants' door. "Where does the door off the kitchen lead?"

"A paved yard. It's used to store the soap buckets and some of the other old things from the kitchen. Cook puts her herb pots out there during the spring and summer."

"Is the yard accessible from the street or the garden?"

"No, you'd have to climb the fence to get in that way.

Besides, during the day there is almost always someone in the kitchen, so whoever killed Mr. McCourt couldn't have gotten in that way, especially when we were preparing a formal tea. Cook never leaves the kitchen then."

"What happened after you checked the linens?"

"I went back upstairs and inspected the rooms," she replied. "The morning room, the drawing room, the halls, the foyer, and the water closets. Mr. McCourt had made it clear that he wanted everything to be perfect."

"So this tea was important to him?" Barnes pressed. "Is that your assessment?"

She hesitated. "Yes, but I've no idea why. Mr. McCourt wasn't one to discuss such matters with servants. But from his manner, it was clear this occasion was very important to him. So I made sure that the rooms were in good order. After that, I went back to the china pantry and got out the dishes to be used. Once that task was completed, it was almost time for the guests to arrive, so I went back upstairs to do one final check."

"Where were Mr. and Mrs. McCourt at this point in time?" Barnes asked.

"Mrs. McCourt was in the study speaking to Mr. McCourt."

"I see. Were you in Mr. McCourt's study today?"

"No. No one is allowed in there except for once a week when the downstairs maid is permitted to go in and clean. Annie cleaned the room today."

"Was that when she chipped his plate?" he asked.

Mrs. Williams sighed. "I'm afraid so. He was utterly furious when he saw the damage. In the girl's defense, she came to me straightaway and admitted what she'd done. But that didn't stop him from being angry. We could hear him shouting at Mrs. McCourt through the closed door of the study. It was a bit embarrassing, as the guests had started to arrive by then. But luckily, Haines had orders to take them to the morning room, so he was able to get them out of the foyer rather quickly."

"So when Mr. and Mrs. McCourt were in the study together, they were arguing?"

She nodded. "I'm afraid so."

"Did you hear the argument?" Barnes asked.

"No, I had to go back to the kitchen to supervise the serving."

"Who hung the mistletoe in Mr. McCourt's study?" he asked curiously.

She blinked in surprise. "Mistletoe? What mistletoe?"

"There was a sprig hanging in the doorway between the study and the drawing room," he replied.

"No there wasn't," she insisted. "I was in the drawing room just as the guests were leaving and there was nothing hanging off the doorframe. I'd have noticed."

Barnes suddenly realized this could be very important. "Are you absolutely certain of that?"

She raised her eyebrows and crossed her arms over her chest. "Of course I am. Mr. McCourt hated that sort of thing and certainly wouldn't have allowed it to be hung anywhere near his study."

Barnes wasn't sure he understood. "But if he hated 'that sort of thing,' then why is the house filled with Christmas decorations? There's greenery hanging on the mantelpiece; there's even a tree with candles and bows—"

"But he loathed mistletoe," she interrupted. "He won't even let us hang it in the servants' hall."

The door opened, and a housemaid stuck her head inside. "Excuse me, Mrs. Williams, but I've a message for the constable."

"Yes, Annie, what is it?"

"The inspector is in the mornin' room. He's finished speakin' with Mrs. McCourt and is goin' to help with interviewin' the staff. He said for the constable to join him there when he's finished speakin' to you and to Cook."

Upstairs, Witherspoon smiled at the young footman sitting across from him. The lad couldn't be more than twelve, and he looked as if he expected to be flogged. His blue eyes were as wide as one of Mrs. Goodge's pie plates, he was pale as a ghost, and his reddened hands were clutched tightly together on his lap. "Don't look so worried, young man," he said kindly. "I'm only going to ask you a few questions."

The boy's lips trembled, but he managed a tiny smile. "Yes, sir. I know. Mr. Haines told me to be on my best behavior."

The inspector sighed inwardly; the poor lad was scared. To give himself a moment to decide the best way to get the footman to relax, he turned his head and gave the room a cursory glance. The walls were papered in cheerful yellow and white stripes, the curtains were made of white eyelet fabric, and the furniture was actually comfortable. "What's your name?" He kept his tone as casual as he could.

"Duncan Malloy, sir," the boy answered.

Witherspoon saw that he'd unclenched his hands. "How long have you been working here, Duncan?"

"Six months, sir. I came at the end of June. My mum passed on, sir, and my auntie couldn't keep me no more, so they sent me 'ere."

The inspector suddenly thought of his new goddaughter and made a silent vow that she'd never spend one day of her childhood working. He'd never really given it a lot of thought before, but there was something wrong with a social system that tossed children out into the world to earn their own living before they were even old enough to shave. "Duncan, I want you to think carefully before you answer my questions. It's very important to tell the truth."

"Yes, sir. I always tell the truth, sir." Duncan dragged a deep lungful of air into his body and straightened his spine. "I go to the Methodist chapel every Sunday with Mr. Haines, and I know it's wrong to lie."

"I'm sure you always tell the truth," Witherspoon assured him. "Mr. McCourt was murdered this afternoon, and I'm certain that's very frightening for you and the rest of the household."

"Yes, sir. It scared me to death when I 'eard."

"I want you to think back and tell me if you saw or heard anything out of the ordinary today?"

"There was the fire, sir. We don't generally 'ave one of them in the afternoons."

"Where were you when the fire started?"

"I'd gone to Beaman's to get the sand, sir." He scratched the end of his nose. Witherspoon noted his knuckles were raw and bleeding in spots. "And it was a jolly good thing I came back when I did. Mr. Haines grabbed the bucket from me and used it to put the flames out."

"Why were you fetching sand?"

"For the Christmas tree, sir," the boy replied. "They were goin' to light the candles as soon as they had tea, and Mrs. McCourt won't 'ave a lighted tree in the house unless someone is standin' there with a bucket of wet sand in case the boughs catch a spark. I don't know why they don't want to use water, but I do what they tell me."

"And where and what is Beaman's?"

"It's the greengrocer's up the road. They bring a load of sand for the households that put up a tree," he explained. "Mind you, they charge a pretty penny, but that's only to be expected. Where else in this neighborhood could ya get a bucket of sand?"

The inspector nodded. "Do you remember exactly what time it was that you came back from the greengrocer's?"

Duncan chewed his lower lip. "No, sir. All I know is that I was late. Mr. Haines 'ad told me to be back by half past four, and I know it was a bit later than that because I heard the church clock strikin' the half hour and I was still waitin' for the sand at the greengrocer's. I waited a good ten minutes, sir, and I was gettin' more and more nervous. Mr. Haines gets right angry if we're late gettin' ready for an occasion."

"How long does it take to get from the greengrocer's to here?" Witherspoon asked. He was trying to determine the exact sequence of events.

"About six or seven minutes, sir." Duncan scratched his nose again, this time with his other hand.

"When you came back, which door did you use?" The inspector struggled to keep his mind on the case, but it was difficult not to stare at the footman's hands. Ye gods, what on earth did they make him do, scrub the lamps with carbolic soap? Didn't they notice his flesh was torn and bloody? Why didn't someone put some salve on his knuckles?

"The servants' door, sir. That's the only one we're allowed to use," he replied. "When I got 'ere, the door was already open and Annie was standin' in the hall screamin' and Mr. Haines was tryin' to put out the flames."

"Exactly where was the fire?" Witherspoon interrupted. "In the servants' hallway?"

"It was in front of the back stairs, sir," he said. "The rug was on fire. Mr. Haines was stompin' at it with 'is feet, but then 'e saw me and shouted at me to bring the sand, so I ran over and 'e grabbed the bucket and threw the sand on it. It put the fire out. By that time, everyone else 'ad come to see what all the fuss was about, and then Mr. Haines started in askin' who'd left the paraffin lamp on the landing with the ruddy door open."

"Is that what caused the fire?" the inspector asked.

Duncan shrugged. "That's what everyone thought. The lamp was lyin' on the floor with all the oil spilled out and the top part all cracked. If you leave the servants' door open, it causes a terrible draft through the hallway. But no one would own up to 'avin' set the lamp on the staircase mantel, now, would they? And I don't think one of us did it. The only ones who handle the lamps is Mr. Haines or Mrs. Williams."

"When you were coming back from Beaman's, did you see anyone who looked suspicious hanging about the area?"

"I didn't notice anyone," he admitted. "But I was in such a rush to get back, I wasn't payin' any attention."

"When the fire had been put out, what did you do then?"

"Mrs. Williams sent me to the kitchen to help take up the servin' trays," he replied. "The sand was spilled onto the rug, and the place was startin' to stink to high heaven, so there weren't no reason for me to go to the drawin' room. It was a shame, too, as I was wearin' my uniform and everythin'."

The inspector couldn't think of anything else to ask the boy, and it was getting very late. "Thank you, Duncan. You've been very helpful. You may go now."

Duncan gave a quick bow of his head, got up from the chair, and started for the door.

"Just a moment," the inspector called. "I noticed your knuckles are so raw they're bleeding. Can't you get the housekeeper to put some salve on them for you?"

Duncan dropped his gaze and stared at the floor. "I don't like to ask, sir."

"Whyever not?" Witherspoon asked. "Your hands are in terrible shape. You could get a nasty infection."

"I don't want to give them a reason to sack me." He looked up at the inspector. "I overheard Mr. McCourt tellin' Mrs. McCourt that she needed to cut back on household expenses, and then 'e said maybe they didn't need a footman. I was scared if I asked for anythin' extra that Mr. McCourt would say I cost too much to keep. If I lose this place, I've got nowhere else to go."

Witherspoon reached into his pocket and pulled out a handful of coins. He'd suspected that the lad had been scared to ask for medicine, and he was disgusted. He stood up and handed the money to the footman. "Here, take this, and tomorrow, I want you to go to the chemist's and get some healing salve for your knuckles."

"Oh, I couldn't, sir," he replied.

"Yes, you can." He grabbed the boy's hand and dumped the coins into his palm.

"I'll pay you back when I get my quarter's wages," he cried. "I promise."

"You don't need to do that," Witherspoon replied. "But when you're grown up, if you ever see someone in need and you can help, then you must pay me back by assisting that person; do you understand?"

Duncan grinned broadly. "Indeed, I do, sir, and thanks ever so much. My knuckles hurt so badly that I can't sleep at night."

Witherspoon was dead on his feet by the time he trudged up the stairs at home. But before he could even get out his key, the door flew open.

"You shouldn't have waited up, Mrs. Jeffries!" he exclaimed as he stepped inside and took off his hat. "It's very late."

"I don't need much sleep, sir." She reached for his bowler and put it on the coat tree. "I wanted to make certain you had a bite to eat before you retired."

He handed her his overcoat and scarf. "That's very kind of you. I must admit, I'm starving."

"Go on into the dining room, sir, and I'll bring your supper right up."

Five minutes later, he was sipping hot tea and tucking into a plate of lamb stew. "It was dreadful, Mrs. Jeffries." He put down his cup and reached for a slice of bread. "Someone had actually used a sword and slashed both sides of the victim's neck."

"That's certainly an unusual way to murder someone," she murmured. "Where on earth did the killer get such a weapon?" She already knew the answer to that question. Wiggins and Smythe had reported in and told them what they'd learned at the pub.

"Oh, our victim was an Oriental antiquities collector, and the sword had been hanging in a display on the wall of his study," the inspector said as he spooned up a bite of stew from his plate. "It certainly made it convenient for the killer. All he had to do was take the sword down off the display. There were three other swords there as well." He popped the food into his mouth.

"The display was within easy reach, then?" she asked.

He shook his head, chewed, and swallowed. "No. Unless the killer was very tall, he or she would have to have stood on something, but there was a wooden stool in the study, and the murderer probably used that. According to what Barnes found out from the servants, the sword was something called a Hwando. It's got a rather long blade and is from the Joseon dynasty."

"It's Korean?" she clarified. She'd always been very inter-

ested in the Far East and had read a number of books and
even attended several lectures on the various cultures in that
part of the world.

He took another bite of stew before he answered. "I suppose it must be," he finally said. "We were so intent on getting the facts of the case that I'm afraid I didn't pay too
much attention to the details. But nonetheless, we gathered
a substantial amount of information." He told her about his
interviews with the widow and the servants.

Mrs. Jeffries listened carefully, occasionally asking a
question or nodding in agreement. "You have learned a great
deal, Inspector," she said when he'd finished his narrative.

Witherspoon shrugged modestly. "I wasn't the only one,
of course. The constables that did the house to house caught
up with us as we were leaving. Unfortunately, no one at any
of the adjacent properties saw or noticed anything unusual.
But that's to be expected; the house next door was empty,
and everyone else had their doors and windows tightly shut
because of the cold."

"And the constables found nothing untoward when they
searched the area?"

He shook his head and reached for his teacup. "Nothing.
Mind you, everyone knew we already had the murder
weapon, and it was dark by the time they began searching.
I've ordered another search for tomorrow morning."

"Do you have any suspects, sir?"

He frowned. "I suppose everyone who was at the tea party
could be considered a suspect."

"I thought most of the guests had already left the premises when the murder occurred," she commented.

"Not all of them." Witherspoon took a sip of tea. "Arthur
Brunel was the one who sent for the police, and Constable

Barnes had quite an interesting interview with one of the housemaids. A young girl named Annie."

"The one who cracked the rim of the Chinese plate?"

He nodded. "She said that when she was bringing up a tray, she overheard a woman asking one of the other guests why on earth he'd come to the McCourt house—" He broke off and grinned. "She didn't like to admit it, but she deliberately stopped and listened. She was in the hallway and heard the man say quite clearly that he only came so that he could see her."

"Who is the 'her'?" She frowned in confusion. "I'm not sure I understand, sir."

"I didn't, either, but then the maid told me that the voice didn't belong to Mrs. McCourt, so the only other woman it could have been was Mrs. Leon Brunel."

"And who was the man?"

Witherspoon sighed. "Annie said she didn't recognize his voice, so we'll have to try and sort it out ourselves. But you must admit, a conversation like that does put the cat amongst the pigeons."

CHAPTER 3

Witherspoon and Barnes were back at Victoria Gardens bright and early the next morning. In the pale light of a cold winter's day, Witherspoon directed a small army of constables in searching the communal gardens and the immediate area surrounding the McCourt home.

Barnes had popped into the kitchen of Upper Edmonton Gardens this morning when he'd stopped to fetch the inspector. He'd had a short but useful chat with Mrs. Jeffries and the cook. When he and Witherspoon had first begun to work together, he'd soon realized the inspector was getting far more information than they were uncovering in the normal course of their police work. It hadn't taken brilliant detecting on his part to realize Witherspoon's household and friends were the ones doing the helping. He'd debated long and hard with himself before he'd revealed to the housekeeper that he was onto them, but the truth was, he admired what they were doing. They were smart and discreet, and they had sources that the average policeman couldn't hope to compete with. All in all, it had worked out nicely.

Constable Griffiths smiled apologetically as he approached Witherspoon and Barnes. "Sorry, sir, but the only things we've found are a couple of old burlap bags, a broken umbrella, and a pencil case. All the items look as if they've been out here for weeks, sir."

"Tell the lads to go over the grounds one more time and then go and help with the house to house," the inspector instructed.

"Yes, sir." Griffiths bobbed his head respectfully and left. As soon as he was gone, Barnes said, "Let's hope we can find a witness from somewhere around here." He pursed his lips. "This time of year with everyone out and about for the holidays someone must have seen something."

"I'd not count on it, Constable," Witherspoon replied. "Half the houses here are probably empty because people have gone to Scotland for Christmas."

"And if you ask me, that makes no sense at all." He shook his head in disbelief. "Scotland is more wet, cold, and miserable than London."

"Agreed, but these sort of people do enjoy imitating the royal family, and the Queen takes her entire brood to Balmoral for the holidays. But let's be optimistic; they can't all have gone north, so perhaps someone will have seen something." Witherspoon glanced at the rear of the McCourt house. "The servants are up by now, and I'd like us to have another word in that quarter before we begin interviewing yesterday's guests." He turned and went down the path, his feet crunching loudly on the gravel.

"Who do we want to speak to specifically?" Barnes asked as they crossed the small paved terrace to the back door.

"I want to speak to the housekeeper again, and I'd like you to talk to the butler. I think a precise time line of everyone's whereabouts could be of value." He stopped and then turned toward the far side of the house. "Let's take a look at that balcony."

Barnes hurried after him.

Witherspoon pointed up at the second floor. "Look, it's quite small, but surely if Mrs. McCourt was standing out there for ten minutes, someone should have seen her."

"Not if all the servants were out in the gardens," Barnes said reasonably. "Not unless one of them had a reason to look for her. You can't see the balcony from out back."

"In any case, let's see if we can find out if anyone did notice her." Witherspoon sighed heavily. "And if none of the servants saw her, let's see if one of the neighbors might have seen her."

As soon as the hansom cab carrying the inspector and Barnes pulled away from the pavement, the others descended upon the kitchen of Upper Edmonton Gardens.

Luty Belle Crookshank and her butler, Hatchet, were the last to arrive. Everyone else was already at the table in their usual spots: Mrs. Jeffries sat at the head with Mrs. Goodge on her right; Wiggins sat beside the cook with Ruth on his other side; Betsy, holding the baby, and Smythe and Phyllis sat on the left side of the table.

"It's all his fault," Luty announced as the two of them swept into the room. "It takes him forever and a day to git movin' in the mornings."

Luty Belle Crookshank was an elderly, white-haired American woman. From the wild west of Colorado, she'd married an Englishman who'd gone prospecting, and they had made a fortune in silver mining. Now widowed, she'd been a witness in one of the inspector's first cases and had realized that his household was snooping about looking for information. After that case had been resolved, she'd come to them with a problem of her own, and ever since, she and Hatchet had insisted on helping them.

She knew everyone who was anyone in London, and despite being unschooled, plainspoken, and of no social pedigree whatsoever, she was welcomed in the homes of cabinet ministers, bankers, diplomats, and aristocrats. She loved bright clothes and even brighter jewelry. Today she wore an emerald green cape with a white fur collar and a matching fur hat.

"Don't be absurd, madam. I was ready a good ten minutes prior to our leaving the house." Hatchet grinned broadly. He was a tall, white-haired man with a regal bearing and a ready wit. He was devoted to his employer and not in the least shy about voicing his opinions. "Good morning, everyone," he said as he helped Luty out of her cloak and went to the coat tree, shedding his own overcoat and black top hat as he walked.

"There's that pretty dumplin'." Luty's pearls swung wildly as she rushed over to where Betsy sat holding the baby. Amanda waved her chubby arms and gave her a wide, toothless grin. "Oh my goodness, look, she's smilin' at me."

"Of course she is, Luty. She knows her godmother," Betsy replied. She was a pretty, blonde-haired woman in her twenties. She was the maid in the Witherspoon household, but in truth, since she'd had the baby, her duties were so light as to be nonexistent. She was now more a housewife than housemaid, and she'd already made up her mind that she was going to have a talk with Mrs. Jeffries about giving up her duties altogether. Taking wages when she didn't feel she'd earned them properly made her feel guilty, and in any case, she didn't need the money. "I'm going to feel very left out now that you've all got a murder," she said as Luty chucked the baby under the chin and then skirted around the table to where Hatchet held out her chair.

"You'll contribute your bit," the cook assured her. "You won't be able to get out and about like before, but that's alright. There will still be bits and pieces that you can do."

Betsy laughed softly. She couldn't believe she'd once feared this moment; once been terrified that after she'd married there would come a time when she wasn't able to do her fair share when they had a murder. She'd dreaded that moment more than anything, but now that it was here and she held her child in her arms, she couldn't imagine why she'd been so frightened. Now the thought of being away from her baby was unthinkable. "That's nice of you to say, but don't worry about me. I'll be fine," she declared. "And now that we've got Phyllis on the hunt with us, she'll be able to take over some of my patch."

"Don't say that!" Phyllis exclaimed. "I don't think I'll be able to find out near as much as you always did. I'll do my best, but I don't want everyone thinkin' I can do as well as you. You're much better with people than I am."

"Nonsense, you'll do just fine," Betsy replied. "You just need some practice, that's all." Betsy was the one who went to the neighborhoods surrounding the murder scene and the homes of their suspects. With her shopping basket over her arm and her sweet smile, she'd become an expert at getting information and gossip out of the local merchants.

"Of course you will, Phyllis, so stop worrying," Mrs. Jeffries reassured her. "Now, let's get started. I'll start by telling Luty and Hatchet what we know, and then I'll tell the rest of you what I learned from the inspector last night and what Constable Barnes told Mrs. Goodge and me this morning." She took her time in the telling and was careful to stick to the facts. When she'd finished, she looked at the faces around the table, hoping that someone would be able to add something to the meager details they knew thus far.

"Daniel McCourt," Luty murmured. "That name sounds awfully familiar, but I can't recollect anythin' specific about it."

"I, too, recognize the name," Hatchet agreed. "But like you, I can't recall in what context I have heard it." He looked at Mrs. Jeffries. "McCourt was a collector of Oriental art? That might be useful, as I've a number of connections in London's art community."

"I'm not so sure he actually collected art." She frowned in confusion. "From what the inspector said, the murder weapon was from the victim's collection, but I'm not sure a sword would be considered art."

Hatchet grinned. "I've got some sources that should be knowledgeable about antiquities as well."

"I'll 'ave a go at the local hansom drivers and the pubs," Smythe volunteered. "We've 'ad a bit of luck on this one; all the tea party guests live close to the murder house, so if they're suspects, at least we won't be runnin' about all over London. But even if they lived close, they'd 'ave probably taken a hansom rather than walked yesterday. It was bloomin' cold."

"And it's going to be just as cold today," Betsy interjected. "So make sure you don't forget your scarf and gloves."

"I'll see what I can suss out from the McCourt servants," Wiggins offered. "And if there's no one about the murder house, I'll try one of the other people. Cor blimey, we've got enough suspects to choose from. 'Ow many people was at the tea party?"

"Mr. and Mrs. Leon Brunel, Arthur Brunel, Charles Cochran, Jerome Raleigh, and Nicholas Saxon." Mrs. Goodge recited the names quickly. "And don't forget Mrs. McCourt. She ought to be a suspect as well. We've only her word that she went upstairs to that balcony."

"None of the other servants saw her up there," Ruth mused. "And they were out in the communal garden."

"We don't know that no one saw her," Mrs. Jeffries reminded them. "Neither the inspector nor Constable Barnes asked that specific question yesterday; they were too busy taking general statements. But I've no doubt they'll take care of the matter today."

"None of these names sound familiar to me," Ruth admitted as she reached for her teacup. "But my women's group is meeting today. I'll see if I can learn anything there."

"I'll get some notes out to my old colleagues," Mrs. Goodge murmured. "And I've got the laundry boy and the butcher's lad comin' round today. Lucky for us the murder was close by. Maybe one of them will have a bit of useful gossip."

Phyllis, who'd been staring at the tabletop, glanced up to see everyone looking at her expectantly. She took a deep breath. "I'll speak to the local merchants," she offered. "I'm not sure I'm goin' to be able to learn anythin', but as I said, I'll do my best."

Wiggins caught her eye and gave her a reassuring smile. "You know, we don't always learn much when we're first startin' a case," he said to her. "Sometimes it takes a few days, so don't be gettin' all miserable if you don't 'ave much luck your first time out." In truth, he didn't think Phyllis was going to learn one blooming thing. She wasn't as pretty or as confident as Betsy, and when she got nervous, she stuttered just a bit over some words. Yet he didn't want to discourage her. She was a nice person, and he hoped he'd be wrong and she'd surprise them.

"That's excellent advice, Wiggins," Mrs. Jeffries said. "As for me, I think I'll take a quick trip and have a look at the murder house. Don't worry; with this cold weather, my bonnet will hide my face well enough to keep any constables from the inspector's station from recognizing me."

"Why do you want to go there?" Betsy asked curiously.

"It was something the inspector said," Mrs. Jeffries replied. "I can't quite recall his exact words, but the gist of the matter is that there are three doors and a number of windows in the McCourt house. Because of the fire, all of them were open. I'd like to see how easy it would be for someone to gain access to the place without being noticed. That's the sort of thing one must see for oneself."

Smythe looked at her, his expression speculative. "You thinkin' the fire wasn't an accident?"

"I'm trying not to form any conclusion until we've more facts," she replied. "We all know how easy it is to get on the wrong track entirely if we make assumptions too early in the case. But on the other hand, it is possible that whoever killed Daniel McCourt deliberately set the blaze. None of the servants would admit to being anywhere near the area where the fire started."

"Of course they wouldn't," Phyllis blurted out. "I mean, most houses aren't like this one. Our inspector is a decent person who wouldn't toss you into the streets for the least little thing. In all the places I used to work, if you made a mistake that caused any damage, you'd be shown the door right quick and without a reference to boot."

Gerald Witherspoon had been raised in very modest circumstances. He was only rich today because he'd inherited this house and a fortune from his aunt. Consequently, he'd never learned to regard servants as objects to do his bidding and actually treated them as human beings.

"She's right," Ruth agreed. "Just because the servants insist they can account for their whereabouts when the fire supposedly started, that doesn't mean they're telling the truth. Lying to keep a roof over one's head is understandable."

"So you're saying the fire could have been a genuine accident?" the housekeeper countered.

"Shouldn't we treat that as an equal possibility?" Hatchet said. "Perhaps the killer merely took advantage of the circumstances. It wouldn't be the first time a murder was committed because someone saw a golden opportunity and didn't want to waste it."

"We don't know enough yet to be speculatin'," Luty declared. "And every time we start thinkin' too much about the case before we've got all our facts, we git in trouble. So I say we ought to just git out there and find out as much as we can."

Mrs. Jeffries laughed and rose to her feet. "Let's see if we can't learn a few facts today. Everyone be back here by half past four for our afternoon meeting."

There was the sound of chairs scraping as people began to move. Smythe looked at his wife. "Are you goin' to stay 'ere or go 'ome?"

Betsy hesitated, unsure of her welcome in the kitchen now that they had a case. "I don't know. Mrs. Goodge has her sources coming and I—"

"Don't you worry about that," the cook interrupted. "You and that baby stay right here. As a matter of fact, you can help me get these lads talkin'. Wiggins"—she looked toward the coat tree where the footman stood putting on his jacket—"can you go into my room and pull the rocker out here, please?"

"Sure." Wiggins headed off toward the cook's quarters on the far side of the staircase.

"Are you certain I won't be in the way?" Betsy asked.

"Don't be daft, girl. I can use the company," the cook declared.

"Mrs. Williams wasn't as helpful as I'd hoped, but she was sure that none of the servants left the back garden," Wither-spoon admitted as he and Barnes got out of the hansom in front of Arthur Brunel's house on Claringdon Crescent. "But thanks to Haines, we do have a better time line of yesterday's events."

"And he also confirmed that the servants stayed in the garden, so none of them could have seen Mrs. McCourt on the balcony." Barnes paid the driver. "So we'll have to wait till we read the house-to-house reports to see if anyone else might have noticed her. Mind you, even if no one saw the woman, it doesn't mean she wasn't there."

"True, but I do want to verify her statement if possible. I don't think she was overly fond of her husband," the inspector added.

Barnes laughed. "You can say that about half the married women in England, sir, but that doesn't mean they'd do murder." His eyes narrowed as he studied the three-story brown brick home belonging to Arthur Brunel. "Wonder what's going on here, sir."

The house sat back from the street behind a small fenced garden. Two workmen blocked the short walkway leading to the front door; one was bent over a set of sawhorses cutting a piece of wood, and the other was on his knees rummaging through a toolbox. He looked up just then and caught sight of the two policemen.

"Pardon me." The inspector smiled politely at the laborer as he opened the creaking gate and went up the walk. "But do you know if Mr. Arthur Brunel is home?"

The workman stopped sawing as his companion stood up. Both men were now staring at them. "He's in there." The taller of the two men wiped the sawdust off his hands and pointed to the front door. "Just bang the knocker."

But they didn't need to do that, as the door opened and a young housemaid stuck her head out. She looked directly at the inspector. "What do you want, sir?" she asked.

"We'd like to see Mr. Arthur Brunel."

"He's not receivin', sir." She started to close the door, but Barnes slapped his hand against the wood and stopped her from slamming it shut.

"This isn't a social call," he said softly. "Tell Mr. Brunel we need to speak with him. If he doesn't wish us to come into his home, he's more than welcome to accompany us to the station."

Behind him, one of the workmen snickered.

The housemaid's eyes widened with fright. "I'm only doin' what he told me to do," she explained. "I'll leave this open and go tell Mr. Brunel what you've said."

She disappeared, and they could hear the murmur of voices from the interior of the house. A few moments later, she reappeared and ushered them inside. She led them across a tiny foyer, past the staircase, and into a drawing room. "He's in here," she murmured softly before hurrying back to the hall.

They stepped farther inside, both of them blinking as their eyes adjusted to the gloom. But there was enough light to see that the walls were papered in an ugly gray green pattern, the curtains were closed, the carpet was frayed, and the furniture was one step away from being decrepit.

From out of the shadows, a man stood up. "I'm sorry to sound rude, but I suffer from terrible headaches. That's why I had the maid say I wasn't receiving. Please come in and sit down."

"I'm Inspector Gerald Witherspoon, and this is Constable Barnes." The inspector squinted as he moved deeper into the room. "We're sorry to barge in like this, but it's important we speak with you. Are you Arthur Brunel?"

"I am." He waved them toward two chairs by the empty fireplace then sat back down on a love seat opposite. He had red hair, a snub nose, and a face full of freckles. "And I do know why you're here. But I assure you, sir, I had nothing to do with Daniel McCourt's murder."

The inspector sat down and then winced as something hard punched directly into his backside. "You were at the McCourt house yesterday for tea, is that correct?" He heard Barnes groan as he sank into the other chair. He glanced over and saw the constable grimacing in pain.

"Yes, I was invited to the house. But I didn't stay long. No one did. There was a fire in the servants' hall, and the place stank to high heaven. We didn't even get to finish our tea, which was very annoying, as I'd told the maid not to bother to make me any supper."

"Can you please tell us what happened yesterday at the McCourt home?" Barnes asked.

Brunel thought for a moment. "Let me see, I think I arrived right on time, which would have been half past four. I don't know why the tea wasn't set for the proper time of five o'clock, but it wasn't. We were kept waiting for some time in the morning room, of all places, and then the butler escorted everyone to the drawing room."

"Do you know exactly when you went into the drawing room?" The inspector shifted his weight. Ye gods, what on earth was in these chair cushions?

"This is just a guess, but I'd say we went in about four forty," he replied. "I can't say for certain, as I don't have a timepiece and didn't look at the house clocks. But we were only in the drawing room for a couple of minutes before we heard the commotion and found out there was a fire. Daniel McCourt assured us that everything was under control and we should have tea, but within moments it was obvious that would be impossible. The house stank something awful. We sat there trying to pretend we didn't notice the smell when all of a sudden Leon exclaimed that it looked as if his wife was going to faint."

"Mrs. Brunel had taken ill?" Barnes clarified.

Arthur smirked. "That's what Leon said, but Glenda looked perfectly healthy to me. As a matter of fact, I happened to look at her just when he made the comment, and I must say, she looked surprised. But obviously, Elena McCourt couldn't have guests keeling over from the fumes, so she asked us all to leave."

"It was Mrs. McCourt who asked you to go?" Witherspoon said.

"Oh yes," he replied eagerly. "Daniel didn't say a word about the smell. He just sat there smiling and pretending that nothing was wrong. But that's just like him. He ignored Leon's comment completely and kept wittering on about how we'd be so surprised by his latest acquisition. He was quite put out when his wife insisted we all leave. But he could hardly object, as everyone literally bolted for the door the moment it was acceptable to do so. The stench was terrible."

"I understand you and Mr. McCourt weren't on the best of terms?" the inspector said.

"That's putting it mildly, Inspector," he replied. "I haven't spoken to him in over three years. Daniel conspired with my half brother to cheat me out of my share of our father's estate." He waved his hand around the darkened room. "You saw the men outside. They're builders, and because of

McCourt, I'm now forced to turn the top floors of my home into flats. That's the only way I can hang on to my property."

"How did he cheat you, sir?" Barnes asked.

Brunel smiled bitterly. "Daniel McCourt is our cousin. He was also the executor of my father's estate. He and Leon, my half brother, have been friends since childhood. Between the two of them, they managed to ensure that I got a mere pittance of what was coming to me. They cheated me."

"Then why did you accept McCourt's invitation?" Witherspoon asked.

"I almost didn't." He shrugged. "Then I changed my mind. The truth is, I was curious. I was surprised to get an invitation. I went to see what he wanted."

"We understood Mr. McCourt had arranged the tea because he wanted to show off his latest antiquity acquisition," the inspector said as he watched Brunel carefully for his reaction. "Was that not the case?"

"That's exactly what the man wanted. I've no idea why McCourt thought I'd be interested in one of those heathen things, but like a fool I accepted his invitation, thinking that perhaps he might have some other reason for wanting to see me. But it was the same old thing: Daniel showing off and being greedy. As soon as he walked into the drawing room, I realized I shouldn't have come. If the fire hadn't started and stunk up the house, I'd have found an excuse to leave in any case. Mr. Saxon and Mr. Raleigh were glaring at each other, Charles Cochran didn't say a word to anyone, Elena McCourt was ill at ease, and Leon's poor wife kept her eyes on the floor as if she wanted to memorize the pattern in the rug. It was most unpleasant."

"Are you saying that none of the guests wanted to be there?" Barnes asked.

"That's how it appeared to me." Brunel laughed harshly. "But luckily, someone set the house on fire, and that gave everyone an excuse to go. Unfortunately for me, I left my wallet in the drawing room, and I was almost home before I realized what I'd done."

"So you went back to retrieve it?" Witherspoon pressed. "Is that correct?"

"Correct. I'd started to go into the pub nearby, and out of habit, I'd patted the pocket where I keep my wallet. It wasn't there." He sighed. "Then I remembered I'd taken it out at the McCourts' house and instead of putting it back into my coat pocket, I'd laid it down on the arm of the chair. So I had to go all the way back to get it."

"Which door did you use when you went back to the house?" Barnes asked.

Brunel blinked, surprised by the question. "Why, the front one, of course. It was standing wide open, so I went straight inside."

"Did you see anyone?" the inspector asked.

"No, so I started for the drawing room, and then I heard another commotion. Well, you know what I found when I went inside. Mrs. McCourt and the butler were standing there, both of them blubbering so badly I couldn't tell what they were saying. Then I saw him lying there." He looked away. "He was a greedy braggart and a thief, but he didn't deserve to die like that."

Barnes stood up. "You could tell he was dead?"

Brunel didn't seem surprised by the constable's sudden move to vacate his seat. "It was obvious. For God's sake, there was blood everywhere. So I immediately ran for help and fetched the constable from the corner. Oh, sorry about the chairs. The cushions got wet a few months back, and now they've gone hard as rocks."

Witherspoon got up as well. "Why didn't you stay and give us a statement? Surely you must have realized that we'd want to speak with you."

"You are speaking with me," Brunel countered. "I told the constable what had happened, I got my wallet, and then I left. I didn't kill the fellow, so I don't see why I should have had to inconvenience myself any further. I hadn't had my tea, and I was hungry and thirsty. I wanted to go home and have a drink."

Samson, Mrs. Goodge's cat, hissed and swiped his paw at Phyllis as she came out of the hallway. But she dodged around the stool where the nasty old tabby perched and went into the kitchen.

"Smack his paws when he does that," Betsy instructed. She was sitting in the rocker that Wiggins had pulled next to the table.

Phyllis cringed visibly and then continued on toward the coat tree. "Oh, I couldn't do that. I don't like hittin'. Even an old mean one like him doesn't deserve to be whacked about." She reached for her jacket.

"I didn't mean for you to beat him," Betsy said as she rocked the baby. She hadn't missed the way Phyllis had reacted. "But a little tap to let him know he's doing wrong won't hurt him."

"Mrs. Goodge loves him dearly, doesn't she?" Phyllis slipped her coat on and reached for her woolen hat. Wiggins had brought the animal home at the end of one of their cases. Samson had been the pet of a murder victim, and the footman had claimed the cat would have starved to death if left at the household of his previous owner.

"Indeed she does," Betsy said. "So we all put up with the nasty old thing." She noticed that Phyllis' shoulders were hunched and her fingers fumbled with the buttons as she fastened her coat. "You're scared, aren't you?"

She didn't reply for a moment, and then she raised her chin. Her eyes were filled with tears. "I'm not goin' to be very good at this; I know it. Everyone's been so nice to me that I'm scared of lettin' you all down. But I'm not like you. I don't know how to put people at their ease and get them chattin'.'."

Betsy weighed her words carefully before she spoke. No one really knew very much about Phyllis' past except that she'd been out and working for her living since she was twelve. She rarely spoke of her family and made only the vaguest of comments about her previous employers. Betsy suspected the girl had gone through some dreadful experiences. Someone had made her feel both worthless and stupid. Of course she wasn't either of those things, but Betsy knew the only way Phyllis would get over her fear was to get out in the world and see for herself that she was just as capable and smart as everyone else at Upper Edmonton Gardens. "When we first started helping with the inspector's cases, I didn't know how to do it, either," Betsy said as she eased the now sleeping baby lower into her lap and propped her elbows on the arms of the chair.

"But you're pretty and you've a nice way about you." Phyllis swiped at her cheeks.

"You're pretty, too," Betsy countered. "And you've a lovely smile. But you've got to have faith in yourself. You're a nice, intelligent, clever girl. You've just got to learn to trust yourself."

"But what if I don't find out anythin'?" she wailed softly.

"Then you'll go out again tomorrow, and you'll keep trying until you figure out how to do it."

"But what if I can't do that?" she persisted. "I hate the

idea that I'm goin' to be the one that can't contribute, and you'll all be ever so polite about it, but I'll still be a failure."

"No, you won't. We've all got faith in you and your abilities. Nell's bells, you're the best forger I've ever seen," Betsy said, reminding her of how her talent had helped solve their last case. "You don't have to be me, Phyllis. You need to be you. Just get out there and do your best; that's the only thing people expect of you."

"Let's hope Mr. and Mrs. Leon Brunel have as much to tell us as Arthur Brunel," Witherspoon murmured as he and Barnes waited in the drawing room of the elegant, five-story red-brick house in Kensington.

Barnes chuckled and gazed at his surroundings. "We did get an earful, didn't we, sir? It's too bad we already knew that Arthur Brunel thought he'd been cheated by the victim. After seeing the difference between his house and this one, I suspect he might be right."

The room was painted a pale cream. White-and-gold-striped curtains were draped across the four windows on the far wall, giving the entire assemblage a stagelike effect. The floors were an intricate parquet wood pattern covered with elaborate Persian carpets. A fireplace with a black marble mantel graced the opposite wall. The furniture was upholstered in various shades of white, gold, black, and crimson. In one corner there stood a four-drawer cabinet with stylized flowers carved on the panels. Directly above that were shelves containing ceramic horses, glazed earthenware pots, incredibly bright vases in a multitude of colors, and, on the very top shelf, a sculpture of a three-tier tower in a brilliant iridescent green.

Witherspoon was gawking at the room as well. His attention fastened on a row of chests and cabinets on the wall opposite the fireplace. He wasn't certain what they might be called, but he knew they were old, valuable, and from the Far East. "Yes, the difference between the two homes is rather startling, isn't it?" he muttered. "But perhaps Mr. Leon Brunel had alternative sources of income besides his inheritance."

On the left side of the fireplace, a door that neither policeman had noticed suddenly opened, and a middle-aged man with thin brown hair, fair skin, and a sharp nose appeared. "I'm Leon Brunel," he announced. "My housekeeper has said you're the police."

Witherspoon smiled politely and extended his hand. "I'm Inspector Witherspoon, and this is Constable Barnes."

Brunel shook hands and then waved both policemen toward the sofa and chair. "Please sit down."

"I'm sure you know why we're here," the inspector said as he and the constable took a seat.

"I do, but I don't know what you think I can tell you. Daniel was alive and well when my wife and I left," he replied.

"Did you notice anyone suspicious hanging about the neighborhood?" Barnes took out his notebook and pencil.

Brunel shook his head. "No, but I wasn't paying attention to the people on the street." He frowned. "Come to think of it, I do recall seeing a rather odd-looking man standing at the corner."

"Can you describe this person?" Witherspoon said.

"Oh, I didn't really look all that closely, but he had bushy black and gray curly hair. It hung almost to his shoulders, and he was wearing some rather disreputable-looking garments, a very long gray overcoat and a greenish colored cap of some sort. His attire looked filthy."

"You seem to have noticed quite a bit about the fellow," the constable said dryly.

Brunel gave him a sharp look but said nothing.

"Where was the man in relation to the McCourt house?" Witherspoon asked.

"He was on the corner of the Kensington High Street and Victoria Gardens." Brunel pulled a gold pocket watch out of his vest pocket, flipped it open, and noted the time with a frown.

"When did you see this person?" the inspector asked. "Was it before you entered the McCourts' or afterwards, when you were leaving?"

"It was when we first arrived. I spotted the man when our cab came around the corner."

"Who was the first of the guests to leave the McCourt home?" Barnes asked.

"We were," he replied. "As I said, the stench was dreadful. I knew it was a bit rude, but I was afraid my wife would become ill from the smell, so I got the both of us out of there as soon as possible."

The door from the hallway opened, and a woman stepped into the room.

"Glenda, what are you doing?" Brunel said irritably. "I told you I would handle this."

The two policemen had risen and were now openly gaping at her. Her hair was dark brown and arranged in a becoming style that framed the perfect bones of her face. She had green eyes with long black lashes, full pink lips, and just the palest hint of color on the ivory skin of her high cheekbones. She wore a maroon and gray day dress that emphasized her small waist and womanly figure.

Witherspoon blinked as he realized he was being rude, but she was one of the most beautiful women he'd ever seen. "I take it you are Mrs. Brunel," he said as she approached.

She smiled and extended her hand. "Yes, and you're the

famous Inspector Witherspoon. I heard the butler announce you."

By this time, Leon Brunel had gotten to his feet. "Glenda, you needn't have bothered to come down here. I can handle this matter."

She ignored him and extended her hand to Barnes. "You must be Constable Barnes. I've heard of you as well."

Grinning with pleasure, Barnes returned her handshake. "Thank you, ma'am, but we just do our duty."

Witherspoon stared at his constable. Barnes was actually blushing!

Still ignoring her husband, Glenda Brunel waved at the seats the policemen had just vacated. "Do sit down. I've ordered tea to be served."

"This isn't a social call," Brunel snapped as he flopped back into his seat. "There was no need to do that."

"Don't be rude, Leon." She took the spot next to Witherspoon. "These men perform a valuable service for this country, and I, for one, am going to cooperate in any way that I can."

The door opened again, and a maid wheeled a tea trolley into the room.

"Bring it over here," she ordered the girl. She turned to the dumbstruck policemen and gave them a brilliant smile. "I'll pour. Now, how do you gentlemen take your tea?"

Wiggins increased his pace as he reached the corner of the Kensington High Street. He'd gotten to the McCourt house just as a young lad whom he thought might be the footman had trotted out of the servants' entrance. Unfortunately for Wiggins, just at that moment, Constable Griffiths had come out of a house a few doors down. Wiggins had jumped behind a postbox to keep from being seen. By the time it had been safe to move, the lad had disappeared around the corner. Wiggins had raced after him, but there was so much foot traffic he had the devil's own time finding him. But now that he had him in his sights, he was determined to follow.

The footman went into a chemist's shop. Wiggins hurried over and watched through the window at the door. The boy stood in front of the counter with his hand extended and his other hand pointing at his knuckles. The clerk nodded, turned, and pulled a small, round tin off the shelf.

"Excuse me," a woman's voice boomed in his ear. "I'd like to go inside."

Wiggins backed away from the door, ducking his head apologetically at the frowning matron. "Sorry, ma'am. I was just wonderin' what was takin' my brother so long in the shop."

The lady swept past him without another word. But the encounter gave Wiggins an idea, and he hurriedly positioned himself so anyone coming out of the shop couldn't see him. A few seconds later, the bell jingled. Wiggins waited a second or two, then charged forward, banging into the lad with enough force to send him flying to the ground.

"Cor blimey, I'm so sorry. I didn't see ya." He extended a hand to the youngster, who glared up at him from the pavement.

"Watch where you're goin'," the boy muttered, but he took the proffered hand.

"I'm so sorry," Wiggins said. "This was all my fault. Are ya alright? Are ya hurt?"

"I'm fine," he said as he dusted the dirt off the back of his dark brown trousers. "I'm more worried about my clothes. If they're torn any, I'll be in for it."

"They're fine. I don't see any tears," Wiggins said quickly. "But I do feel a right idiot. Let me make it up to ya."

"Make it up to me?" He eyed him warily. "What are you talkin' about?"

Wiggins had an answer at the ready. It was a trick he'd used on other occasions, and it usually worked. "It were my fault for knockin' you down, lad. It's just I've 'ad such good news it sent me wantin' to fly." He chuckled. "Let me buy ya a cup of tea and a sweet bun. There's a café just over there. I feel real bad, and I'm superstitious, too. It'd be a bad omen if I did somethin' wrong when I've 'ad such good news."

"Can I 'ave any kind of bun I want?" He licked his lips.

Wiggins knew he had him. "You can even 'ave two of 'em if you like. Come on, it's just up 'ere."

A few moments later, they were sitting at a window table at the café.

"My name is Albert Jones," Wiggins said conversationally as he pushed the plate of pastry toward the lad. "What's yours?"

"I'm Duncan Malloy." His eyes widened and he smacked his lips. "Are all those for us?"

"They are," Wiggins assured him. "'Elp yourself. I told ya, I 'ad good news today and I'm glad I've found someone to celebrate with. If I'd not run into you, I'd be on my own."

Duncan reached for a treacle tart and took a huge mouthful. "What kinda news?"

"I'm goin' to Canada," Wiggins lied. "My uncle sent me a ticket and some travel money. He owns a hotel in Halifax. I'm to work for 'im, and that means I'll never 'ave to bow and scrape to the likes of the toffs in this town again. I've been workin' as a footman since I was ten, and I'm bloomin' sick of it. But I gave notice today, and they were right annoyed that I was leavin'."

Duncan swallowed his food. "You're lucky. I wish I 'ad

an uncle like that. I'm a footman, too, and I bloomin' well 'ate it."

"Is your guv a mean one, then?" Wiggins asked. He was a bit ashamed of himself, but he told himself he was lying to the boy in the service of a good cause.

" 'E's not so much mean as 'e is real strict." Duncan licked the crumbs from his fingers. "I mean, 'e was real strict." He stared at a sticky bun covered with walnuts.

"Was?" Wiggins repeated. "Did somethin' 'appen to 'im?" He jerked his chin at the plate of treats. "Go on, then, 'ave another one," he ordered.

Duncan snatched the bun as if he were afraid it might disappear. "Somethin' 'appened, alright. Mr. McCourt was murdered yesterday. We've 'ad the police around and everythin'."

Wiggins feigned surprise. "Murdered? 'Ave they caught who did it?"

Duncan took a bite, shook his head, chewed, and swallowed. "Nah, no one knows. But Mr. McCourt 'ad his throat cut with one of them swords he was always collectin'. Mind you, it was real scary, and just thinkin' about it gives me nightmares. I think it's givin' all of us bad dreams. I 'eard Annie—she's one of the maids—tellin' Mrs. Williams, the housekeeper she was sure she 'eard someone walkin' out in the side passage last night."

"Maybe Annie should tell this to the police," Wiggins suggested.

Duncan nodded eagerly. "That's what I thought, but when Mrs. Williams suggested it to the mistress, she said Annie was bein' fanciful and nervous because of the murder."

"How would she know that?"

"Mrs. McCourt's room is just above the passageway between the houses," he explained. "And she claimed she'd not slept a wink all night and she'd not 'eard nothin'."

CHAPTER 4

Phyllis took a deep breath, gathered her courage, and stepped into the greengrocer's. Her chat with Betsy had given her renewed confidence, and she'd taken Betsy's advice and walked the entire length of the street, peeking into the shops to find the youngest clerks. The girl standing behind the potato bin didn't look more than fifteen. She was thin and pale with crooked teeth and hunched shoulders. She wore a frayed pair of fingerless red mittens on her hands and a limp green scarf wound around her neck. Phyllis hoped she was the chatty type.

"May I help you, miss?" the clerk asked as Phyllis approached.

"Yes, thank you." Phyllis gave her a wide smile but got only a somber stare in return. "I'll have half a dozen of those rutabagas." She pointed to a bin on the wall.

"Yes, miss." She grabbed a sheet of newspaper from underneath the counter. With a deft turn of her hand, she twisted the paper into a cone shape and began tossing the vegetables into the center.

Phyllis cleared her throat. "Er, I'm wonderin' if you know of a family named McCourt that live near here."

"Never 'eard of 'em." She looked over her shoulder. "Do you want anything else, miss?"

"I'll have a cabbage," she replied. "Are you sure you've never heard of them? They're supposed to live nearby, and they do their shoppin' in this neighborhood."

"I've just said I've never 'eard of 'em."

Phyllis felt tears spring into her eyes. She knew she wasn't going to be good at this, and later this afternoon, when the others were all there, they'd know she couldn't do it. Embarrassed, she ducked her head and stared at the countertop.

"Wait a minute. Are they the people that had the murder?" the girl said.

Phyllis lifted her chin and noted that her thin face had softened. "That's them. My mistress gave me a letter of condolence to take to the house, and I can't remember the address. She's goin' to sack me if I don't get that ruddy letter to Mrs. McCourt." She was making it up as she went along.

"Look, I'm sorry. I know what it's like to work for hard people." She glanced over her shoulder toward a curtain on the wall behind her and then back at Phyllis. "I didn't mean to be rude before," she said, dropping her voice to a whisper, "but I've gotten in trouble for bein' too familiar with the customers. Mrs. Beaman will have my guts for garters if she catches me chattin' with you."

"I don't want to get you in trouble," Phyllis blurted out.

"It should be alright today. She went upstairs with one of her headaches, and that means she'll have gone to bed by now. The McCourts shop here, alright. Leastways their household does. I've never seen either of them myself, but I heard that Mr. McCourt had his throat cut."

"That's what I heard, too." Phyllis leaned forward eagerly. "I don't suppose you know their address?" she asked, remembering to stay in character with the lie she'd told.

The girl grinned, and her face was transformed. "Number twelve Victoria Gardens. My brother does the delivery to the house. He says that it's no wonder Mr. McCourt was murdered; he's a right nasty fellow. Their footman was here yesterday gettin' a bucket of wet sand, and he was ever in such a state. We were real busy, and he had to wait his turn. We're the only ones that brings in sand, you see."

Phyllis wasn't certain she did, but not wanting to stop the flow of words, she merely nodded.

"Duncan's a nice lad, and I could tell by his expression he was worried. I asked him what was wrong, and he told me that the McCourt house was in a right old mess. He said Mr. and Mrs. McCourt was fightin' like cats and dogs and that one of the housemaids was certain she was goin' to get the sack."

"I wonder what the McCourts were fightin' about." Phyllis hoped she was saying something that would keep the girl talking.

"I don't know." There was a scraping sound from behind the curtain, and an expression of alarm crossed the girl's face. "Let me get you that cabbage," she said loudly as footsteps pounded down a set of stairs from the inner reaches of the building.

"Thank you," Phyllis said. "And I'll have a pound of carrots as well," she added just as the door opened and a stout, dark-haired woman with a stern visage stepped into the shop.

* * *

Witherspoon held the silver-and-pink-patterned teacup with care. It was of the thinnest, finest porcelain and looked as if a good sneeze could shatter the delicate china into pieces. "Thank you, Mrs. Brunel. Did you see anyone suspicious looking when you were either arriving at the McCourt home or when you were leaving?"

She shook her head. "No, Inspector, I didn't."

"Surely you remember that man I pointed out when we came around the corner to Victoria Gardens," Leon said to his wife. "He was most certainly suspicious looking."

"Of course he wasn't," she replied. "We've seen the man on previous occasions. Don't you remember that we saw him when we went there for luncheon in October? I think he must live in the neighborhood."

Leon frowned. "Yes, of course, dear, you're right. We have seen him before." He glanced at Barnes. "That's probably why I was able to describe him so easily."

The constable smiled noncommittally. "What time did you get to the McCourt house yesterday?"

"We arrived a few minutes after half past four," Leon replied.

"Were the other guests there when you arrived?" Witherspoon asked, even though he already knew the answer.

"Everyone else was in the morning room when we got there," Leon replied. "As a matter of fact, the room was so crowded, I stepped out so that it would be more comfortable for the others."

"It wasn't that uncomfortable," Glenda Brunel interjected. "There were plenty of chairs, and we weren't in there more than five minutes."

"Oh dear, you've caught me." Leon chuckled indulgently. "Alright, I'll confess that I wanted to have a closer look at the vase in the foyer. It is a Ming and it is exquisite."

"Are you a collector as well, sir?" Barnes asked.

"Indeed, I am," Leon replied. "As a matter of fact, my interest in Oriental art and artifacts superseded Daniel's. I've been collecting for years. He was always interested, but he wasn't able to afford it until after he married Mrs. McCourt."

"And now his collection is bigger than yours," Glenda added as she smiled sweetly at her husband. "That's rather unfair, don't you think?"

Leon shrugged. "Not really." He looked at Witherspoon. "Daniel McCourt was our family solicitor before his marriage."

"He's also a cousin," Glenda supplied.

"How long have he and Mrs. McCourt been married?" Barnes asked curiously. He'd gotten the impression from the servants that the McCourts had been married for a number of years.

"They celebrated their fifteenth anniversary this past October," Glenda said quickly. "But it is common knowledge that it was Mrs. McCourt's fortune that allowed Daniel to indulge himself in his passion for collecting."

"Now, now, Glenda. You mustn't speak ill of the dead. Daniel's behavior was no different than most men of our class." He smiled ruefully. "He's been a good husband to his wife and provided her with everything."

"He hasn't provided her with anything," she snapped. "It was her family's money that has kept them all these years. If Daniel hadn't married her, he'd still be a mediocre solicitor working for Cochran and Stevens."

"Please, dear." Leon patted his wife's hand. "Let's not be uncharitable. He's been a good husband to Elena."

Glenda Brunel looked as if she wanted to continue the argument, but she changed her mind and clamped her mouth shut.

"Cochran and Stevens. Would Charles Cochran be affiliated with them?" Witherspoon inquired.

"Definitely," Leon answered. "Charles' father started the firm, and as far as I know, Charles is still with them. Daniel resigned from the firm after his marriage."

"Mr. Cochran and Daniel McCourt stayed in contact with each other after he left the firm . . ." The inspector took a sip of tea. "Is that correct?"

"I presume so," Leon replied with a shrug. "He'd been invited to tea."

"I don't think they remained friends," Glenda argued. "We've never seen him at a social function at the McCourt house."

"He was at the funeral for Elena's late aunt," Leon countered. "And at the reception."

"Of course he was there. Charles Cochran is the Herron family solicitor, and the funeral reception was held at the Herron home, not the McCourt house." She smiled smugly. "As a matter of fact, Daniel McCourt wasn't even present when Natalie Herron's will was read. He was specifically told he couldn't go into the Herron drawing room when Charles read out the will. He had to wait outside in the garden."

Leon Brunel drew back slightly, his gaze on his wife. "How on earth do you know that?"

"How do you think I know?" She laughed. "Elena told me when we were at lunch earlier this week. We're friends, you know."

"How long were you in the morning room?" Witherspoon asked.

"I don't know, exactly, but it was no more than five or perhaps six minutes," Glenda said. "Then we went into the drawing room."

"Did either of you notice any mistletoe hanging from the doorframe between the drawing room and the study?" Witherspoon asked.

"I certainly didn't." Leon sniffed dismissively. "And I can't imagine Daniel allowing such a heathen practice in his household."

"I didn't see any, either, but I don't understand how you can be so sure that Daniel wouldn't have allowed it," Glenda said to her husband.

"Because he hated nonsense like that," Leon shot back. "If there was any mistletoe about the place, it was put up by either Elena or one of the servants."

"You don't know that." She glared at him. "The rest of the house was beautifully decorated. There was even one of those Christmas trees."

"Lots of households have a tree," Leon muttered. "If I'd known you were so fond of them, I'd have had one put up here."

"I don't want one," she replied. "They're more trouble than they are worth."

"Did Mr. or Mrs. McCourt explain why they wanted you all to go into the drawing room at the same time?" Barnes asked. He knew it couldn't have been because the tree was lighted. At that point the footman wasn't back with the sand. "Was it just to show off the Christmas decorations?"

"I don't think so," Leon said.

"You know very well why, Leon." Glenda crossed her arms over her chest. "Tell the truth. Daniel wanted to make his big announcement. He'd bought something for his collection and wanted to show it off and—"

"Glenda, please," Leon interrupted. "The poor man is dead. Let's not cast aspersions on his character."

"Did he say what it was he'd acquired?" Barnes asked

quickly. "You're not the first to mention that Mr. McCourt wanted to show something off, but thus far, no one knows what that something might have been."

"I don't know. Everyone left before he could finish telling us." Glenda's brows drew together in a confused frown. "Have you spoken to Jerome Raleigh? He appraises everything before Daniel buys. Surely he'd know what the object was."

"Thank you, Mrs. Brunel, we'll do that." Witherspoon glanced at Mr. Brunel. "Do you know?"

"I'm not certain, but I think it might have been a Hwando sword. I'd heard that Daniel had only recently bought one and they're somewhat rare. But I can't be sure that's what he wanted to show us."

Barnes glanced at the inspector, who gave the barest nod of his head. "It was a Hwando that was used to murder him," he said.

"Oh dear God." Leon closed his eyes briefly. "The papers only said it was a sword. I'd no idea it was the Hwando."

"You didn't know the Hwando was hanging in his study?" the constable pressed. "The doors between the study and the drawing room were wide open."

"I know that, Constable, but Daniel kept his swords displayed on the wall in the study, and one didn't go there without an invitation," Leon replied. "You couldn't see it from where we were in the drawing room, and I've not been in his study for months."

Witherspoon put his cup down on the table. "How long were you actually at tea before the fire broke out?"

"We'd only just started," Glenda said. "Elena had poured and the maid had lifted the stack of plates off the bottom rack of the trolley when all of a sudden there were people shouting from below stairs. Naturally, Daniel and Elena excused themselves and went to see what was wrong. They came back a few moments later and announced there had been a small fire by the back staircase but that everything was now fine." She smiled ruefully. "But within five minutes, it became obvious that it wasn't over. The room seemed to fill with the most dreadful smell."

"Was it paraffin?" Barnes asked.

She frowned prettily. "At first, that's what it seemed to be, but then it wasn't."

"I'm sorry, Mrs. Brunel, but I don't understand exactly what you mean," the inspector said.

"It's difficult to explain, but it was almost as though there were two separate odors, and both of them were paraffin. At first we all pretended not to notice, but honestly, within a few moments, it simply couldn't be ignored. I felt so sorry for Elena; she was so humiliated, and I know we're not supposed to speak ill of the dead, but Daniel only made the situation worse. He kept pretending that nothing was wrong."

"But my dear, what else could he have done?" Leon asked reasonably.

"He could have kept quiet long enough for her to do something. But he kept talking and talking about what a wonderful acquisition he'd made." She gave a discreet, ladylike snort. "Elena finally interrupted him after you commented that I appeared to be about to faint. She stood up and ordered the maid to open the windows. Then she apologized for the awful smell and told us we could leave. Well, it was dreadful, so everyone got up and started for the hallway to get their hats and coats."

"What was Mr. McCourt doing at this point?" Witherspoon asked.

"He was upset," Leon said, "but trying hard not to let it show."

"And that's when everyone left?" Barnes pressed.

"As I've already said, we were the first to leave, so I can't say when the others might have gone."

"Arthur Brunel and Mr. Saxon were right behind us." Glenda gave her husband a sharp look. "We heard them talking."

"Yes, but we didn't actually see them leave," he argued. "Unless, of course, you looked back. Did you?"

"Why would I?" she said irritably. "But we did hear them."

"Did you summon a hansom or walk home?" Witherspoon asked.

"We went to the corner and got a cab. I put my wife in it and presumably"—he gave her a quick, assessing look— "she came straight home."

Witherspoon glanced at the constable. "You didn't return home with Mrs. Brunel?"

"No, I had an errand of my own to run," Leon said. "I'd planned on doing it this morning, but as our social engagement ended so abruptly, I decided to take care of the matter immediately."

"Where did you go, sir?" Witherspoon asked. He noticed that Mrs. Brunel was watching her husband closely.

"I went to see my solicitor, Inspector." He broke off and smiled at his wife. "I had some rather urgent business."

Glenda Brunel stared solemnly back at her husband.

Witherspoon wasn't an expert on marital relationships, but he sensed that something wasn't right between these two. But that wasn't his concern. He turned his attention to Leon. "You do understand we'll need to know the name of your solicitor and the time you arrived home last night."

"He got home at eight o'clock, just in time for dinner," Glenda said. "And the solicitor's name is Jonathan Harwood. He has offices at number six Warwick Way in Pimlico." Even though she was answering the inspector, her eyes never left her husband's face.

Smythe entered the Dirty Duck Pub and stopped inside the door. It was just past opening time, and the place wasn't crowded yet. He scanned the room and spotted his quarry sitting alone at a table near the fireplace. He headed toward him.

Blimpey Groggins glanced up and grinned broadly as he saw Smythe. Blimpey was a short, portly fellow with ginger-colored hair, red cheeks, and a round face. "Hello, hello! It's always nice to see one of my favorite customers. Are ya here for business or are ya just stoppin' in to wish me a Merry Christmas?"

Smythe raised an eyebrow as he yanked out the stool and sat. "Come on now, Blimpey, pull the other one. You know good and well why I'm 'ere."

"'Course I do, but that don't mean we can't be civil and wish each other the best of the holiday season." Groggins held up two fingers toward the barman. "You'll 'ave a pint. So, yer guv caught the McCourt case."

"'E did. Seems like every Christmas 'e gets a real tangled one to sort out." Smythe wasn't surprised that Blimpey already knew why he'd come. It was Blimpey's job to know everything that went on in London. He was an information dealer, and Smythe was one of his best customers.

Groggins had once been a thief, with second-story work as his specialty. But after an unfortunate fall from an upper-floor balcony that resulted in a painful dog bite to his backside, he'd decided to find another way to make a living. Blessed with a phenomenal memory, Blimpey realized that with a bit of thought and effort on his part, he could put his ability to good use and make a handsome livelihood. He had sources in all the police stations, the courts, the financial district, the different commercial districts, the banks, the docks, and even the newspaper offices. His clients ranged from insurance companies looking to make sure a fire had been an accident to thieves wanting to know whether their latest fence was trustworthy. Blimpey treated all of his clients with both discretion and respect while charging them an arm and a leg. Smythe wasn't lazy, and he did do a fair bit of investigating himself, but his philosophy was that it would be foolish not to avail himself of an expert when he could well afford to do so.

As a much younger man, Smythe had been the coachman for Euphemia Witherspoon, the inspector's late aunt. He'd saved his wages and, with the blessings of his employer, gone to Australia to try his luck at prospecting and his luck had been very good. He'd come back to London with more money than he'd ever dreamed of and stopped in to pay his respects to his former employer. He'd found Euphemia Witherspoon lying in a sickbed. By her side was a very young footman named Wiggins, the only one of her many servants trying to take care of her. Smythe sent him for a doctor, but not before the lad had told him that the other servants had been stealing from their mistress and selling the goods. Smythe had used the threat of the law to send them packing. The doctor did his best, but despite his professional care, the woman was dying. Before she passed away, she'd made Smythe promise to stay on in the house and ensure that her nephew, Gerald Witherspoon, wasn't taken advantage of as she'd been. Smythe had honored that promise, and in doing so, he'd ended up richer in family and friends than he'd ever thought possible.

The barman put their pints on the table, and Smythe nodded his thanks. He waited till the barman was out of earshot before he continued speaking. "I've got a list of names for you," he began.

"You mean the guests that 'ad come for tea." Blimpey picked up his beer and took a sip.

"Cor blimey, you are good." He laughed. "But you knew I'd be comin' round, didn't you?"

"As soon as I got the word yer inspector 'ad been called to the murder house, I 'ad my people on it. But you'll be wantin' to know what I know about the victim, Daniel McCourt."

Smythe nodded.

"Before he married his missus, he was a solicitor at Cochran and Stevens. He wasn't a very good one, either. Then about fifteen years ago, he up and married Elena Herron. Her family 'ad money and settled a pretty penny on them when they wed. He quit the firm right before the weddin' and 'asn't done a day's work since." He took another quick sip of his drink. "Spends his time collectin' Oriental art and antiques. That's all I know, but like I said, I've already got my people workin' on findin' out more. Now, what are these names you've got for me?"

"You mean you don't know who was there?" Smythe grinned and took another swallow from his glass.

"I know that Nicholas Saxon was one of the guests, but my source wasn't able to get the rest of the names. I did find out somethin' interestin' about Saxon. You'll never guess who he was engaged to before she up and married someone else."

He put his beer down. "Elena McCourt?"

"Nah, she's a bit too old for him. Saxon was fixin' to marry one of London's real beauties, a Miss Glenda Norris. But he made the mistake of introducin' said Miss Norris to Leon Brunel at an exhibition of Chinese art, and before ya could say dance a jig and play a tune, she'd broken off with Saxon and her engagement to Brunel was announced."

"'Ard luck for Saxon. Did 'e make a fuss about it?"

Blimpey shrugged. "My source didn't know that, but even if 'e did, it weren't Leon Brunel that were murdered; it was Daniel McCourt. But I know 'ow you and yer lot like to know every little detail, so I thought I'd give ya this one for free. Now, tell me who else was at the tea party?"

"Mr. and Mrs. Leon Brunel, Arthur Brunel, Charles Cochran, and Jerome Raleigh," Smythe replied.

"Raleigh?" Blimpey laughed. "God, I've not 'eard that name in donkey's years."

"You know 'im?"

Blimpey nodded. "Oh yes, I know all about Jerome Raleigh. 'E used to be an appraiser at Goodison and Bright. But they sacked 'im for takin' a bribe. It seems that for the right price, Raleigh would underestimate the value of a piece, thus allowin' John Q. Public, or to put it another way, the person that 'ad given 'im the lolly, to pick up said piece for a pittance of its real worth."

"Are you jokin'? He's a ruddy crook?"

"I'd not trust the bloke farther than I could toss 'im. If a man can take a bribe once, 'e can do it twice."

Smythe raised an eyebrow but said nothing.

Blimpey gasped. "Don't look at me like that! I'll 'ave ya know I was a damned sight more honorable than Jerome Raleigh. I was a thief," he insisted. "And bein' a thief is different than takin' bribes. It's a matter of trust."

"Blimpey, don't take me so seriously. I didn't mean to offend—"

"But I do take it seriously," he interrupted. "Once you 'ire me to find out somethin' for ya, I wouldn't take any money, no matter 'ow much I was offered, to give ya false information."

Smythe held up his hand. "Come on, Blimpey. You know I'd trust you with my life. Everyone knows that once you give your word, it's set in stone."

Blimpey's expression softened. "Ta, I'm a bit raw about my past. My Nell tells me that 'alf the ones in the House of Lords 'ave their seat 'cause their ancestors robbed, raped, and murdered the poor, but as long as they were doin' it in the name of the King, that was supposed to make it right."

"Your Nell's a smart lady," Smythe said quickly.

Blimpey waved his hand impatiently. "I know, I know, that's why I married 'er. But what the toffs once did doesn't make me feel any better about what I once 'ad to do."

"We all 'ave a few bits in our past that we feel bad about," Smythe murmured. "But we do what we got to do to survive in this old world. Now, back to business. How come the auction house didn't 'ave Raleigh arrested?"

Blimpey laughed. "Cor blimey, for a man of the world you're an innocent. They kept it real quiet; made 'im leave London and promise to keep 'is mouth shut about the incident. If people found out the auction house 'ad been usin' appraisers that weren't honest, their business would dry up in a heartbeat. Goodison and Bright is one of the oldest auction houses in England, and they value their reputation."

"I see what you mean." Smythe frowned. "But if they made him promise to leave London, what's 'e doin' back here?"

"Well, this 'appened ten years ago, so maybe he thought the statute of limitations would protect 'im. 'E was never stood in the dock, so the crown weren't involved, and there were never any formal charges filed," Blimpey explained. "But this is all speculation. I'll find out what I can about 'im and what 'e's been up to lately."

Smythe drained his glass and stood up. "I'll check back in a couple of days."

"I'll 'ave somethin' for ya," Blimpey said. "You can count on it."

Nicholas Saxon lived in a five-story row house on a small street off the Edgware Road. He'd obviously been anticipating their visit, as the door opened only seconds after Barnes banged the knocker.

"Do come in, gentlemen." He stepped back, opening the door wide. He was a tall man in his late thirties with wavy brown hair, brown eyes, and full lips. His nose was straight and his gaze steady.

"Are you Mr. Nicholas Saxon?" Witherspoon asked.

"I am, and you're the police. Please come in. I've been expecting you."

Witherspoon introduced himself and the constable as they stepped inside the house.

The foyer was a good ten feet by ten feet with a patterned parquet floor covered by a huge, brightly colored Persian carpet. Against the wall was a long, low table with ornately carved legs. Three vases were arranged along the top. Perfectly balanced in shape, pattern, and color, the display caught the gaze of both policemen.

Saxon smiled proudly. "That's celadon pottery from the Joseon dynasty. Exquisite, isn't it?"

"They're very beautiful," Witherspoon said.

"They are three of the best pieces from my collection." Saxon stepped around the policemen and moved down the hall past the wide staircase to a set of double doors. "The drawing room is through here. We'll be more comfortable there."

The drawing room was as beautiful as the foyer; again, a huge, multicolored exotic carpet covered the parquet floor, the walls were painted a pale gold, and brilliant red curtains hung at the three long windows. Two tall matching vases in red and yellow stood sentry by the fireplace, and between them was a bronze-colored fire screen with a copper-colored dragon etched on the surface of the metal. But as they moved toward the settee, Witherspoon noticed the faint outline of empty spots on the wall that hinted of paintings and portraits coming down and being sold off. Exotic Oriental statues, ceramics, cabinets, and chests were placed decoratively about the room. A brilliant blue and white tea set graced the top shelf of a three-rung cabinet, but he noticed that the bottom shelf was bare and the middle shelf held only a tiny brass figure of a sitting Buddha.

Saxon sat down in a chair opposite them. "Would you care for a cup of tea?"

"No, thank you," Witherspoon replied. "We're sorry to disturb you, but as I'm sure you're aware, Daniel McCourt was murdered yesterday."

Saxon smiled faintly. "I'm aware of it, Inspector. But I don't know what I can tell you about the man's death. He was alive when I left."

"How long have you known Mr. McCourt?" Barnes asked.

"I met him at an exhibit of Oriental art and furnishings at the British Museum about five years ago."

"You've been friends since then?" Witherspoon asked.

Saxon smiled faintly. "We were never friends, Inspector. My relationship with McCourt is, or I should say was, one of business."

Barnes looked up from his notebook. "What kind of business, sir?"

Saxon sighed heavily. "Oriental art and artifacts. He buys them; I sell them."

"You're a dealer, then?" Barnes was fairly sure the man wasn't, but he wanted to get the fellow talking a bit more freely.

"No, I'm not. What I am is broke." He laughed harshly. "My family has been in the Far East import/export business for years, and we'd done very well for ourselves. But times being what they are, for a number of reasons, some of them our fault, some of them no one's fault, the business began to fail. But you're not here to learn about my family history. What is important is that my uncle collected Oriental art and artifacts. My family hasn't been blessed with many members of my generation, so when he died, I inherited everything of his. But by then, the business was bankrupt, and all I had left was this house and his collection." He smiled sardonically. "I've been selling it off for the past five years. That's how I came to be acquainted with McCourt. He bought a number of items from me."

"Did he acquire any swords from you?" the inspector asked.

"Yes, two; one was a Japanese Katana and the other was a Chinese Won dynasty piece."

"You didn't sell him a Hwando?" Witherspoon hoped he was pronouncing the word correctly.

Saxon's eyes widened in surprise. "Certainly not. I didn't even know he had a Hwando."

"We think he might have only recently acquired it," Barnes said as he looked up from his notebook.

"I knew he'd acquired something; that's why we were

there yesterday. But the way he went on about it, I'm surprised it was just a Hwando."

Witherspoon's eyes narrowed. "Isn't that a valuable piece?"

"It's valuable, yes, but it's not terribly rare. I've two in my collection that I've deliberately held back from selling because there's a number of them on the market right now. You must understand, Inspector, it's only a small group of us that collect or sell Oriental artifacts. Most of us know one another, and we know what's being offered. The way Daniel was going on and on about his latest acquisition made one think he'd acquired a piece from the Goryeo dynasty or even something from the Three Kingdoms period."

The inspector nodded in understanding. "So the sword wasn't particularly rare. Is there any other characteristic that might impart value to such an object?"

"If the sword had historical significance, say there was a marking or something on the weapon to indicate it had been used by one of the great kings of the Joseon dynasty, that might increase the value, or if it had been made by a master swordsmith of the era, that could increase its worth," Saxon explained. "But I've not heard of anything like that coming on the market recently. Take my word for it, gentlemen; if a Hwando belonging to any of the great kings was for sale, it would have taken more money than Daniel McCourt had to acquire it."

Barnes said, "Is it possible that Mr. McCourt didn't know his sword wasn't all that special?"

Saxon shook his head. "McCourt hadn't been collecting as long as Leon Brunel, but he was no fool, and the individual that used to appraise for him would certainly have known it."

"Are you referring to Jerome Raleigh?" Witherspoon rubbed his hands together to ward off the chill.

"Yes, at one point, Daniel didn't buy anything without Raleigh having a look at it first." He smiled cynically. "Of course, from what I've heard, the two of them have parted ways."

"What do you mean?"

"One doesn't like to repeat gossip, Inspector, but I did hear that they'd had a falling-out recently." He grinned broadly. "There are rumors that Raleigh deliberately under-values or overvalues pieces depending on who has, shall we say, made it worth his while to be less than truthful."

Neither policeman said anything for a moment, but then Barnes fixed Saxon with a hard stare and said, "Let's stop dancing about, Mr. Saxon. Just tell us what you know."

Saxon's grin disappeared. "If you insist. Two weeks ago, McCourt took a set of Yuan dynasty vases to Goodison and Bright to be sold. But he didn't leave them there, because their appraiser told him the pair weren't worth nearly what McCourt thought they ought to fetch at auction. When Mc-Court mentioned that his own appraiser, Raleigh, had val-ued them much higher, they laughed at him. McCourt was so furious he made a terrible scene. That's how I found out about it."

"Yet McCourt had invited Jerome Raleigh to tea," Barnes mused speculatively.

"Indeed, and he was as nervous as a kitten in a roomful of bulldogs," Saxon said with relish.

"Did you dislike Mr. Raleigh as well?" the inspector asked.

"I don't dislike the fellow, but then again, he's never cheated me. I do all my own appraising. My uncle taught me well."

"If Mr. Raleigh was as nervous as you seem to believe he might have been, why would he have accepted McCourt's invitation?" Barnes inquired.

"He was scared not to come, Constable. Staying away would have looked very much like an admission of guilt," he explained. He leaned forward, bracing his elbows on his knees. "You must understand, appraising Oriental art and antiquities isn't a precise endeavor. Even the most expert appraiser can make mistakes or be fooled. I suspect Raleigh accepted the invitation so he could plead his case to McCourt directly and try to convince him that even if he'd overvalued the Yuan vases, it had been an honest mistake. Unfortunately for him, the afternoon turned into a disaster and everyone left."

"When you were there yesterday, did you see any mistletoe hanging down from the doorframe between the drawing room and the study?" Witherspoon asked suddenly.

Saxon drew back in surprise. "No, I can't say that I did. But I wasn't paying that much attention."

The inspector nodded, satisfied that thus far everyone's statement confirmed the mistletoe hadn't been there during the tea.

"You left the McCourt house just after Mr. and Mrs. Brunel, is that correct?" Barnes wanted a sense of where everyone was at any given moment. Something Mrs. Jeffries had mentioned this morning had suddenly popped into his head. She'd made the point that if every door and window in the place was open, anyone from outside could have slipped into the house without being noticed.

"That's right. I followed them out of the house. The Brunels turned toward the hansom cab stand on the corner, and I went in the opposite direction."

"Did you walk home?" Witherspoon asked.

"Yes, I wanted to clear that awful stench out of my lungs," he replied. "And I didn't want to waste money on a cab."

"Do you have servants here, sir?" Barnes asked.

Saxon hesitated. "I have a cleaning lady that comes in twice a week, but other than that, I'm alone here."

"You cook your own meals, sir?" the constable persisted. In his experience, men of Saxon's class wouldn't even know how to light the cooker, let alone prepare food.

Saxon's mouth compressed into a thin, angry line for a moment. "No, I take most of my meals at the café around the corner. It's quite cheap, and the food isn't bad."

"Did you have dinner there last night?" Witherspoon asked.

"No, I wasn't particularly hungry," he replied tersely.

"So even though you'd had nothing to eat, you came home," the constable pressed. "Is that correct?"

"That's right. As I said, I wasn't hungry. It hadn't been a pleasant occasion and I hadn't wanted to go in the first place, so that fact and the miserable stench made me lose what little appetite I had."

"Was there anyone here when you came home?" Witherspoon asked softly.

"No, I was quite alone. As I told you, I don't have servants."

"After you arrived home, did you stay in all evening?"

"Yes, I had a whiskey or two, read for a time, and then went to bed."

"Did any of your neighbors see you?" Barnes continued. "Did you speak to anyone on the street who might be able to verify the time you arrived home?"

"I didn't speak to anyone," he snapped. "Good lord, I didn't like McCourt, but I had no reason to murder him."

Witherspoon regarded him thoughtfully. "If you hadn't

wanted to go to the McCourt home, why did you accept the invitation?"

"I was curious, Inspector." He laughed. "I was going to send my regrets, but I ran into Mr. and Mrs. Brunel, and both of them encouraged me to go. Leon said he suspected Daniel had something special to show us, and Mrs. Brunel claimed I ought to go because it was Christmas."

"Leon Brunel knew what it was?" Barnes asked quickly. He glanced at Witherspoon.

"No, I specifically asked Leon, and he admitted he didn't know." He sighed. "I was hoping it was to be a Goryeo sword. My sources in Hong Kong claimed that there was one available and that the owner was going to sell it, so even though I never really thought McCourt could afford such an expensive item, I went along just in case he'd actually bought it."

"I take it this sword is more valuable than the Hwando?" Witherspoon clarified.

"Oh yes, it's extremely rare and worth a great deal of money." Saxon shrugged and got to his feet. "Elena McCourt has just inherited a fortune, so I thought Daniel would have had the resources to make such a purchase."

"But he couldn't afford a Hwando sword?" Barnes queried, thinking of what Saxon had told them less than ten minutes ago.

"He couldn't afford a Hwando sword used by one of the great kings of the Joseon era," Saxon corrected. "Something like that would be a museum piece." He began to pace back and forth in front of the unlighted fireplace. "But a Goryeo sword could be had for less. I'm not an expert on that period—no one outside of the Far East is—but I do know that the age alone would be enough to make the piece valuable even if it were in terrible condition."

"What about Mr. Leon Brunel?" Barnes pressed. "He's a collector, too. Could he have afforded either object?"

"Most definitely. Leon Brunel certainly isn't poor," he replied, his tone suddenly harsh and bitter. He stopped with his back turned to them so that neither man could see his face. "I know that well enough."

The two policemen glanced at each other but remained silent, both of them hoping he'd elaborate on his own.

Saxon said, "Even if he were poor, if he wanted something, he'd find a way to acquire it. He's the kind of man who always wants what someone else has, and once he owns something, he never lets it go."

CHAPTER 5

Mrs. Jeffries was the last one back for their afternoon meeting. She swept off her hat and cloak as she rushed into the kitchen. "I'm so sorry to be late, but I have had the most trying day."

"We've only just sat down," Betsy said.

"I've poured the tea." Mrs. Goodge picked up the big brown teapot, tipped the steaming brew into a cup, and put it down in front of the housekeeper's chair.

"Nell's bells, Hepzibah, you look like you've been runnin' miles!" Luty exclaimed as Mrs. Jeffries took her seat at the head of the table.

"Gracious, I think I have." She smiled gratefully as she reached for her cup. Taking a sip, she looked down at her lap and sent up a silent, heartfelt prayer of thanks to the Almighty that she'd not been caught. When she lifted her head, they were all staring at her. "I have had an adventure."

She grinned sheepishly. "I'll tell you about it as soon as I've had a moment to catch my breath. Why don't you all give your reports first?"

"I ain't got much to tell." Luty snorted in derision. "Half of London is gone, and I wasted the whole danged day goin' from one source to another only to find out the person was in Scotland or the south of France. But I did run into Lucille Fenwick when I stopped at the Alexandria Hotel in Knightsbridge."

"Good gracious, madam, how very unfortunate for you. How long did it take you to get away?" Hatchet chuckled.

Luty shot him an impatient frown. "Wipe that grin off yer face; I'll have you know that for once, she had somethin' useful to say."

He laughed even harder. "And you believed her?" He looked at the others. "Lucille Fenwick is notorious for exaggerating, and believe me, I'm being kind in using the word 'exaggerate' instead of 'lie.'"

"I'll admit she's not the most trustworthy of sources," Luty conceded. "But she only tells real big lies when she's talkin' about herself, and today she was gossipin' about Daniel McCourt."

"What did she say?" Mrs. Jeffries asked quickly.

"She claimed she'd seen Daniel McCourt just a few days before he was murdered."

"Seen him where?" Betsy asked.

"In the lobby of the Alexandria." Luty grinned. "She said McCourt was meetin' a blonde woman who'd just stepped out of the lift. I asked her if she knew who the woman was, and she said she didn't."

"And she was certain McCourt was meetin' this person?" Smythe asked.

"She was. She said when the lift doors opened, McCourt

jumped up from his seat and hotfooted it across the lobby to her."

"She saw all that as she was leaving the hotel?" Hatchet asked in disbelief.

"Well, she did mention that she'd peeked back in while the doorman went to fetch her cab," Luty said. "And she saw the two of them with their heads together; thick as thieves was how she put it."

"I wonder if his wife knew he was meeting another woman," Ruth mused.

"We don't know that he was meeting anyone!" Hatchet exclaimed. "Madam, you know as well as I do that Lucille Fenwick isn't just an unreliable source; she's been accused on more than one occasion of making things up out of thin air. Have you forgotten the Kaiser Wilhelm incident?"

"Kaiser Wilhelm?" Wiggins repeated. "The German Emperor?"

Hatchet stared at his employer. "Will you tell them, or shall I?"

"I'll tell 'em." Luty sighed. "Much as I hate to admit it, Hatchet's right. A few years back, she claimed she'd had tea with the Kaiser when she was in Berlin, but what had actually happened was she was drinking tea in a café when his carriage rolled past. But just because she's a habitual liar doesn't mean she doesn't tell the truth sometimes. I think this is a worthwhile bit of information."

"I agree, Luty," Mrs. Jeffries said. "And if McCourt was in that hotel lobby, I'm sure someone else will have seen him. We must find out what he was doing there."

"I can't go back," Luty said glumly. "Lucille is stayin' there until her new house is finished, and I don't want to risk runnin' into her again. If she heard me askin' more questions about McCourt, she'd realize there must be a reason. She might be a lyin' chatterbox, but she's not stupid. There's already too many people who know what we git up to whenever the inspector has a murder case."

"True, but most of them can be trusted," Mrs. Jeffries pointed out.

"Yeah, well, Lucille ain't one of them. She'd blab it all over town."

"I can 'ave a go at it," the footman volunteered. "I can nip over tomorrow."

"See if you can also find out exactly what day it was that McCourt was there," Mrs. Jeffries added.

"Why thank you, Wiggins." Luty smiled gratefully. "Now, let's just hope that Lucille wasn't lyin' through her teeth this time and the mysterious blonde lady is still there. Anyways, that's all I found out. But I'm goin' to dinner at Lord Farleigh's tonight. Maybe I can pick up somethin' interestin' there."

"Take heart, madam," Hatchet said. "My day wasn't much better than yours. I, too, had to rely on a source that, shall we say, isn't very reliable. But beggars can't be choosers. I did find out a few tidbits about our victim and his wife."

"What did you learn?" Mrs. Jeffries helped herself to a slice of brown buttered bread.

"Elena McCourt's just inherited a fortune from her aunt," Hatchet replied. "Apparently, as soon as the will was read, she made it clear to several of her friends that she was taking control of her money."

"What does that mean?" Wiggins asked.

"I suspect it means she wasn't going to let her husband get his hands on it," Ruth interjected. "Oh dear. I'm sorry, Hatchet. I didn't mean to interrupt your report, but it does dovetail nicely with what I found out."

Hatchet waved off her apology. "Actually, I'm delighted you were able to verify my information. As I said, my source isn't the most trustworthy person."

"Did your source know how much she inherited?" Betsy asked.

He shook his head. "He didn't mention an exact figure, but he did say she was the sole remaining heir of the Herron family, and they are known to be very, very rich."

"That's what my source said as well," Ruth added.

"Why don't you go next," Mrs. Jeffries suggested to her.

"Alright. As I've already mentioned, several people at my Women's Group meeting commented about her inheritance and the fact that she's been very forthcoming about controlling her own money. But I also heard something else from Joanne Wells, who is a member of our group and an acquaintance of Elena McCourt's. Joanne told me that the day after the reading of Mrs. McCourt's late aunt's will, they ran into each other when both of them were out shopping. Joanne made some comment about spending too much money and how her husband was going to complain, and Elena just laughed. She said she didn't have to be concerned about that anymore, and from now on, it was her husband's turn to worry. Joanne asked her what she meant. She just shrugged and said that she'd be the one controlling the purse strings and that she wasn't disposed to be generous."

"I don't understand; does that mean McCourt had no money?" Mrs. Goodge frowned in confusion. "But that doesn't make sense. How could he keep up that big house and all those servants?"

"Perhaps their living expenses are paid for out of her marriage settlement money," Mrs. Jeffries speculated. "Or perhaps he wasn't completely destitute. After all, he just purchased something for his antiquities collection." She glanced at Ruth. "Did Mrs. Wells make any other comments?"

Ruth smiled ruefully. "Despite my best efforts, I couldn't get anything else out of her. But I might have something for our morning meeting. Like Luty, I'm going to a dinner party tonight."

"I'll go next," Smythe volunteered quietly. He was holding the baby, who'd fallen sound asleep. "I went to the hansom stand closest to the McCourt house and 'ad a word with a couple of the drivers. One of 'em told me that the only fare he 'ad around the time the tea party ended yesterday was a lady. 'Er husband put her in the hansom and gave him the address, but as soon as the rig went round the corner, the woman insisted 'e stop, and she got out and scarpered off."

"Did he remember the address he'd been given?" Mrs. Jeffries asked quickly.

"He couldn't recall the name of the street; just that it was in Kensington."

"That's not much help. Everyone at that tea party lives in that neighborhood," the cook complained.

"True, but it is a very interesting piece of information," Mrs. Jeffries said. "Don't forget, by the time the guests had gone, the servants at the McCourt house were outside and all the windows and doors were open."

"Meanin' any of the guests could have gone back, grabbed the sword, and murdered the victim," Phyllis said thoughtfully. "Includin' the mysterious lady who got out of the hansom cab."

Mrs. Jeffries nodded approvingly at the maid and then looked at the coachman. "Was the driver able to describe what she looked like?"

Amanda squirmed and made a mewling sound but didn't awaken. Smythe waited till she'd settled before he answered.

" 'E only got a peek at her when she climbed out of the cab, but 'e told me she was dark-haired and wearin' a rust-colored cloak with a fur collar and a matchin' hat. From the glimpse 'e got of her face, 'e said she was pretty."

"Sounds to me like he got more than a glimpse of the woman." Betsy laughed softly. "Mrs. Brunel was the only woman other than Mrs. McCourt who was at the tea. If she's young and pretty, all we need to find out is if Mrs. Brunel has a rust-colored cloak."

She glanced at Amanda, sleeping in her father's arms. Listening to the others give their reports hadn't been as hard as she'd thought. She'd been afraid that the meeting might make her wish she could be out and "on the hunt" again, and though it did cause a tiny pang of regret, she was glad she'd stayed with her baby. Today hadn't been difficult. She tried her best to stay out of Mrs. Goodge's way, especially when the cook had someone in the kitchen, but she'd soon gotten bored, and using the baby as an excuse, she'd spent the afternoon at home, returning only a few moments before the meeting.

"I'll make it a point to ask the inspector," Mrs. Jeffries said. "Who would like to go next?"

"I've got a bit more to report," Smythe said quickly.

"Oh, sorry, do go on," Mrs. Jeffries said.

"I 'eard somethin' about Jerome Raleigh and Nicholas Saxon," he continued. He told them what he'd learned from Blimpey, without, of course, mentioning Blimpey.

"Glenda Brunel was once engaged to Nicholas Saxon!" Mrs. Goodge exclaimed. "Gracious, Smythe, you've found out more than any of us."

"Nah." He shrugged modestly. "I just got lucky today, that's all."

"But it wasn't Leon Brunel that were murdered; it was

Daniel McCourt," Wiggins pointed out. "And seems to me that we ought to be takin' a real close look at Jerome Raleigh. If 'e tried to pull the same fraud on McCourt that he pulled on his old employers, then McCourt might 'ave found out. He'd probably 'ave wanted Raleigh prosecuted."

"Which would give him a motive for murder," Mrs. Jeffries said.

"But only if he tried to cheat McCourt," Mrs. Goodge argued. "And we don't know that he did. He might have learned his lesson ten years ago."

"That's true." Smythe nodded in agreement. "My source 'adn't 'eard anythin' about him bein' up to 'is old tricks. But I'll keep snoopin' about and see what I can find out."

"If you're done, can I go next?" Wiggins asked. At the coachman's nod, he told them about his meeting with the footman from the McCourt house. "After he was finished tellin' me about the maid who 'eard someone outside in the passageway last night, I found myself wonderin' if she was bein' fanciful or if there's somethin' to it."

"You're thinking she might have really heard someone walking about outside?" Hatchet said.

"That's right, and what's more, maybe the reason Mrs. McCourt didn't want Annie sayin' anythin' to the police was because she was the one outside doin' the walkin'."

"Then why wouldn't she simply tell the housekeeper that the maid had heard her walking? Mrs. McCourt said she'd not been able to sleep, and perhaps she went outside for some air," Betsy said reasonably. "It's her house, and she can do what she likes."

"It's the middle of winter," the footman protested. "It's cold. No one in 'er right mind would go out unless she 'ad a reason."

Enjoying herself, Betsy crossed her arms over her chest.

"What kind of reason? Come on, Wiggins. What are you getting at?"

"I don't know what I'm gettin' at." Wiggins frowned. "But I think it's mighty suspicious that she didn't want the maid to tell the police what she'd 'eard. Maybe she was hidin' somethin'."

"What could she be hidin'?" the cook asked as she reached for the teapot. "The murder weapon was found next to the body. Maybe she didn't want the girl sayin' anythin' to the police because the maid is a nervous ninny who jumps at her own shadow."

"We're getting off course here," Mrs. Jeffries said. "Though I must say, both arguments are somewhat valid. Wiggins, can you find a way to speak to Annie and learn what she may or may not have heard?"

Wiggins grinned. " 'Course I can. It'll take a bit of doin', but Albert Jones will make sure 'e finds a way to speak to the girl."

Phyllis looked at Wiggins, her expression confused. "Albert Jones? Who is he?"

" 'E's the name I use when I'm on the hunt," Wiggins confessed. "People talk, and it wouldn't do for a constable or even the inspector to overhear one of the servants mentionin' they'd been knocked over on the 'igh street by a fellow named Wiggins."

Phyllis' eyes widened. "Oh, I never thought of that." She frowned, trying to remember whether she'd mentioned her name or where she worked while she was out today. She was fairly sure she hadn't.

"I did 'ear one more thing from Duncan," Wiggins added quickly. "Just as I was fixin' to leave, the lad took some salve out of his pocket and smeared it on his knuckles, which were in a right old mess. When he saw me lookin' at his 'ands, he said the police inspector who'd come to the house 'ad given him the money to buy the salve."

There were murmurs of approval from around the table, but it was Phyllis who spoke up. "Inspector Witherspoon is such a good man. I hope I never have to leave here," she declared.

"Yes, he is a good man," Mrs. Jeffries agreed. "And that's one of the reasons we all work so hard to help him. Why don't you go next."

She took a deep breath. "I didn't learn much, but I did have a quick chat with the girl at the greengrocer's on the high street." She repeated what she'd heard, taking her time and trying to recall every single word. She didn't want to get it wrong. "And that was the only bit I found out. I know it's not very much, but I only managed to do the shops on one side of the street today, so I'll do the other side tomorrow."

Betsy started to clap her hands and then stopped when the baby's little fists jerked. "Bravo, Phyllis," she whispered. "I knew you could do it." She pushed back in her chair and took Amanda out of Smythe's arms. "Let me put her down for a nap. I'm afraid I'm going to wake her."

"But I ain't had a chance to hold her," Luty hissed. Betsy hesitated, but Luty waved impatiently. "Let the baby go to bed, but I git to hold her first at our mornin' meetin' tomorrow."

"We've got a deal," Betsy agreed before she hurried off toward the cook's suite. Mrs. Goodge had insisted they put a crib in her room so the baby could nap there during the day.

"I wish we knew what the McCourts were squabblin' about," Wiggins mused. "I'll see if I can get any more information out of the maid. It must 'ave been a real nasty argument. Too bad Mrs. McCourt didn't tell the inspector exactly what they was arguin' about."

"You'll sort that out soon, lad," Mrs. Goodge said confidently. She pushed a plate of raisin scones toward Phyllis. "You've done well, Phyllis, and I'm sure you'll do even better tomorrow. You've all done better than me; I've not found out anythin' at all from my sources today. But an old colleague is visitin' in the mornin', and I expect she'll have a few bits of information that might come in useful."

Betsy had returned as the cook was speaking. She slipped back into her chair. "Now it's Mrs. Jeffries' turn to tell us about her adventure."

Mrs. Jeffries winced slightly. "To begin with, I'll admit that my 'adventure' almost gave me heart failure."

"Cor blimey, what 'appened?" Wiggins asked eagerly.

"As you all know, I went to Victoria Gardens to see the 'lay of the land,' so to speak. My bonnet was pulled down low over my face to prevent any constables I might run into from recognizing me, and all seemed to be well. I walked past the front door of the McCourt home without mishap, and no one paid any attention to me. But then I realized that from the front of the place, you couldn't see the back or side doors, so I thought I'd be clever and try to get into their communal garden. But the only gate that I could find was locked. So I went back out to the street. Just then, I saw a delivery boy going to the house two doors down. He'd left the service gate open, so I nipped in and dashed through the passage to the garden. I'd just gotten directly behind the McCourt house when four constables suddenly appeared, so I turned to run back the way I'd come, but then I saw another two constables."

"Oh my goodness, that must have been terribly frightening!" Ruth exclaimed. "What on earth did you do?"

"The only thing I could; I ran into the passageway in the house next door to the McCourt home and prayed they weren't going to search there. There wasn't even anyplace to hide. The flower beds along the fence were completely bare, and there wasn't as much as a bush I could jump behind. So I stood just inside the gate as the constables approached, but when I heard them talking, I realized they were going to come in. Honestly, if I'd had time, I'd have burrowed under the pine mulch, but I didn't have a moment to spare! They were getting closer by the second, and being caught hiding in the house next to the murder house would have been ten times worse than being seen in the communal garden."

"How is that worse?" Phyllis asked.

"At least if she'd been in the communal garden she could always say she was looking for our inspector," Betsy explained.

"But as it was, I was now effectively trapped," Mrs. Jeffries clarified. "Getting into the passageway from the communal garden end was easy; those gates are often unlocked so family and servants can come and go as they please. But the gate at the street end is always locked. I'd no choice. When I realized they were coming inside, I ran toward the street. As I feared, the gate was locked."

"What did you do? 'Ow'd you get away?" Wiggins asked eagerly.

"I threw myself against it hard as I could." She rubbed her shoulder. "And I'm sure I'll pay for that with a multitude of aches and pains, but it worked! The gate flew open and I ran outside." She sat back and looked at the faces around the table. Their expressions ranged from amused to shocked.

"Bloomin' Ada, Mrs. Jeffries, that's a good way of gettin' out of a bad spot!" Smythe exclaimed.

"You broke the lock on their gate?" Mrs. Goodge asked incredulously.

"It was already broken. It must have been," the house-keeper said defensively. "A good lock shouldn't have given way as easily as that one did."

"I don't know," Betsy mused. "You're a strong woman; you could do a lot of damage." She ducked her head to hide her smile.

"I didn't do any damage!"

"Although it does sound as if you destroyed private property," Hatchet said primly, but his eyes twinkled, and he was struggling not to laugh.

"I'm going to pay for the lock!" Mrs. Jeffries exclaimed indignantly.

"Just the lock?" Wiggins asked. "'Ave you gone back to look at the gate? If ya slammed yourself into it 'ard enough to bust it open, you might 'ave knocked it clear off the hinges."

"Of course I didn't go look at it!" Mrs. Jeffries yelled. "I was too busy running away—" She broke off as she realized they were all having a good chuckle at her expense. "Very funny," she said as everyone began to laugh. She crossed her arms over her chest and glared at them. "I'll have you know I was terrified."

"I'd have been frightened, too." Ruth giggled. "But you got away, and that's what's important. It was quick thinking on your part."

"It sure was," Luty agreed. "And you ain't the first one of us to have to do somethin' undignified when we're out on the hunt. I once had to hide in a closet. We're not makin' fun of ya; we're just havin' a good laugh because it finally happened to you."

"You were lucky one of their servants didn't catch you." Mrs. Goodge chuckled.

"Indeed I was," she said before laughing ruefully.

"Maybe they were gone," Luty said cheerfully. "Just like all my sources."

Witherspoon was tired by the time he and Barnes entered Jerome Raleigh's ground-floor flat. He lived in a modern block on a cul-de-sac off Brook Green.

Raleigh was a tall, thin man with a broad face and blond hair brushed back from his high forehead. He was wearing a heavy woolen brown and blue plaid dressing gown. A pair of wire-rimmed spectacles framed his watery blue eyes. He gestured at two balloon-back chairs by the fireplace. "Please sit down, gentlemen," he offered as he flopped down on the sofa opposite them. "As you can see, I'm not well, so I've got to lie down."

"We'll be as brief as possible, sir," Witherspoon replied as they took their seats. Like the other houses they'd visited today, this one also boasted a huge array of gorgeous Oriental objects. Chinese ceramics, brass statues, vases of every color and description, wooden boxes inlaid with mother-of-pearl designs, and half a dozen sets of teapots with matching cups were arranged on the shelves along the walls. A faded Oriental rug covered the space between the gray love seat and the two chairs, and the middle of them was a brilliantly polished low table with carved legs. "I'm sure you know why we're here."

"Of course." He pulled a white handkerchief out of his pocket and rubbed the bottom of his nose. "Terrible business, just terrible. But I don't know what you think I can tell you. Daniel McCourt was alive when I left his home."

Barnes took out his notebook. "We're speaking to everyone who was there yesterday afternoon."

Witherspoon nodded in agreement. "What time did you arrive at the McCourt home?"

"Half past four. I don't believe in being fashionably late. That's a foolish affectation and it's also rude."

"Were the other guests on time?"

"Yes, we were all punctual, though Leon Brunel disappeared as soon as they arrived." He rubbed the handkerchief across his upper lip.

"How did you get to the McCourt home?" Barnes asked.

"I walked. It's not far, and this time of year, it's more trouble trying to get a hansom than it's worth," he replied.

"Did you notice anyone suspicious either when you went into the McCourt home or when you left after the fire?" Witherspoon asked.

"You know about the fire, then." He waved off his own question. "Of course you do. But in answer to your question, no, I saw no one who struck me as being suspect in any way."

Witherspoon gestured at the objects on the shelves. "You've quite a collection here."

"I'm a dealer, Inspector. Unfortunately, the warehouse where I used to store my goods has been plagued with burglaries, so I'm forced to house the most valuable pieces here."

"Which warehouse would that be, sir?" Barnes asked softly.

"It was a small concern off Commercial Road in Whitechapel. I don't think they're still in business. Now, can we get on with this? I'm really not feeling well."

"You're an antiquities dealer, sir?" Witherspoon commented. "We were told you were an appraiser."

"I do both, Inspector," he replied. "Most appraisers also have their own collections."

"Do you work for any of the local antiquity auction houses?" Barnes asked blandly.

"No, I'm independent and my clients come to me through referrals."

Witherspoon said, "Do you know if Mr. McCourt had any enemies?"

Raleigh blinked in surprise at the sudden change in topic. "He wasn't a particularly well-loved man, but I don't know of any actual enemies he might have had."

"What about Mr. Arthur Brunel?"

Raleigh blew his nose again. "What about him? The men weren't close anymore, but he'd been invited to the house, so there must have been some sort of reconciliation."

"Then you know they were estranged?" Witherspoon pressed. He wanted to see how widespread this information had been.

"Everyone knew it. Arthur Brunel has told most of London that McCourt conspired with Leon Brunel to cheat him out of his fair share of their father's estate." He leaned all the way back, causing the sofa to squeak. "Look, Inspector, is this going to take much longer? I'm very tired. Oh dear, wait a moment." He straightened back up again. "I've told you a fib. There was someone outside the McCourt house. Gracious, I must be running a fever. I completely forgot. There was a lady standing there."

"You saw a woman?" Barnes asked patiently.

"She was on the other side of the road, and she was staring at the house. When she saw that I'd spotted her, she walked away. But I saw her again when I came out. I noticed particularly because she was quite attractive and very well dressed. She had on a forest green jacket with a matching hat."

"What did she look like?"

"She had blonde hair and very fine features, but she wasn't young. I'd guess she was in her early forties."

"And where was she when you saw her after leaving the

McCourt home?" Witherspoon asked. He noticed that a line of perspiration had appeared on Raleigh's upper lip.

"At the corner opposite the hansom stand," he replied. "And when she knew I'd seen her for the second time, she turned and walked away. Don't you think that's suspicious?"

"Perhaps she was simply out shopping in the area," Barnes suggested. He wasn't sure he believed him. No one else had mentioned this woman, and there was something about Raleigh that got his back up. "And she was alarmed by your staring at her."

"I wasn't staring," he snapped. "I simply glanced in her direction, and both times, when she saw me, she trotted off like the hounds of hell were at her heels. Besides, if she'd been shopping she'd have had a boy with her to carry her packages."

"We can see you're unwell, Mr. Raleigh," Witherspoon said. "But there is one other matter we need to ask you about."

"What's that?"

"You appraised for Mr. McCourt," Witherspoon said. "You advised him on what pieces to buy and on what the real value of particular pieces might be; is that correct?"

Raleigh had gone a bit pale. "That's right."

"Did you advise him as to the value of a set of Yuan dynasty vases that he recently took to Goodison and Bright for auction?"

Raleigh drew a sharp breath. "I did advise him on those particular pieces, but as I'm sure you already know, I made a mistake. It wasn't my fault. They were supposed to have been genuine Yuan, but it turned out they were copies from a much later period."

"We understand McCourt made a scene at the auction

house when he found out he'd overpaid for the pair?" Barnes said.

"He was furious," Raleigh admitted. "He came to see me directly from their premises. He said I'd never work for him again. I tried to tell him that it was simply a mistake and that even the best person could be fooled."

"Did he think you'd been paid to deliberately overvalue the piece?" Witherspoon suggested.

Raleigh's mouth flattened to a thin line. "Why are you asking me this? I'm sure you already know the answer. He accused me of taking money from the seller, but that's nonsense. I didn't even know the man. I simply made a mistake."

"And Mr. McCourt isn't known for being forgiving of mistakes, is he?" Barnes said. "If he was angry at you, why did he invite you to his house for tea?"

"Isn't it obvious?" He snorted derisively. "He invited me to show off his latest acquisition. He wanted to rub my nose in the fact that he'd acquired something without my help or expertise."

"Why did you accept the invitation?" Witherspoon asked curiously.

"Oh, that's simple, Inspector. I accepted because I fully intended to cast doubt on the authenticity of whatever it was that he was going to exhibit." He smiled slyly. "I'm still enough of an expert that people seek my advice. In fact, Daniel's own cousin was picking my brain for information just a few days before the tea."

Barnes looked at him. "You know what he was going to show everybody?"

"Not really, though I suspect it was some sort of weapon." Raleigh laughed. "But whether it was genuine or not wouldn't have been the point. Whatever the object was, I was going to make just the sort of comment to cast doubt on its authenticity. McCourt would have hated that, and I wanted to watch the bastard squirm."

Mrs. Jeffries shoved the bolt home on the top of the front door and then wandered into the drawing room. Tired as she was, she couldn't go to bed; she knew she'd not sleep a wink. Her mind was racing. She flopped down on the settee and stared at the lamp she'd put on the mantelpiece so she'd have light to go upstairs. The household was quiet, and everyone, save her, was abed. The inspector had already gone up, and she had no doubt he'd fallen asleep as soon as his head hit the pillow. The poor man had arrived home as tired as a pup. But they'd had a sherry together, and she'd kept him company while he ate his dinner and told her all the details of his day.

Gracious, she thought, no wonder he was so exhausted he could barely finish his pudding; he'd questioned almost every single person who'd been at the tea and had gotten an earful from all of them.

She closed her eyes as she tried to make sense of everything. Nicholas Saxon had been engaged to Glenda Brunel, but did that have anything to do with McCourt's murder? As had been pointed out, it wasn't Leon Brunel who'd been killed. And what about Jerome Raleigh? Their assumption that he'd gone to the tea to try and make amends with McCourt was utterly wrong. From what Witherspoon had been told, Raleigh had gone to exact a petty and personal revenge on the deceased.

She leaned her head back and stared up at the ceiling. Why would Raleigh admit such a thing to the inspector? Wouldn't it have been far safer to simply say he'd gone to apologize in hopes of keeping McCourt's future business?

She sat up, wincing as the sudden movement jarred her tender shoulder. Maybe Raleigh wasn't so keen on keeping McCourt's custom because he knew there wasn't going to be much future business. Perhaps he'd already heard that Elena McCourt was telling everyone she knew that it was now her husband who had to worry about money.

Moving slowly, she got to her feet. She had to get to bed, even if she didn't sleep. She walked across the darkened room and picked up the lantern. She had a lot of information, but she couldn't make sense of any of it, and the more she tried to force the facts into some sort of comprehensible pattern, the more she was convinced that nothing they'd learned thus far pointed to the killer.

Luty and Hatchet were the last to arrive for their morning meeting. Both of them were grinning from ear to ear as they hurried into the kitchen.

"Looks like you two must have found out somethin'," Mrs. Goodge said cheerfully.

"I can't speak for Hatchet, but I know I got an earful last night!" Luty exclaimed as she snapped open the gold clasp of her sapphire blue cloak. Hatchet swept off his black top hat and simultaneously caught her cloak as it slipped off her shoulders. "And I expect he heard somethin', too, because he's been whistlin' all the way over here." Luty's smile faded as she stared at the empty chair beside Smythe. "Where's Betsy and my goddaughter?"

"She wanted to come, but she 'ad a bit of a cough this mornin', and as it was lookin' like rain, I didn't want 'er goin' out in the wet," Smythe said apologetically. "But if it clears up, she and the baby will be along this afternoon."

"Is it serious?" Luty asked anxiously.

"It's just a slight cough; she'll be fine," he assured her.

Mrs. Jeffries waited till they'd taken their seats. "Before we hear Luty and Hatchet's information, I'll tell you what I learned from the inspector last night. He got home rather late in the evening because he managed to speak to almost everyone who'd been at the tea party. I think the only one he didn't interview was Charles Cochran, and he'll be seeing him this morning. Constable Barnes popped in as well this morning and added a few details." She told them everything she'd heard, taking care not to put emphasis on any one fact or statement.

"What's he going to do after he takes Cochran's statement?" Hatchet asked.

"He's going to speak to Daniel McCourt's solicitor to see how much his estate is worth and who inherits it. Then he said something about broadening the scope of the investigation by speaking to other collectors."

"Is there any way to guide the inspector toward questioning the help at the Alexandria Hotel?" Hatchet asked.

"I mentioned it to Constable Barnes this morning," she replied. "Why? Is it important?"

"I certainly think so," Hatchet replied. "As madam mentioned yesterday, we went to a dinner party last night at Lord Farleigh's, and I started making some discreet inquiries amongst the footmen and coachmen who were in the servants' hall. I found out a bit more about McCourt's meeting there."

"So Lucille wasn't just blowin' hot air," Luty cried triumphantly.

Hatchet ignored her. "Apparently, before the lady in question appeared and stepped out of the lift, McCourt had been in the lobby for some time, and at one point, he jumped behind a large potted fern to avoid being seen by someone else who'd entered the lobby."

"How could anyone see somethin' like that?" Luty argued. "Maybe he slipped behind that plant to adjust his clothin'."

"Don't be absurd, madam. My source was utterly sure of what he saw," Hatchet shot back. "He said McCourt stood well out of sight for a good two minutes and then came back out into the open."

"Did your source see who it was that McCourt was hiding from?" Ruth asked.

"I'm afraid not, but he saw something that Lucille Fenwick missed." He grinned at Luty. "Our mystery woman was accompanied by a Chinese servant. Once he arrived, the three of them left the lobby."

"Did they go to her room?" Mrs. Goodge asked. "I wouldn't have thought the hotel would allow such goings-on."

"I don't know exactly where they went, but no one on the hotel staff stopped them, as it's a very respectable place," he replied. "Oh, and I also found out that the house next to the McCourts' is empty. The Crandalls have gone to Scotland for Christmas."

"No wonder I wasn't caught yesterday," Mrs. Jeffries murmured. "I thundered down that passageway loud enough to wake the dead." She tried to absorb this new information, but for the life of her, she couldn't think what it might mean.

"I'll bet the mystery woman is the one that Jerome Raleigh claims he saw," Wiggins speculated eagerly. "You know, the one he said was 'angin' about outside."

"Come on, lad, you know better than that," Smythe chided. "No jumpin' the gun until we've got all the facts. We've gone down that road before, and we're most always wrong."

"Besides, we don't even know if Raleigh was tellin' the truth," the cook added. "He may have been makin' the whole thing up to get the inspector off of him."

Luty looked at Hatchet. "Are you done yet?" she asked plaintively. He nodded, and she plunged ahead. "You weren't the only one who heard somethin' good last night. I got an earful, too."

"Oh, do tell, madam," he said dryly.

Luty laughed. "I found out that Daniel McCourt was fixin' to sue Arthur Brunel for slander. Seems that for the past three years, Brunel has been tellin' everyone who stood still for thirty seconds that McCourt used a bunch of legal shenanigans to cheat him out of his share of his and Leon's father's estate."

"Is that a rumor, or did your source know for certain the lawsuit was going to go forward?" Mrs. Jeffries asked.

"It was more than a rumor." Luty grinned broadly. "My source was the wife of one of the partners in the legal firm that McCourt had hired for the case. Not only that, but she told me that McCourt had been quietly goin' around London gettin' the names of people willin' to testify against Brunel."

"Cor blimey, now that McCourt's dead, I guess there won't be a lawsuit," Wiggins murmured.

"But why would McCourt sue Arthur Brunel?" Mrs. Goodge frowned in confusion. "Didn't the inspector say that the fellow was in such a bad financial situation he's bein' forced to turn the top two floors of his house into flats?"

"Indeed he did," Mrs. Jeffries murmured thoughtfully. "But perhaps McCourt didn't care."

"Or maybe 'e just wanted to shut the fellow up," Smythe added. "Maybe 'e was sick and tired of Brunel slingin' mud at his reputation."

"But how could McCourt afford to sue Brunel?" Hatchet drummed his fingers on the tabletop. "From the comments that Elena McCourt has made recently, it sounds as if her late husband had no money at all. Didn't she say something to the effect that 'it was now his turn to worry'? It takes financial resources to bring a case against someone."

"If he was quietly going about London looking for people to testify on his behalf," Mrs. Jeffries said, "then perhaps he started the suit before he realized he couldn't depend on his wife for financial support."

"There's somethin' I don't understand," Phyllis said quietly.

"What's that?" Mrs. Jeffries reached for the teapot.

"Well, from the gossipy bits we've all heard, it seems as if it's only been recently that Mrs. McCourt has stood up to her husband, and it seems as if she only stood up to him because she's now the one with the money, right?"

"To date, that is how it appears." Mrs. Jeffries eyed the girl speculatively. "What are you getting at, Phyllis?"

Phyllis chewed her lower lip thoughtfully. "If Mr. McCourt was now havin' to depend on his wife financially, where did he get the money to buy whatever it was that he was goin' to show all the guests at the tea party?"

CHAPTER 6

"Of course I'll answer your questions and cooperate any way that I can, Inspector." Charles Cochran smiled politely at the two policemen as they took their seats in front of his massive desk. He was a short, slender man with graying hair, hazel eyes, a long, bony face, and a mustache. "I want you to catch Daniel's killer."

Cochran's office was on the third floor of a rust-colored brick building on a road off the Marylebone High Street. It was half past nine in the morning, but heavy clouds had rolled in from the west, and the light coming in through the windows was gray and dreary.

"You and Mr. McCourt were close friends," Witherspoon began.

"Not at all," Cochran interrupted. "I did see Daniel at the reading of the Herron family will, of course. But for a good number of years now, we've only seen one another if we hap-

pened to accidentally meet. We have some mutual acquain-
tances, and sometimes we'd run into one another at a social
function. I was very surprised to receive an invitation to tea.
However, I am morally opposed to murder."

"Aren't most people opposed to murder?" Barnes was intrigued by Cochran. He was different from what he'd expected. To begin with, his office, though filled with shelves
of law volumes and file boxes, also housed two fat tabby cats
sleeping on thick rag rugs in front of the small fireplace, and
on the edge of the desk was a stack of brochures from the
Royal Society for the Prevention of Cruelty to Animals. Instead of the usual portrait of Her Majesty over the mantelpiece, there were two framed charcoal drawings, one of
William Wilberforce and one of Thomas Clarkson. Just
above the pictures was a framed copy of Abraham Lincoln's
Emancipation Proclamation.

"Yes, but their opposition isn't based on morality or ab-
solutes of right or wrong; it's based on personal self-interest
and an overwhelming need for law and order," Cochran explained earnestly. "Governments hang people and send
young men off to war and don't consider it murder. Taking
a life in defense of property either by a private citizen or an
agent of the law isn't considered a crime, and colonial governments acting on England's behalf commit atrocities
against native peoples frequently, yet no one hauls the local
English governors up before the court."

"But the taking of life isn't necessarily murder," Witherspoon interjected.

"That's my point, Inspector; it should be," Cochran
chided gently. "And much as I personally found Daniel Mc-
Court an objectionable person, no one had the right to take
his life. But you gentlemen didn't come to debate the ethical

nature of law and governments with me. You have questions you want to ask. Please, go ahead."

Witherspoon stared at him in annoyance. It didn't seem right that the fellow should snatch the moral high ground without an argument. But he was correct; there were questions to be answered. "Considering that you and Mr. Mc-Court were not friends," he said, "why do you think he invited you to his home?"

"At first, I was mystified by the invitation," he replied. "Not only had I not seen nor heard from Daniel in ages, but we had absolutely nothing in common."

"You're not a collector of Oriental art or weapons?" Barnes asked.

"Not at all."

"Mr. McCourt worked here, didn't he?" Witherspoon glanced around the office to give himself a moment to think. Something important nudged the back of his mind, and over the years, he'd learned to trust this "inner voice." But he couldn't catch the little imp, and the feeling evaporated as quickly as it had come.

"Yes, for a few months when he first qualified. But he resigned shortly before his wedding," Cochran replied. "He met his wife when he took some papers to her family home."

"You were their solicitors?"

Cochran shook his head. "Not at that time. When I first met the Herron family, we represented the sellers of a piece of property Mr. Herron wished to acquire. It was several years later when their family solicitor died that we were asked to represent the Herrons. By then Daniel had been gone from our firm for years. We did, however, draw up the papers for the marriage settlement between Elena Herron and Daniel. But we were acting on McCourt's behalf at that time, not the Herron family. Since he left the firm, the only time we've met is if we ran into one another by sheer chance."

Barnes said, "Was the tea party the first time you'd been to his home?"

"Yes."

"You just said, 'At first, I was mystified by the invitation.'" The inspector repeated Cochran's words. "Does that mean you later came to your own conclusions as to why you received the invitation?"

"It does." He hesitated. "But you must realize I'm only speculating as to why he wanted me there. I could be wrong, and the man is dead; he can't defend himself."

"We understand that." The inspector nodded in encouragement.

"Fine. He invited me because he wanted to intimidate his wife," Cochran declared. "But that's only my opinion. McCourt neither said nor did anything to confirm my suspicions."

"That's a very odd assumption, Mr. Cochran." Barnes stared at him expectantly.

"I know. Daniel had never invited me to his home, and he never would have done so without a reason. But it wasn't until a day or so afterwards that I had an inkling of what he was hoping to accomplish. His wife had just inherited a fortune, and I'd heard that she was telling her friends she was taking control of the money. You must understand, under the terms of the original marriage settlement, Daniel had complete authority over the finances, but now she was to be the one in charge. But even then, it wasn't until I walked in the front door and heard the two of them shouting at each other that I really understood." He grimaced. "He wanted me there so she'd believe that he'd sent for me to consult with him. I drew up the original documents for the marriage settlement. I suspect the invitation was simply a ruse to frighten her into believing that there was something in that original document that might affect control of her new inheritance."

"Is there?" Barnes asked curiously.

"Of course not." Cochran laughed in derision. "But that's the sort of stupid thinking that would have occurred to Daniel. He was a dreadfully bad solicitor and an equally bad husband. He'd bullied Elena Herron from the moment he'd married her, and now he was desperate to bully his way back into controlling her money."

"What about the original marriage settlement?" Witherspoon said. "Wouldn't he still control that money?"

"He would if there were any of it left. But between his collecting and bad investments, it's gone. I've heard from a number of reliable sources that McCourt was broke. If he hadn't been murdered, he'd have had to declare bankruptcy to pay his debts."

Mrs. Goodge put a slice of her seedcake onto a plate and handed it to her guest. "Here you are Mollie. As I recall, you were always fond of seedcake."

Mollie Dubay laughed. "And you always had a remarkably good memory." She was a tall, gaunt, gray-haired woman with rough-hewn hands, broad shoulders, and a straight spine. She and Mrs. Goodge had once worked together in the same house, but she'd been sacked from her last position as a housekeeper to Lord Fremont and had now retired. She owned a small home in Colchester and took in lodgers to help make ends meet.

"I was so pleased to get your note, and as I was coming to London anyway, I decided to take you up on your kind offer. You were by far the best pastry chef I'd ever seen." She forked up a bite of cake and popped it into her mouth. Her eyes closed in pleasure as she chewed. "You haven't lost your touch. This is wonderful."

"Why, thank you." The cook beamed in pleasure. She hesitated for a brief moment, not sure how to proceed. She'd not invited Mollie here as a source, but as a friend. She'd sent Mollie the invitation to come for tea before they had a case. Her old colleague had gone through some tough times and had no family, and Christmas was often a hard season for people like her. Mrs. Goodge was so very grateful for her situation that she was mindful of those who'd spent their lives in service and ended up in their last years all alone. Mrs. Goodge knew that if she'd ended up anywhere but here, she'd be very much in the same situation as Mollie Dubay. "So, how many lodgers do you have?"

"Two ladies, Miss Kellogg and Miss Fields. They were both in service just as we were. They're near our age and glad to have a decent place to live," she explained. "I don't charge very much, and I'm glad of the company."

"Are you goin' to do a bit of shopping while you're here in town?"

Mollie stuffed another bite into her mouth, shook her head, and chewed greedily. "No, I've got to see a solicitor. Your invitation came at just the right time. I've been left a legacy, and you'll never guess who left it to me. The very one that sacked me!"

"Lord Fremont?" Mrs. Goodge laughed. "I remember the day he let you go. You came here, and we put our heads to-gether and came up with a plan."

"I was in such a state," Mollie declared. "Being let go was so shocking that I just wandered the streets for a bit and found myself on your doorstep. You were so kind to me that day. I'll be forever grateful."

Mrs. Goodge shrugged modestly. Fred lifted his head from his spot by the cooker, saw that all was well, and then went back to sleep. "Nonsense, anyone would have done the same. But I thought Lord Fremont died last summer."

"He did, but the family fought over the will, and none of the legacies were distributed." She made a face. "They've finally come to some agreement, so I'm going to collect my two hundred pounds."

Mrs. Goodge gaped at her. "He left you two hundred pounds?"

"He left all his old servants the same amount." She snickered. "And apparently, there are quite a number of us, so it added up fairly quickly. His family was furious but finally realized none of them could get their share of the estate unless they stopped fighting."

"I wonder why he did it," the cook murmured. "He wasn't known for bein' a kind or even a halfway decent man."

"He wasn't, but he was sick a long time before he finally passed, so he had plenty of time to think of where he might be headed once he left this world," she declared. "At least that's my idea. Now, enough about me. Is there any way I can help you? Has that inspector of yours got himself another case?"

Mrs. Goodge had given up worrying about people discovering they helped the inspector with his cases. She'd finally come to the conclusion that if their activities came to be known, she could always claim that all she did was gossip a bit in the kitchen. "Yes, he got saddled with the McCourt murder. Did it make the papers in Colchester?"

"Indeed it did," she replied. "And I also read the London papers. I was especially interested in that case because my lodger used to work for the Herron family."

"Oh my goodness." Mrs. Goodge couldn't believe her

luck, or perhaps it wasn't luck but divine providence that had sent Mollie here for a reason. "Did she know anythin' about the McCourts?"

"That's all she's talked about the last two days, which was one of the reasons I was glad to escape to London," Mollie chuckled. "I shouldn't have said that. Miss Kellogg is a very nice person, but she does tend to go on and on about things. She's told me every detail she can remember."

"Gracious, do you think any of those details might be useful to the inspector?" Mrs. Goodge fully intended to get everything there was to be had from the woman, even if she had to bar the back door to keep her from leaving.

"I don't think so. Miss Kellogg worked for them over fifteen years ago." She paused. "But then again, she was there when Daniel McCourt proposed to Elena Herron. Mind you, from the way she tells it, half of London was visiting the Herron estate that Christmas. But that's not important. Miss Kellogg was the downstairs maid, and she'd gone to the drawing room to polish the furniture. The house was decorated for the holidays, and there were candles and ribbons and greenery everywhere. Just as she went into the room, she saw Daniel McCourt go down on his knee and ask Elena Herron for her hand. Miss Kellogg says it was ever so romantic. He'd proposed to her under a sprig of mistletoe."

Phyllis followed the maid. She hoped she was doing right, but Betsy had told her to follow her instincts, and right now, her instincts were screaming at her to stay away from the shops! The girl slowed her pace, and Phyllis adjusted her footsteps accordingly. Discouraged after her disastrous attempt to find out anything from the shopkeepers and clerks near the McCourt home, she'd trudged the half mile to the Brunels' neighborhood hoping her luck would change and that she'd run into a friendly clerk who wouldn't mind a quick gossip about Leon or Glenda Brunel. As she'd come abreast of the Brunel house, the servants' door opened, and this young maid stepped out and started walking. Thinking the girl was going on an errand for her mistress to one of the shops, she'd followed. But the maid turned away from the commercial district and went down a residential street.

She rubbed her hands together to keep warm as a cold wind slammed into her. The girl suddenly veered into the gateway of a churchyard. Surprised, Phyllis stopped and tried to think what she ought to do. A moment later, she charged after her quarry.

She stepped inside the gate and spotted the girl sitting at the top of the short stairway leading to the church door. She was staring down at the ground, her shoulders slumped and her legs splayed out on each side. Her gray broadcloth skirt had hitched up, revealing black stockings that had been patched on the shins with thick white thread. Her feet stuck out and pointed up at the sky. Her high-topped shoes were scuffed, and the one on her left foot had a hole as big as a tartlet on the bottom sole. Just then, she glanced up, and their gazes met.

Phyllis froze. But before she could think what she ought to say, her mouth opened and the words poured out. "Don't be scared." She edged away from the entrance. "I'm not follocin' you. Well, I am, but only because I could see you looked so upset. Is there anythin' I can do to help?"

"How did you know I was upset?" she challenged. She didn't look alarmed; only annoyed. She was skinny as a rail and had stringy reddish hair tucked up beneath her maid's cap.

"Your eyes are red from cryin', and your face is so long your chin will hit the ground if you're not careful."

"Why should you want to help the likes of me?"

Phyllis noted that her coat was so old and worn you could see the lining on the front placket. "Because someone once helped me," she replied. "And I think you could use a bit of assistance right now." By this time, Phyllis was at the foot of the church steps. "May I sit down? My name is Phy . . . Millicent Burns." She avoided using her real name just in time.

"Go ahead, it's a public place." She shrugged as if she didn't care and looked away, but Phyllis had seen the flash of hope in her eyes.

Phyllis plunked down as close to her as she dared and gave her a wide smile. "What's your name?"

"Harriet Adamson," she mumbled.

"Won't you tell me what's wrong? Sometimes talkin' helps."

The girl stared at her for a long moment, and then her eyes filled with tears. "It won't help me. I'm goin' to be sacked and I've no place to go."

"You're losin' your employment." Phyllis gazed at her sympathetically. "That's terrible. Have they told you when you have to get out?"

"Not yet." She was crying in earnest now. "I know Cook is goin' to tell the mistress that it was me that took the bottle, but it weren't, it weren't. I've not even been in the storage room for ever such a long time, and Cook keeps the spice cabinet locked as tight as a maiden's corset, so how could I have stolen anythin'?"

"What happened?"

She sniffed. "Someone stole one of Cook's spices, and she's raisin' a right old fuss about it. But it wasn't me! But I'm the one that's goin' to get the blame, and they're goin' to sack me for sure."

"But if the cabinet was locked, how can you be blamed?" Phyllis asked reasonably.

"Because two days ago I had the keys to the cabinet." She sniffed and wiped her nose with the hem of her skirt. "Cook had to borrow the housekeeper's set when she was fixin' breakfast, so she sent me up to fetch them from Mrs. Murray. When Cook gave the keys back to me, I stuck 'em in my pocket and got so busy I didn't think to give 'em to Mrs. Murray until late that afternoon. Today when Cook went to get her little glass jar of saffron out of the cabinet, it was gone, and I overheard her tellin' Mrs. Murray that I must've taken it."

"What on earth would you do with saffron?" Phyllis exclaimed. "Are you a cook?"

"No, but my cousin is an apprentice chef, and Cook claims I stole it for him." She sobbed harder. "When Mrs. Murray spoke to me about the matter, I told her I didn't even like my cousin. But the saffron is gone, and they're blamin' me. Even though I'm innocent, I offered my wages to replace both the jar and the spice if she'd not say anythin'. But she said she had to because there'd been another petty theft from the storage cupboard—a tin of lamp oil—so she couldn't let this go. She had to report it to the master and mistress."

Phyllis patted her arm. "I'm so sorry. Is there a chance they won't sack you?"

"If it were up to the mistress, I might be safe. She'd not be concerned about a tin of lamp oil and a pinch of saffron; she's not as hard as he is," she replied. "But it's not up to her. It'll be him that makes the decision. He makes all the decisions in that house. Oh God, I don't know what I'm goin' to do or where I'm goin' to go."

"How about this cousin of yours. Can he help?" Phyllis was no longer concerned about arriving back at Upper Edmonton Gardens without anything useful to report; this poor girl being tossed out on her ear was far more important than chatting up a few shopkeepers.

"I doubt it. He doesn't much like me, either." She sighed and looked at Phyllis. "It was nice of you to speak to me. You were right; talkin' did help just a bit." She got up and gave Phyllis a tremulous smile. "I'd better get back and face the music. At least if they sack me, they'll have to give me my wages. It's almost the end of the quarter."

Phyllis brushed the damp dirt from the stairs off her skirt as she stood. "I'll walk you to the gate," she offered. She was thinking hard, wondering whether she dared. She found she did. "Look, if you do get sacked, there's an address you can go to in Knightsbridge. It's a big house owned by an American named Luty Belle Crookshank. I've heard she's a decent sort, and she's always in need of domestic help."

The legal firm of Denton and Wiles was located on the ground floor of a building off the Kensington High Street. Witherspoon and Barnes waited in the outer office while one of the clerks went to announce them to McCourt's solicitor. They had come there directly after stopping in at the station for a report from the station sergeant.

"At least we don't have to go and see Leon Brunel's solicitor," Barnes remarked.

"Thank goodness," Witherspoon said. "I almost cried with joy when Sergeant Powers told us that Harwood confirmed Brunel was there. That means his alibi is now confirmed."

"But is it, sir? The report said Brunel didn't get to Harwood's office until they were ready to lock up for the day."

The constable watched while the clerk stuck his head in an office on the far side of the room. "It was almost six o'clock. If Brunel put his wife in a hansom at four fifty or thereabouts, he should have gotten to the lawyer's office by half past five at the latest."

"It's Christmas, Constable," Witherspoon reminded him. He'd so wanted at least one suspect to be eliminated. "And the traffic is terrible this time of the year. It probably took longer than usual to get there."

The clerk closed the door and hurried toward them. "Mr. Denton's been expecting you." He ushered them across the room and into the inner office.

A dark-haired man of late middle age rose from behind a desk and nodded politely at the two policemen. "I'm Oliver Denton, Daniel's solicitor." He gestured at two straight-backed chairs facing the desk. "Please, have a seat."

"Thank you, sir," Witherspoon said as they took their seats. "I'm Inspector Witherspoon, and this is Constable Barnes."

Denton took his chair and reached for a box file on the side of his desk. "I understand why you're here, Inspector. You're investigating Daniel McCourt's murder, and you probably want to know who is going to inherit his estate."

"That's the main reason we've come," Witherspoon replied. "But there are some other questions we'd like to ask you. First of all, how long have you been McCourt's solicitor?"

Denton paused, his fingers resting on the top of the file. "It's been about fourteen years."

"You became his lawyer after he married his wife?" Barnes asked.

He raised his eyebrows. "Yes, I think it was about then. We've not done much work on his behalf, but we did draw up his will. Other than that, I've not had many dealings with the fellow."

"That's unfortunate." The inspector smiled. "I was hoping you might know if Mr. McCourt had any enemies? Was he involved in any lawsuits, that sort of thing?"

Denton hesitated. "Oh dear. I was afraid you were going to bring that up, and the truth is, I'm not altogether sure of what I ought to say on the matter. McCourt hadn't actually asked me to file the lawsuit. I told him we were still in the process of gathering evidence."

"But we have it on good authority that he'd decided to move forward on the matter," Barnes interjected. He was bluffing, but the lawyer didn't need to know that, and he didn't want the fellow clamming up on them now.

Denton sighed. "Well, I did advise him that it was going to be decidedly difficult to prove in court and that it was going to be very expensive. He said he was tired of Brunel's slanders; that he'd done nothing wrong with the estate and certainly hadn't conspired with Leon Brunel to cheat Arthur out of his share."

"Did Arthur Brunel know that McCourt was going to sue him?" Barnes asked.

Denton's mouth flattened into a thin line. "He did. I told Daniel to be discreet about the matter, but apparently, he wasn't."

Witherspoon thought of what he should ask next. "How did you find out Arthur Brunel knew about the pending lawsuit?"

"Daniel told me when I ran into him last month at my club." Denton shook his head in disgust. "One hates to speak ill of the dead, but he was laughing about the matter and saying that Brunel had come to him, gotten down on his knees, and begged him not to sue. Now Daniel's dead—"

He broke off. "I'm certainly not implying that Arthur Brunel murdered him. I was simply making a comment about what I had observed of McCourt's character." Denton was back in full legal mode. "It amused him to have people under his thumb." He pulled the file box over, untied the black ribbons on the side, and flipped open the lid. "Now, I don't wish to keep you longer than necessary, so let's get to the contents of his will." He reached in, drew out a sheaf of documents, and began riffling through the pages.

Witherspoon wanted to ask more questions, but he had the feeling that this particular well had run dry. However, there was one additional thing he had to ask. "I take it that Mrs. McCourt was aware of the pending lawsuit against Arthur Brunel?"

Denton looked up. "Yes, she was. She had to be; she was going to have to pay for it. McCourt had no money of his own. He lived off a marriage settlement when he married. But his investments weren't always wise, and that money is almost gone. He was desperate for more cash. As I'm sure you know, he'd become a fanatical collector of Oriental artifacts and needed money to keep buying. Actually, I might as well tell you, despite McCourt's insistence we sue, if he'd not died, I wouldn't have done any more work on his behalf without payment."

"Why is that?" the inspector asked.

"Because I have it on good authority that his wife had already made it clear she wasn't going to give him any of her money, and I know how much a suit like this will cost."

"So who inherits his estate?" Barnes asked. "Or does he even have an estate?"

"Now that he's dead, he does." Denton picked up the sheaf of papers and scanned the contents as he spoke. "He is the sole owner of his Oriental art and artifact collection, and it's very valuable." He picked up one of the sheets and handed it to the inspector. "Here's an itemized list. I've had my clerk make a copy. Except for his personal property and his clothes, this constitutes his entire estate."

"Who gets it?" Barnes asked bluntly. "And what's the current estimated value?"

"Except for a few pieces from his collection that are bequeathed to his cousin, Leon Brunel, McCourt left everything to his wife, and a conservative estimate would be in the area of thirty thousand pounds."

Luty grinned at John Widdowes as she took the chair opposite his desk. Behind him, the view of the Thames was magnificent, and she knew that was why the head of Widdowes and Walthrop, Merchant Bankers, kept his back to it. "Thanks for seein' me without an appointment. I know you're a right busy man."

Widdowes smiled back at her. He was a handsome man of middle age, and beneath his perfectly tailored blue suit jacket were broad shoulders and a muscular build. He had thick graying blond hair, a neatly trimmed beard, and dark brown eyes. "Even if you hadn't switched some of your business my way, I'd still take time to see you. Your visits are always, shall we say, interesting. By the way, how are Inspector Witherspoon and his household?"

Luty laughed. Widdowes was one of the few bankers she trusted. On a recent case, she'd come to him and tried to wheedle information out of him. He'd seen through her ruse but helped her because it was the right thing to do, and he made it clear he was honest and ethical in his business dealings. "He's just fine, and I'm sure you already know he caught that McCourt murder case."

His clerk entered carrying a tea tray, which he put down

on the edge of the desk. He grinned at Luty and then with-drew. "I'll pour," Widdowes offered. "Sugar or cream?"

"Both," she replied. She waited patiently till he fixed the tea and handed her the cup and saucer. "Now, about that McCourt murder."

"I'm afraid I don't know anything about Daniel Mc-Court." He picked up his cup and took a sip. "But when I heard your inspector got the case, I made a few discreet in-quiries just in case you dropped by to see me."

"Bless your heart. What did ya hear?" she asked eagerly.

"Not very much, and most of it is just average, ordinary, run-of-the-mill gossip," he replied.

Luty looked at him archly. "You'd be surprised how many times some little nugget of gossip has caught a killer. It's always the small things that give 'em away."

He brightened. "In that case, I'll try to recall everything I heard. You know, of course, that he's a collector of Orien-tal art?"

"Yup." She nodded encouragingly, hoping she'd hear something she didn't already know.

"Ah, good," he continued. "I'll bet you didn't know that McCourt has no money of his own, he lives off a marriage settlement from his wife's family, and there are rumors the marriage isn't a happy one."

"Most of 'em aren't," Luty muttered. "But do go on."

"He was engaged to another woman when he was ap-proached by Milton Herron with an offer of his daughter's hand in marriage, and he immediately broke off the engage-ment. The woman was so humiliated she left the country."

"What was her name?" Luty asked.

Widdowes frowned. "Now that, my source didn't know. But he did know that the woman's brother was so outraged by the shabby way his sister had been treated that he accosted McCourt at the opera in front of his new bride and vowed revenge. But I don't think he's your killer; it was over fifteen years ago."

"There's a huge difference between the mind of a collector and the mind of an artist," Reginald Manley told Hatchet.

Hatchet had come to the elegant Mayfair mansion of Reginald and Myra Haddington Manley. They were not only two of his favorite people; they were also a source of information. The three of them were having morning coffee in front of a cozy fireplace in one of the smaller sitting rooms of the house. The couple had known immediately why Hatchet had come to see them and were, as always, delighted to be of help in the cause of justice. Hatchet, for his part, knew they were discreet and could be trusted.

"And what would that difference be?" Myra smiled at her husband. She was a middle-aged woman with a narrow face and brown hair graying at the temples. She was always dressed in the most flattering and fashionable of clothing, and today was no exception. She wore a fitted turquoise blue dress with an elaborate onyx and gold brooch coupled with a single strand of pearls and matching earrings.

Myra was from one of the wealthiest families in England, and she'd braved substantial disapproval from her own set when she'd married Reginald Manley, an artist who'd spent most of his life being supported by willing women rather than selling his paintings. But the marriage was a happy one. Once he was wed, Reginald Manley had devoted himself to his wife, and Hatchet had observed that he genuinely loved her.

"To begin with, artists aren't insane," Reginald said with relish. "Once we finish a piece, we're quite content to sell it if we can find someone to buy it, or we stuff it in the back of a cupboard or paint over it if we can't. But a collector, on the other hand; once he's acquired something, he's loath to let it go."

"Would you say that Daniel McCourt was that kind of collector?" Hatchet reached for his coffee cup and took a sip.

"Good lord, yes. He only sold things when he wanted to buy something else, and he only did that to get the upper hand over his cousin," Reginald replied.

"You mean Leon Brunel?"

"Both men are fanatical collectors and very competitive with each other," Reginald said. "But McCourt would occasionally part with something. I don't think I've ever heard of Brunel selling anything. But I think that before he died, McCourt got the upper hand over Brunel."

"What do you mean?"

Reginald grinned broadly. "The gossip I heard was that he managed to buy an old and valuable artifact from one of the ancient kingdoms of Korea right out from under his cousin's nose. But what I don't understand and what no one else seems to know is where he acquired the funds to get these items."

"His wife's aunt passed away and left her the entire Herron fortune," Myra said. "Poor Elena McCourt was always such a mouse that I imagined he bullied her into giving him an advance against her estate." She shook her head. "I pity any woman married to the men in that family. The whole lot of them were a miserable bunch. Elena Herron was set to enter a convent, but her father was desperate for a grandchild, so he forced her to marry McCourt. Glenda Norris was engaged to Nicholas Saxon when she had to marry Leon Brunel. Thank goodness Arthur Brunel never married; it saved some poor female from having a terrible life."

Hatchet put his coffee cup down. "What I don't understand is why the Herrons would pick Daniel McCourt for a son-in-law. I understand that Mrs. McCourt is an attractive woman. Couldn't the Herrons have found someone from their own class to marry her off with? That's usually how those things are done."

"McCourt was available and willing. Old Mr. Herron wanted a grandson, and Elena was no longer a young girl. At the time of the marriage she must have been close to thirty years old."

"If having a grandchild was so important, why did he wait so long before forcing her to wed?" Hatchet asked.

"Because Elena had an older brother named Henry. He'd done his duty and married a nice, wealthy young woman from a good family, but before they had children, Henry died, leaving Elena the only one left to carry on the family line."

"But any of their children would have carried the Mc-Court name, not Herron," he pointed out.

"Yes, that does seem odd, doesn't it? Perhaps Mr. Herron was less concerned with the name dying out than he was with his own bloodline disappearing." She smiled in amusement. "I always thought it poetic justice that the McCourts were childless."

Arthur Brunel stuck his head out and frowned. "What do you want?"

"We'd like to come in, sir," Witherspoon said politely.

"Why? I've already answered your questions." He tried to close the door, but Barnes flattened his hand against the wood and pushed back. The constable had seen the flash of panic in Brunel's eyes and knew without a shadow of a doubt that he'd realized they'd found out about the lawsuit.

"What are you doing?" Brunel's voice rose to a high, hysterical pitch. "How dare you barge your way into my home!"

"We're not in your home, sir." Barnes fixed him with a hard stare. "And we've come across some information that is quite damaging to you. You can either let us in or you can accompany us to the station. It's your choice, sir."

All the fight left the man, and he stood back, opening the door wide. He nodded for them to enter. Silently, they filed back into the sitting room. Remembering the hard cushions on the chairs, both men hurried toward the sofa and, without waiting for an invitation, took a seat.

Brunel remained standing and stared at them sullenly. "I don't know what you could have possibly heard. I've done nothing wrong, and Daniel McCourt was alive and well when I left. I've told you that already."

"No one at the pub remembers seeing you," the inspector said. This wasn't quite true. He'd not had a chance to speak to the constables who had gone to the pub to check the fellow's alibi.

"It's no wonder no one recalls seeing me." He crossed his arms over his chest. "It was crowded and I was only there a few moments before I realized my wallet was missing and had to go back to the McCourt house."

"Why didn't you tell us that Daniel McCourt was suing you?" Witherspoon asked softly.

Brunel took a deep breath and closed his eyes briefly. Then he straightened his spine and raised his chin. "The lawsuit has nothing to do with McCourt's murder. You didn't ask me about it, and I saw no reason to volunteer the information."

"You've admitted that you thought McCourt conspired with your half brother to cheat you out of an inheritance," the inspector continued. "That alone is reason enough to show that you've a motive for the man's death. You can't be sued by a dead man."

"I wasn't worried about being sued. He'd agreed not to go ahead with it, and even if he changed his mind, I wasn't worried about being dragged into court by him."

"He'd told you this?" Barnes asked, his expression deliberately incredulous. "He was just going to drop the suit out of the kindness of his heart?"

"Of course not. Daniel didn't have a heart." Brunel laughed harshly. "He agreed to drop the suit because I blackmailed him into it."

"Blackmailed him how?" Witherspoon demanded.

"I saw him with another woman, Inspector, and not just any woman. I saw him with Lydia Kent, and I threatened to tell his wife," he replied.

"Lydia Kent?" Barnes inquired. "Who is she?"

"She was once engaged to Daniel. He broke it off with her so that he could marry Elena. McCourt always kept poor Elena under his thumb because he controlled the money. But she just inherited a fortune, and this time, she's the one in control. Daniel hated it, but there was little he could do about the situation. He didn't dare let her know he'd been seen in a London hotel going into a suite of rooms with an old paramour."

"Is this woman in London?" Barnes asked.

He shrugged. "I have no idea. But if she is, you might want to ask her what she was doing when he was murdered."

"Are you implying she might know something about his death?" the constable pressed.

"Oh, I wouldn't go that far." Brunel was clearly enjoying himself now. His entire demeanor had changed since he'd seen them on his doorstep. "But I imagine it's likely. Daniel's always been a fool when it comes to understanding human beings. I'm no saint, Constable, but I never took pleasure in watching another human being debase himself, no matter what he'd done to me. But you asked about Lydia Kent, not me. I'm sure she hated him. He publicly humiliated her, and no matter how much time passes, one never forgets that. I saw her on the day of the tea. I had to walk there, you see. I couldn't afford a hansom cab, and I saw her standing on the corner, staring at the McCourt house."

Witherspoon said, "Did you see her after you came out of the house?"

"No," he admitted. "But then again, if she killed Daniel, she'd have taken care to make sure to stay out of sight."

"When did you see Mr. McCourt and Miss Kent together?" the constable asked.

"A few days before the murder," he replied. "I was in Knightsbridge and saw him and Lydia coming out of the Alexandria Hotel. There was a Chinaman with them carrying a large, flat box."

"I thought you said you saw them going into a 'suite of rooms.'" The constable repeated Brunel's own words.

"Oh, that's what I told Daniel when we had our little chat later that afternoon, and, of course, it must have been true, because he immediately agreed that the lawsuit was a terrible idea."

"Did you have any other reason for not worrying about the lawsuit?" Barnes asked.

He laughed again. "He had no money, Constable, and his wife assured me that despite his foolish threats, she'd make certain she didn't pay for a lawyer to drag me into court. You see, after I had my little chat with Daniel, I made it a point to run into his wife the very next morning when she was out shopping."

"Will Mrs. McCourt verify your statement?" Wither-spoon's head was spinning as his mind tried to process all the information he'd learned thus far.

"I expect so, but you'll really need to ask her yourself."

Mrs. Jeffries looked around and made sure no one was watching before she shoved open the gate and stepped into the passageway. She'd come back to Victoria Gardens for two reasons: one, to inspect the damage she might have done to the Crandalls' gate; and two, because she couldn't get the thought of mistletoe out of her mind.

She eased the gate toward the post without closing it so she could take a good look at the lock. Dark clouds had drifted in and blocked the feeble winter daylight, so she bent close and stared at the mechanism sticking out of the side. She touched the protruding stub of metal that inserted into the post plate. It wiggled easily. Closing the gate all the way, she tugged it gently back and realized it was so loose that it wasn't holding at all. She jiggled the gate and heard what sounded like metal bits rattling around in the lock proper. It was broken, but had she done it? She really had no idea. As Wiggins had pointed out, she was a strong woman and could easily have slammed into it hard enough to break it. But on the other hand, it appeared to be good and sturdy. Drat, it was impossible to tell. Which left her with only one course of action: She had to think of a way to pay for repairing the wretched thing without anyone knowing she was responsible for its destruction.

She sighed heavily and put the problem out of her mind. Right now, she had other fish to fry, so to speak. Turning, she walked purposely up the passageway toward the garden. Respectably dressed in her best bonnet and her good brown cloak, she doubted any of the residents would accost her.

Her only concern was being spotted by a constable who might recognize her. But she didn't think that likely to happen, as this morning Barnes and the inspector both confirmed the lads had completed all the local searches and house-to-house inquiries.

The path across the garden was worn with long use. She skirted a hedgerow and began looking hard at the trees in the center of the space. Her gaze stopped at a yew tree and then quickly moved on, past a pine and another yew. She turned, looking at the copse of trees from a variety of angles and spots along the path until she saw what she had come here to find.

Mistletoe. It grew as a small bundle in the barren, low-hanging branches of an oak tree and would easily be missed if you didn't look closely. But there it was, close enough to the ground that anyone with a small stool could reach it. Everyone assumed that mistletoe was easy to obtain, but she wasn't so sure. One generally didn't purchase it in a shop, and often it grew so high up in trees that unless one had a very tall ladder or was exceedingly good at climbing, it would be difficult to obtain. Mrs. Jeffries had no idea why she was so obsessed with this aspect of the case, but it had haunted her since it was apparent it had to have been deliberately put up by the killer. And the killer had to have gotten it somewhere.

She headed toward it, wanting to have a closer look, to see if it was possible to determine whether any clusters or leaves had been recently cut off the plant, but just as she started toward the oak, she heard voices coming from the McCourt home, and a moment later, she recognized the distinctive tone of Constable Griffiths. "We'll have one more quick hunt around the garden, lads," Griffiths said cheerfully. "The Home Office is putting pressure on our inspector to have this one solved by Christmas, so we'll have a final look here, just in case we've missed something. We need to be sure we've been thorough."

She didn't waste any time dodging toward the trunk of the thickest tree she could see and then making a quick, and hopefully silent, run back the way she'd just come.

CHAPTER 7

Barnes struggled not to smile as he caught sight of the hotel manager's expression when he and Witherspoon stepped through the double oak doors of the Alexandria Hotel. It was an elegant and expensive establishment on a quiet street off the King's Road in Knightsbridge. The manager gawked at them, his eyes widening with horror at the sight of a uniformed policeman crossing the marble floors of the lobby. Two bellboys, one of them loaded down with luggage, froze and stood gaping at them as the policemen skirted a brown velvet circular tuffet with an enormous fern sprouting from its center.

Witherspoon smiled politely as they reached the reception desk. "Is there a Miss Lydia Kent registered in your hotel?"

"We have a guest by that name. If you would care to wait over there, please." The manager pointed to a large potted

tree in the corner behind which was a tiny white metal bis-
tro table with matching chairs. "I'll send a bellman up to see
if she's available."

"That won't be necessary, Mr. Weedon," a woman's voice
said from behind them. "I'm already here."

Witherspoon and Barnes both turned and came face-to-
face with an attractive middle-aged woman. She had blonde
hair and clear blue eyes. She was dressed to go out in a fitted
forest green jacket and a matching hat decorated with short,
spiky feathers. "I was wondering if you would be coming to
have a chat with me." She gave them an amused smile. "You
found me faster than I thought you would."

"You know why we're here, ma'am?" the inspector queried.

"Excuse me." The manager glanced nervously at the
guests who were now openly staring at the threesome. "If
you'd like to speak with Miss Kent, the dining room is
available. I'll have tea sent in."

"Thank you, we'd appreciate that very much," Witherspoon said before turning his attention to Lydia Kent. "Is
that acceptable to you?"

"That will be fine," she replied.

A few moments later, the policemen had introduced
themselves and the three of them were alone in the empty
dining room and seated at a table covered with a heavy white
linen tablecloth.

"We're here about Daniel McCourt," Witherspoon began. "I understand you knew him."

Barnes pulled out his notebook and pencil. He put them
on the table and then looked up as the door from the kitchen
opened and a waiter appeared. He carried a silver tray loaded
with the tea things as well as a plate of sandwiches.

"Mr. Weedon said you were to have this," the waiter said.

He put the tray in the center of the table. "Would you like me to serve?"

"If you'll just pass out the plates, please, we'll serve ourselves," she replied.

"Very good, ma'am." He did as she ordered, nodded respectfully, and then hurried back to the kitchen.

Lydia reached for the silver pot and poured the steaming liquid into cups. "In answer to your question, Inspector, yes, I most certainly did know him. As I'm sure you are already aware, I was once engaged to him and he threw me over for a better catch." She gave them a dazzling smile as she handed them their cups. "But it turned out to be a blessing in disguise." She helped herself to cream and sugar. "I've had a wonderful fifteen years traveling the Far East, and he's been living in London with a woman that can't stand the sight of him."

Barnes nodded his thanks as she pushed the plate of sandwiches closer to him. He helped himself to the top one. "When was the last time you saw him?" he asked.

"Almost a week ago," she replied promptly. "We had business together."

"What kind of business?" Witherspoon took a sip of tea and then reached for a sandwich.

"I sold him a very valuable and very old sword."

"You're an antiquities dealer?" the inspector asked.

"No, but I was suddenly in a position to acquire something that was exceedingly valuable and that I knew I could sell in London. As I was coming here for a fortnight's visit, I thought I'd combine my trip with an opportunity to make a profit." She laughed when she saw the expression on their faces. "Don't look so surprised, gentlemen. Speaking candidly about money and one's need for it is quite acceptable in the Far East, especially Hong Kong."

"You came all the way from Hong Kong to stay here for a fortnight?" Witherspoon said in disbelief. The voyage took such a long time, people generally stayed far longer than two weeks.

"London is only my first stop. Paris is next. I was supposed to leave last Thursday to stay with friends, but thanks to Daniel, I was forced to stay on. Now that he's gotten himself murdered, I expect I'll be stuck here even longer."

"Did you acquire this sword with the intention of selling it to Mr. McCourt?" Barnes asked.

"Good gracious, no!" she exclaimed. "I'm not a dealer, but I am a businesswoman. News travels quickly in the small English community in Hong Kong, so when I heard that a Korean dealer I know to be trustworthy had acquired this artifact, I bought it from him. I was lucky to get it as well, because he'd already been contacted by agents acting for several London collectors."

"You offered more money?" Barnes helped himself to another sandwich.

She smiled proudly. "Oh no, both the other offers were more than I was willing to pay, but I showed up with cash, and in that part of the world, cash in hand is always going to win over paper promises."

"Was Daniel McCourt the only person you notified that you had this sword available for sale?" Witherspoon asked.

"I offered it to the British Museum, and they were interested, but they hoped I'd donate it. When I declined their kind request, I sent Daniel a note telling him it was for sale."

"You didn't contact Leon Brunel or any of the other London collectors?" The inspector thought that rather odd.

"Now, why would I do that"—she smiled slyly— "when I knew that all I had to say to Daniel was that if he wasn't interested, I was offering it to his cousin next. It worked like a charm. Once I mentioned Leon's name, the haggling stopped and he agreed to my price." Her easy manner disappeared, and she was suddenly serious. "But it appears as if Daniel will have the last laugh after all."

"Why is that?" Witherspoon asked.

"Because I assumed that despite his many faults, Daniel cared about his reputation as a collector. I was wrong. I foolishly let him take the sword with him without taking payment. He promised to bring me the money within a day or two. He offered me a letter of credit, but I wanted cash. So he signed a promissory note, and I let him take the sword. When Daniel didn't appear with my money, I decided to stay and find out what had happened."

"Did you go to his home?" the inspector asked.

"Yes, I did. I was going to confront him. I'd heard some very ugly rumors about his financial situation, and frankly, I was somewhat alarmed about his ability to pay what he owed."

"When did you go to see him?" Barnes asked.

"The afternoon that he was murdered," she replied. "I arrived there, and the first thing I saw was a man going inside. A few moments later, a couple went in, and that made me realize there was a social event of some sort going on. I walked to the end of the street, trying to decide if I ought to just barge in or not. But I didn't want to embarrass his wife, so I decided I'd wait awhile and then go back."

"What did you do while you waited?" Witherspoon asked.

"I went to the shops. But frankly, I couldn't enjoy myself. I was too worried about my money. You see, when Daniel hadn't shown up with the payment, I'd made some inquiries and hadn't liked what I'd heard. So as much as I was not in favor of making a scene, I went back to his house, but by that time, it was obvious something dreadful had happened."

"How did you know he'd been murdered?" Witherspoon asked.

"There were constables, and I heard someone in the crowd that had gathered say he'd gotten his throat slit with a sword. At that point it seemed rather tacky to harass the widow for the money."

The inspector tried to keep it all straight in his head. They'd learned so much today that he was getting confused.

"How much did he owe you?" Barnes asked.

"Five thousand pounds."

Wiggins hadn't had any luck at the Alexandria Hotel. He'd managed to speak with two bellboys in the mews behind the building but had learned nothing. So he'd decided to try his hand at speaking to Annie, the McCourt housemaid. Unfortunately, his luck there was just as bad. He'd walked up and down the street a half dozen times, but no one had come out of the servants' entrance. He was determined the day wouldn't be wasted, so he'd taken the advice he'd given Phyllis and moved along, heading to Leon Brunel's street.

There wasn't much traffic besides a hansom cab dropping off a fare and a grocer's delivery van pulling up to the pavement ahead. He moved casually, checking the addresses as he walked until he found the Brunel house. He continued past it until he got to the end of the road, where he crossed to the other side and went back in the direction he'd just come. He did this twice, taking care to keep his attention on the servants' entrance. On his third pass, he noticed a stern-faced old woman watching him from the second-floor window of a house.

"Blast a Spaniard!" he thought to himself. It looked as if he'd have nothing to report. He couldn't hang about here anymore with that old biddy watching him.

He was almost at the end of the street when a young girl came out of the side of the Brunel house.

His spirits soared; she was a housemaid. He could see the brown broadcloth dress hanging from beneath the girl's three-quarter length black coat. He ducked around the corner and crossed the road out of the sight of prying eyes. Bending down, he pretended to be tying his shoelaces. The maid rounded the corner and headed in the direction of the local shops.

Wiggins stood up and followed her, taking care to stay far enough back so that she wouldn't spot him, while also taking the added precaution of remaining on the opposite side of the street.

He saw her turn onto the local high street, and she disappeared from view. Not wanting to lose her in one of the shops, he charged toward the corner, emerging onto a street crowded with well-dressed ladies, housewives with shopping baskets, street urchins, and vendors. Wiggins stood on tiptoe, looking frantically up and down the high street before spotting his quarry less than fifteen feet from him.

She stood in front of a baker's shop and stared at the display in the front window.

Wiggins sidled up next to her. The girl didn't notice; her attention was fixed on a plate of treacle tarts. She was licking her lips. "Those look ever so good, don't they?" he murmured.

"They do." The maid gave him a quick half smile. She was a thin girl with dark blonde hair tucked up beneath her green knitted cap.

"Are ya goin' in there to do a bit of shoppin'?" He gave her his best smile.

She gave him a sidelong glance, her expression wary. "I'm not supposed to speak to strangers."

"Sorry, miss." He bobbed his head deferentially. "It's just that I'm in service and thought you might be as well. It's my afternoon out, and I don't know anyone in London. You looked like a nice girl, and I was hopin' you'd speak to a lonely country boy who's not 'ad a kind word spoken to him in the three weeks 'e's been in London. I beg your pardon for botherin' you, miss." He turned on his heel and walked away, praying silently that his pathetic act worked. He'd almost made it to the corner and had decided that today wasn't his day, when she spoke.

"Wait," she cried.

He turned and gazed at her hopefully. "You're not angry at me, miss? I'm not usually so bold with young ladies, but you 'ave such a kind face."

She smiled, and her thin, rather homely face was transformed into something close to loveliness. "I'm not angry at you. I'm just not used to anyone speakin' to me. I didn't mean to be rude."

"You weren't rude." He returned to the baker's shop. "I was bein' forward. Are you goin' in there?"

She blushed and looked back at the plate of tarts. "No, I was just lookin'."

Wiggins was no expert on women, but he knew they generally liked to look at pretty dresses or fine lace or fancy hats and ribbons. When they were staring at food, it meant they were hungry. He knew what he had to do. For a brief moment, his conscience fought a quick surge of guilt and anger; guilt that he was going to take advantage of her hunger, and anger that they lived in a world where so many had to go hungry. "I was lookin', too." He forced a smile. "It's the first day out I've 'ad since I come to London, and as I've a bit of coin, I was goin' to treat myself. It's not like they feed us all that much where I work."

Seeing a kindred spirit, the girl grinned broadly. "They're not generous with food where I work, either. They sent me out to get more salt, but as the housekeeper is shut up with the mistress plannin' a reception, no one will miss me for at least an hour, so I thought I'd take a bit of time for myself."

"What about the cook. Won't she tattle?" he asked. It was easy to pretend to be another hardworking servant. London was full of them.

"No, she's taken to her room for a lie-down. My name's Abigail Cross. What's yours?"

"I'm Albert Jones." He put his hand in his pocket and fingered the shilling piece he always carried. "It's wonderful to 'ave someone to chat with. There's a small park with benches on it not far from 'ere. What do you say I get us a couple of treacle tarts and we'll go 'ave a sit-down and a chat."

Abigail looked doubtful. "I don't know."

"It's been ages since I've 'ad anyone young to talk to." He pleaded. "I promise I'm a decent sort. It's just a couple of buns and a bit of company that I'm after."

"Alright then." Abigail grinned. "I'll wait here while you go in and get the tarts for us."

Five minutes later, the two had found a dry bench and were munching on their pastries. "This is ever so nice of you," Abigail said. "It's a real treat for me. It's been horrible at my household. No one is even lookin' forward to Christmas or Boxing Day."

Wiggins swallowed the bite he'd just taken. "I'm sorry to 'ear that. 'Ave they been workin' you too 'ard then? Is that what's wrong?" He knew it wouldn't do to jump right in and start asking questions about the McCourt murder.

Abigail nibbled off the edge of her tart. "They always work us like slaves. But lately, the master and the mistress have been at odds, and he's cut the household allowance. You know what that means."

Unfortunately, Wiggins did know. "So the mistress is makin' it up by cuttin' back on the amount of food she lets the cook order." He snorted in disgust. "No wonder you were hungry. Did they even let you 'ave an egg for your breakfast?" Even though he'd never experienced it himself, he knew it was common practice that the first thing cut back when the money dried up was food for the servants.

Abigail shoved the last of the tart into her mouth and chewed vigorously. "We're eatin' porridge these days except for Sundays, when they let us have an egg but no bacon. The housekeeper told us that come January, we've got to start payin' for our own tea and sugar as well. It's not fair. Why should we be punished because Mr. and Mrs. Brunel can't get along."

Wiggins was genuinely upset for the girl. But he had to find out if the discord between the Brunels had anything to do with McCourt's murder. "That takes a big chunk out of your quarterly wages, doesn't it? But why are your master and mistress fightin' so much? 'Ave they always been at odds?"

Abigail bobbed her head. "Who knows. It's gotten worse lately, though. Mr. Brunel's cousin was murdered, and ever since then, they've been goin' at it like cats and dogs. They don't even care that the entire household can hear them."

"Someone was murdered?"

"It's been in all the papers," Abigail said eagerly. "We've had the police around, and that caused an even bigger row than usual. You should've heard them go at it as soon as the policemen left. Mr. Brunel was shoutin' at her that he wished to God he'd never married her, that she was disloyal and treacherous." Abigail brushed the crumbs off her lap and stood up.

"Cor blimey, that's awful." He wished he'd gotten her more to eat.

"Mrs. Brunel screamed right back that it was his own fault for tryin' to lie to the police, and he shouted that she was no better, that he knew for a fact she'd not come straight home after he put her in that hansom cab, and where had she gone. Why didn't she tell the police about where she'd gone, because she'd not come straight home."

He pretended to be shocked. "Was it true?"

"Oh, she'd come home but it was much later than she let the police believe. I know because I overheard her speakin' to that inspector. Just before he and the constable left, the constable asked what time she got home and she said she wasn't sure, but she thought it was close to five fifteen. But that's not true. She didn't get home till after seven o'clock."

"You give me that baby right now," Luty demanded as she charged into the kitchen of Upper Edmonton Gardens for their afternoon meeting. Without even bothering to shed her cloak, she flopped down into her spot, scraped her chair back, and patted her lap.

"Here you are." Betsy gently placed Amanda into Luty's arms. "I'm glad you got back on time, as she's almost ready for her nap."

"I knew that," Luty murmured, turning her attention to her namesake. "That's why I paid the hansom driver double to git me here quick as could be."

"That's not wise, madam." Hatchet clucked his tongue and tried to look stern. "Driving at high speeds through the city is dangerous."

Luty snorted but didn't look up. "Yeah, like you haven't done it whenever it suited you. I swear this baby gets prettier and prettier every day. Oh my goodness, she's grinnin' at me."

Mrs. Jeffries, who'd gone to the wet larder to get another jug of cream, put the pitcher on the table and took her seat. "Are we ready to begin?"

"I can hold my darlin' while we talk," Luty declared. Amanda gurgled in response. "See, she wants to be at our meetin', too."

"Who would like to go first?" Mrs. Jeffries asked. She was eager to give her own report but could tell from the general air around the table that most everyone had something to share.

"I'll go," Hatchet volunteered. He told them about his meeting with the Manleys. "I'm afraid my source merely confirmed what we already knew. Elena McCourt was going to use her inheritance to gain the upper hand in the marriage."

"But why would she kill him now?" Betsy ventured. "Especially as she had all the money and she was going to be in charge. I'd think she'd want to keep him alive so she could get a bit of her own back."

"Unless she was just sick of the feller and fed up with him," Luty murmured. "That happens. Remember, we know they was fightin' right before the tea party. Maybe he pushed her too far and as soon as she got shut of the guests, she killed him."

"And she was the one that insisted everyone leave," Phyllis added.

"I find it more interestin' that Glenda Brunel had once been in love with Nicholas Saxon," Mrs. Goodge said.

"It might be interestin', but that don't give either of them a motive for killin' McCourt," Wiggins said.

"We don't know that for a fact," Ruth said. "What if Mrs. Brunel and Mr. Saxon were planning on running away together and McCourt found out about it. He could have threatened to tell Leon Brunel, and from the gossip I heard from my sources, Leon Brunel never lets something go once it is his. Oh dear—" she broke off and flushed in embarrassment. "I'm sorry," she apologized to Hatchet. "I should have waited to see if you were through."

"That's quite alright," he replied. "I was finished with my report."

Mrs. Jeffries looked at Ruth. "Why don't you go next, then?"

"Thank you. As I said, I did hear some gossip, but I don't know if it's going to be useful or not. I had tea today with an acquaintance of mine whom I felt sure would have heard of some of our principals in this case, and I got very lucky. She didn't know much about Daniel McCourt, but she knew the Brunels socially. Like Brunel, she and her husband are collectors. When they were having dinner at the Brunel home, he showed them a carved jade pagoda from the Ming dynasty."

"When was this?" Mrs. Jeffries asked quickly.

"Sometime in October," Ruth replied. "Olivia couldn't recall the exact date. But what's interesting is that her husband specializes in collecting jade; he's advised the British Museum on some of their acquisitions for the Oriental collection. As they were driving home that night, he told Olivia that he didn't think the carving was a genuine Ming at all. He said it was a badly done reproduction and certainly not old." She stopped and took a breath. "I don't know what this could possibly have to do with McCourt's murder, but I thought it worth repeating."

"All information is worth repeatin'," Mrs. Goodge stated

firmly. "If Ruth is finished and no one has any objections, I'll go next." She told them about her visit from her Mollie Dubay.

"He proposed to her under the mistletoe," Betsy murmured when the cook had finished. "And Mrs. Jeffries told us that Constable Barnes had reported the McCourt butler made it clear that the victim couldn't stand the sight of mistletoe. I wonder if there's a connection."

" 'Course there is." Smythe grinned at his wife. "It probably reminds 'im of the silly way 'e asked her to marry 'im. They didn't exactly become an 'appy couple, now, did they?" He glanced at Luty, pushed back from the table, and got up. "Looks like the lass is sleepin'. Let me take 'er. Your arms must be about ready to fall off."

Luty kissed Amanda's forehead and handed him the baby. He headed off toward the cook's quarters. "But Betsy has a point," Mrs. Goodge continued. "Why was that mistletoe hangin' over the body? Mrs. McCourt wouldn't have put it up. It points too much toward her as the killer."

"Maybe she did it just to spite 'im," Wiggins suggested. "It sounds as if now that she didn't 'ave to depend on 'im for money, she was gettin' a bit of 'er own back."

"Yes, but then the question would be when did she put it up, before he died just to niggle him, or after he died because he was dead?" Ruth mused.

Mrs. Jeffries felt as if they'd all stolen her thunder. But then she told herself not to be childish. Just because she'd been worrying about why that mistletoe was there didn't mean the others hadn't considered the question as well. "Would you like to go next, Luty?"

"Indeed I would." She hesitated, waiting until Smythe returned to his seat at the table. "I had a nice chat with a banker friend of mine, and I'm sorry to say that most of what

I heard was what we already know." She told them about her visit to John Widdowes.

"The woman that he humiliated, the one he was engaged to," Betsy said. "Your source said her brother threatened McCourt?"

"That was fifteen years ago." Luty brushed that aside. "Seems to me that despite our efforts, we ain't learnin' much about this case."

"Yes, it seems like the only thing we've discovered of any value is that everyone in London knew that Elena McCourt now controlled the money and she wasn't going to share it with her husband," Mrs. Jeffries said.

"So why kill him when she could make him dance to 'er tune like she's 'ad to do for him all these years?" Wiggins said thoughtfully. "But then again, sometimes I think married people do a lot of things just to spite each other, not because it makes any sense. Today, I 'ad miserable luck. I couldn't find anyone at the McCourt house to talk to, and the Alexandria Hotel wasn't any better. But I did 'ave a nice chat with a maid from the Brunel house."

"Which Brunel?" Luty asked.

"Leon and Glenda Brunel," he replied. "And from what I 'eard, those two are right miserable with each other." He repeated the conversation he'd had with Abigail Cross.

"Glenda Brunel didn't get home until seven o'clock," Phyllis commented. "That's interestin'. At least you found out somethin' different. I didn't hear much of anythin' when I had my chat with a maid from the Brunel household."

"Tell us what you did hear." Mrs. Jeffries gave her an encouraging smile.

Phyllis told them about following the young maid and their meeting on the church steps. "I'm sorry," she finished.

"I know I should have asked her more questions, but she was so scared she was goin' to be gettin' sacked." She looked at Luty. "And I'm sorry I gave her your address, but she was in such misery. I couldn't think what else to do."

Luty waved off her apology. "You did right by sendin' her to me if she gets sacked. If I can't use her in my household, I'll bully one of my banker friends into hirin' the girl."

"You did very well, Phyllis. You were kind to the girl, and that's important. Now, if all of you are finished, I'll go next," Mrs. Jeffries said. She told them about her trip to the communal garden.

"At least this time you didn't track in pine mulch," Mrs. Goodge commented when she'd finished.

"Did I track it in yesterday?" Mrs. Jeffries laughed. "Gracious, I didn't even notice."

"Even if the mistletoe came from the communal garden, I don't understand why the killer hung it up," Betsy said. "Wouldn't he or she be taking a risk? Constable Barnes said it was hung from the doorframe, and unless the murderer is seven feet tall, he or she would need to stop and drag a chair or something over to get it up that high."

"There was a stool in the study," Ruth reminded them.

"Even so," Betsy argued, "why take the time to do it? The only connection we know of is that he proposed to his wife under a sprig of the stuff. So unless the killer wanted to point to Mrs. McCourt as the killer, why take the risk of staying there one moment longer than necessary?"

"Maybe the killer *was* pointin' the finger at Mrs. McCourt," Wiggins suggested.

"But that would only work if people knew about the proposal," Ruth said. "Mrs. Goodge's source was a housemaid who just happened to walk in. But we don't know if anyone else knew the story, and we've not heard it from any other source."

"Perhaps the killer was just muddying the waters," Mrs. Jeffries suggested, her expression thoughtful. "Then again, there's something about this case that suggests the killer didn't mind taking risks. Besides, if the killer didn't put it up there, then who did?"

The inspector was late for dinner that night. He and Mrs. Jeffries were in the drawing room having a glass of sherry, and he was in the midst of telling her about his day. "It's quite annoying, Mrs. Jeffries. According to the reports, no one in the neighborhood saw or heard anything. Now, I ask you, if someone is getting his neck sliced by a great big sword, wouldn't he make a bit of a fuss?"

"One would think so," Mrs. Jeffries replied. But she wasn't so very sure of that fact. The truth of the matter was, she really should have gone to speak with their good friend Dr. Bosworth. She'd no idea how someone would react upon having an artery or a vein severed. She made up her mind to go along to St. Thomas' Hospital the next morning. "But then again, perhaps a body goes into shock and is quite unable to utter a sound when such an injury occurs. Have you spoken to the police surgeon about it?"

Witherspoon frowned. "No, I haven't, but that's a jolly good idea. Mind you, I'm not sure the neighbors would have noticed anyone lurking about the area in any case; not with all the comings and goings of the tea guests."

"And none of the neighbors saw anything?"

"No." He sighed heavily. "So we can't even verify that Mrs. McCourt was out on the balcony when the murder was taking place. As a matter of fact, when I interviewed Miss

Kent, she mentioned that she'd walked past the other side of the house during the period when the murder must have happened. I asked her if she'd seen the balcony, and she said she had but that it had been empty."

"You don't think Mrs. McCourt is guilty, do you sir?"

"No, why should she kill him now? She has the upper hand."

"Well, it certainly sounds as if you've had a very full day, sir," she said cheerfully. "What else did you learn?" She listened carefully as he recounted the rest of his interviews. "So Lydia Kent claims that Daniel McCourt owed her five thousand pounds? That's a huge amount of money."

Witherspoon frowned. "I thought so as well, but Miss Kent assured us this isn't merely an old sword, but a valuable artifact from one of the earlier kingdoms of that part of the world."

Something nudged at the back of her mind but was gone before she could grab the wretched thing and make sense of it.

He put his empty glass on the table. "Nonetheless, whatever we might think about the value of the Hwando, it does give her a legitimate excuse to have been in the area."

Mrs. Jeffries rose and picked up his glass. "Would you like another sherry, sir? Mrs. Goodge has supper in the warming oven, so there's no rush." She wanted him to keep talking. The more he spoke, the more likely it was he'd recall additional details of his day.

"I'd love one." He smiled. "And pour another for yourself. I do hope we get this case closed soon. I don't know why we always seem to get a difficult investigation at this particular time of the year. It's most unfair. I want to enjoy the season," he complained. "Lady Cannonberry was going to have a dinner party, but she's put it off because of this wretched murder. Oh, I suppose I ought not to feel so hard done by; there are so many in London that have so little. But I still haven't had time to buy Amanda her present."

Mrs. Jeffries stood at the window and stared out at the street. The house was silent, as the others had gone to bed. She'd told Wiggins she'd do the locking up and sent him and Fred up to their room at the top of the house. She tried to marshal the facts of this case into some kind of cohesive order, but it was difficult. They were learning the same few facts over and over. Everyone had found out that Elena McCourt had been dominated by her husband but now had control of her own money because of an inheritance. They had learned that Arthur Brunel felt cheated by his half brother, Leon, and Daniel. Now, thanks to the inspector, there was another suspect who hadn't even been at the tea: Lydia Kent. Where did she fit into the picture? Was there any meaning to the mistletoe over the body, or was the killer simply trying to muddy the waters? She sighed audibly and let the curtain she'd been holding fall back into place. Questions, so many questions, and she couldn't answer any of them. She picked up the small hand lantern she'd put on the table and went up to her rooms.

As she climbed the stairs, her mind raced with possibilities. They needed to learn more about everyone at that tea party. Mrs. Jeffries stopped at the landing and stared into the darkness. They were going around in circles, and it was time to stop.

The next morning, Witherspoon and Barnes found themselves back at Victoria Gardens. They waited in the foyer as the butler went to get Mrs. McCourt.

Barnes walked down the hallway and stuck his head into

the drawing room. "There's no sign of mourning here," he said to the inspector. "The tree is still up and so are the decorations."

"Not everyone believes in draping black crepe all over the house." Witherspoon stared at the ornate mirror on the foyer wall. "The old custom of covering the mirrors hasn't been observed, either."

"And it won't be, Inspector." Elena McCourt appeared from behind them. She'd come in the front door. "I fail to see how covering a mirror or draping the house with black crepe will do the slightest bit of good when there's been a death in the family. But do come into the drawing room and sit down. When Haines told me you were here, I took the liberty of ordering coffee for us." She went past them, the material of her dark green dress whooshing as she led them into the drawing room. "Please make yourselves comfortable." She pointed to the sofa and took the chair opposite.

"I'm sorry to disturb you again, Mrs. McCourt," he began as they sat down.

"Don't be," she interrupted. "You're neither of you fools, so I know you've both guessed there was no great love between my husband and me. But he didn't deserve to be murdered. I'm quite prepared to answer any questions you have, so please don't worry about damaging my feelings. Now, what is it that's brought you here today?"

Witherspoon's mind went completely blank. After his chat with Mrs. Jeffries this morning at breakfast, he'd thought of dozens more questions for the widow, and that was the trouble. He simply couldn't decide where to start.

Luckily, Barnes had no such problem. "Do you know a Miss Lydia Kent?"

"Yes, she and Daniel were once engaged," she replied. "I

believe when he broke off the engagement she went to the Far East with her brother."

The inspector smiled gratefully at the constable and then asked, "Were you aware she'd recently sold your husband a sword?"

"No, I wasn't. But it doesn't surprise me. Daniel bought items from lots of different sources," she mused. "But that's quite odd, really."

"Why is that?" Witherspoon asked.

"Well, he told me that he'd acquired the sword through Jerome Raleigh, not Lydia Kent."

The inspector wasn't quite sure how to phrase his next comment. "Erh, uh, perhaps he thought he was sparing your feelings. Some women wouldn't appreciate their husband having business dealings with a former fiancée."

She laughed heartily. "Don't be absurd. Daniel never bothered to spare my feelings in anything, and lately, he's been so angry at me that if he could hurt me, he'd have done so with relish."

Witherspoon stared at her wordlessly. He shouldn't be so surprised. After all the murders he'd investigated, he knew it was often the case that family members ended up loathing one another. Nevertheless, he was still shocked.

"Why was your husband angry with you?" Barnes asked.

The butler entered, pushing a trolley with a silver coffee service on it. He stopped next to Mrs. McCourt. "Would you like me to pour, madam?"

She waved him away. "No, I'll do it. How do you take your coffee, Inspector?"

"With cream and sugar, please," he replied.

She poured out three cups and glanced at Barnes. "Constable?"

"Cream and sugar as well," he said.

She fixed their coffee and handed round the cups. They were delicate, paper-thin white porcelain with blue flowers and a gold rim. Witherspoon held his saucer carefully as he waited for the drink to cool.

She took a quick sip and then sat back in her chair. "In answer to your question, Constable, Daniel was furious with me because I wouldn't agree to let him control my money. He wasn't used to me standing up to him, but then again, men rarely are."

Barnes smiled slightly. "Has something changed recently in your circumstances, ma'am?"

"How very coy you are." She laughed. "I'm sure our solicitor has already told you that I've recently come into an inheritance from my late aunt. She was very rich, and Daniel naturally assumed I'd hand everything over to him. He was furious when I didn't."

"Was there a reason you didn't want him to handle your financial affairs?" The inspector took a sip of coffee and then struggled not to make a face. He didn't care for it at all.

She put her cup on the table and sat up straight. All traces of amusement had vanished from her face. "When we married, fifteen years ago, my family settled this house and a huge amount of money on us. It was enough for us to live comfortably for the rest of our lives, but Daniel made one foolish investment after another, and if I hadn't inherited from my family, we'd have been out on the street. So I ask you, why should I have given him my money? He'd just fritter it away on stupid investments and his wretched collection."

"You didn't approve of your husband's collecting?" Barnes pressed.

"At first I didn't mind, but he's spent thousands and thousands of pounds on these stupid objects," she said as she gestured toward the study. "And he doesn't even know whether he's buying junk or jewels."

"I thought you said he had everything appraised by an expert," the inspector commented. He tried another sip of coffee, but it tasted no better than the first.

"Jerome Raleigh's been hoodwinking Daniel for years." She sneered. "He's no more an expert than I am, and Daniel had finally realized it as well."

"Yet he invited Mr. Raleigh to tea to show off his new sword," Witherspoon continued.

"No, he invited him here to expose him as the fraud he was, and I think the man knew it. He was decidedly nervous. Daniel kept watching him and going on and on about his latest acquisition. He only did that because he'd acquired it without Raleigh's help."

"So he didn't have the newest item he'd acquired appraised by an expert?" Barnes was getting a bit confused as well.

"Oh, he did," she replied. "But it wasn't Raleigh. It was someone else. I must say that Mr. Raleigh looked very relieved when the fire started and the tea was abandoned. He couldn't wait to get out of here."

Witherspoon was curious. "Excuse me, Mrs. McCourt, but if you had told your husband you weren't going to let him control the money, how did he think he was going to be able to pay for his acquisitions?"

She shrugged. "I assume he had some money put aside for them. He knew I wasn't giving him any more."

"But he'd not put any money aside, he'd signed a promissory note for his latest acquisition," Witherspoon said.

She frowned heavily. "What do you mean? I saw the bill of sale for the Hwando myself, and it was marked paid in full."

"Then I wonder why Miss Lydia Kent says your husband owed her five thousand pounds for it."

Smythe knocked softly on the door of the Dirty Duck Pub. It was too early for opening, but he wanted to speak to Blimpey Groggins. Mrs. Jeffries told all of them to dig a bit deeper, and Smythe knew she was right. They'd been going around in circles now, all of them finding out the same facts over and over.

A barmaid opened the door, saw who it was, and then waved him inside. "Blimpey's at 'is table 'avin' a cup of tea. You want one?"

Smythe nodded and pulled off his cap and gloves. "That would be very welcome. It's so cold outside it feels like my bones are freezin'."

Blimpey waved him over. "Good mornin'. Come and sit yerself down. We've a nice warm fire burnin'."

Smythe stopped and rubbed his hands together in front of the fireplace for a moment before pulling out the stool and settling down. By then, the barmaid was back with a steaming cup of tea. "Thank you," he said. He waited till she'd gone back behind the bar before he began speaking. "I 'ope you've got somethin' good for me. We're not makin' much progress on this one, and it's almost Christmas."

"Don't worry so much." Blimpey laughed. "'Ave I ever disappointed ya? As it is, I've got plenty to tell ya. For starters, Glenda Brunel is 'avin' a romance with her old friend Nicholas Saxon."

"And if it were Leon Brunel that'd been murdered, that would be really 'elpful." Smythe grinned broadly and took a sip from his mug.

"Don't be daft. My point is this: Daniel McCourt knew about the affair."

" 'Ow the devil did you find that out?"

Blimpey raised his eyebrow. "I've got sources everywhere, and ya know I don't divulge them. But let's just say that in the weeks before the murder, street urchins 'ad eyes sharp enough to spot the likes of Daniel McCourt followin' Glenda Brunel to Saxon's house."

Smythe considered it carefully. "Which could mean that either Glenda Brunel or Nicholas Saxon murdered McCourt to keep him from tellin' her husband about the affair. But we've heard that Mrs. Brunel doesn't care much what 'er husband thinks of 'er."

"Don't believe it," Blimpey scoffed. "A woman may scrap with 'er husband and indulge in a bit of name-callin', but she'd not want to be out in the streets. Saxon's got a big house and part of 'is collection left to sell, but the house is encumbered with a mortgage, and once the word about the fake antiquities hits the market, no one will pay much for his collection even if it's genuine."

"What fake antiquities?"

Blimpey chuckled. "Jerome Raleigh 'adn't just made a mistake with those Yuan vases. He's been sellin' fake bits and pieces to McCourt for some time now, and McCourt 'ad found out about it. He was goin' to go public with it and 'ave Raleigh prosecuted, which means that Saxon wouldn't be able to sell diddly-squat to anyone for a decent amount of cash until the scandal died down."

CHAPTER 8

Mrs. Jeffries walked into St. Thomas' Hospital and stopped at the porter's station in the main hall. "Is Dr. Bosworth here today?"

The porter, a burly man with a ruddy complexion, gave her a quick, assessing glance and then opened the ledger on his desk. "Let me check for you, ma'am," he said. She'd worn a gold and brown plaid day dress rather than her brown bombazine housekeeper's attire under her good brown cloak; she had also put on her best hat and had taken the added precaution of wearing her amber and gold brooch to ensure the hospital staff cooperated readily with her inquiries. People were always far quicker to help when you were well dressed.

She waited while his pudgy fingers ran down a list of names. She'd been here many times before and could easily have gone to Dr. Bosworth's office, but the truth was she didn't want to walk down two flights of stairs unless she knew for a fact he was in the building.

"He's here today, ma'am." The porter stood up and started to come around the desk. "Let me show—"

"I know where it is," she interrupted with a smile. "Thanks very much for your help."

She was out of breath by the time she reached his office, so she slowed down to give herself a moment to recover. His door stood open, and he was seated behind his desk reading a file. Bosworth, a red-haired man with a pale complexion and deep-set hazel eyes, was so engrossed in his reading that he didn't look up as she approached. She knocked lightly on the doorframe.

Annoyed at being interrupted, he frowned as he looked in her direction, but then his bony face broke into a broad smile. "Mrs. Jeffries, I've been expecting you. Come in and sit down. Shall I get us tea?"

"Not for me, Dr. Bosworth." She saw that his office hadn't changed very much since she'd last been here. His desk was covered with stacks of books and periodicals, the cabinet beside the door remained full of bottles, vials, and jars filled with various colored liquids, and the linoleum on the floor was still cracked.

He grabbed a stack of files from the chair in front of his desk. "I'm delighted you came by. If you hadn't, I was going to drop by Upper Edmonton Gardens to see you." She sat down on the spot he'd just cleared and watched him dump the files next to his desk.

"I've read the postmortem report on Daniel McCourt." He gave her an inquiring look as he flopped back into his seat. "Inspector Witherspoon did get that one, didn't he?"

Bosworth had helped them on several of their previous cases. He had spent several years in San Francisco, where he'd worked with an American physician. Together the two men had made a study of fatal wounds caused by various kinds of weapons, mainly guns. Apparently, there was no shortage of bullet-riddled corpses in California. Bosworth had also come to the conclusion that a thorough study of the body at the murder scene could yield very interesting and useful results. His ideas weren't accepted universally, but he'd told Mrs. Jeffries that more and more police surgeons were coming to consult with him.

"He did," she replied. "You've read the postmortem report?"

He laughed. "As soon as I heard the victim had been killed with a sword, I asked for a copy of it. It was very interesting. That sword must have been sharp as a razor to inflict the kind of damage it did. Now, I know you had a reason for coming. Do you have some specific questions?"

"I do, but I'm not certain you can answer them," she said. "They are the sort of questions that perhaps no one can answer."

"Now you've got me intrigued." He tapped the top of the file on the side of the desk. "Ask whatever you like, and then I'll tell you what I've found in the postmortem report."

"Alright, according to what the inspector told me, the victim had both sides of his neck uh . . . sliced through." She grimaced.

"That's correct. Both his jugular vein and carotid artery were severed."

"Does that mean he would have died quickly?"

Bosworth made a steeple with his hands under his chin and leaned back in his chair. "That depends on how you define 'quickly.' My estimate would be that he would have died within three or four minutes."

"Would he have been capable of speech?" she asked. "He

was alone in the house, but there were people nearby. I keep wondering why he didn't scream for help."

"I don't think he would have been capable of speech. Both of the wounds were deep, and he probably went into shock as soon as the first blow was struck. Even if he'd tried to call for help, his vocal cords were stunned from the blow and he probably couldn't have managed more than a squeak. Unless there was someone close by the poor fellow, he wouldn't have had a chance."

"Everyone else was outside," she said. "Would there have been a lot of blood?"

"Oh yes." He leaned forward, resting his elbows on the desk. "Blood would have splattered, but if he'd collapsed immediately, the blood would have then pooled around the body."

"Then shouldn't the killer have been covered in bloodstains?" she asked.

"Normally, yes, the killer should have gotten blood on his or her clothes," he replied. "However, I understand this weapon is a sword called a long Hwando. When I read the postmortem, I contacted a friend of mine who knows something about Oriental swords, and he claims that the long Hwando was exactly as the name implied—long, and also very heavy."

"Too heavy for a woman to use?"

He looked uncertain. "I doubt that. I've seen some very strong women. Furthermore, my friend said that if the killer wielded the sword correctly when he or she murdered the victim, then the culprit could have been standing far enough away to avoid any blood that spurt from the wound."

"But how does one learn to wield a sword correctly?" she asked thoughtfully.

"Come now, Mrs. Jeffries," he chided. "Surely you're not

serious. Fencing is very popular, and I believe the Queen's household guards still carry swords."

"Of course they do," she agreed. "But fencing is usually done with a rapier, not a great heavy sword like the one you described, and even for the Queen's household, swords are mainly ceremonial these days. No one uses them as weapons."

"Your killer did."

"What do you think, sir?" Barnes asked the inspector. They were in a hansom cab heading toward Jerome Raleigh's rooms.

Witherspoon grabbed at the handhold as the cab hit a pothole. "I'm not sure what to make of the situation," he replied. "Mrs. McCourt answered our questions with a candor that was most surprising, so I can't think why she'd lie about whether or not the sword had been purchased or whether the money was still owed. What's more, I'm not certain the issue has anything to do with the murder." He sighed audibly. "I know one shouldn't complain, but I'd so looked forward to Christmas this year. I've a godchild now, and I wanted to spend some time getting her a few nice presents. Lady Cannonberry was helping me and we were having a jolly good time looking at all the fancy things in the shops. Oh, don't mind me, Constable. I'm just feeling sorry for myself."

Barnes looked away to hide his smile. After Witherspoon's mother had passed away when he first joined the force, he had very little family and had spent a number of years alone. But his life had changed greatly, and now he had a family of sorts: a godchild, a household that cared about him, and a dear lady friend who was becoming increasingly important to him. The good inspector was now no different than the rest of the working people in London; it was Christmas, and he wanted to spend time with the ones he cared about. "You're entitled to complain a bit, sir," he remarked. "It's not something you do very often."

Witherspoon laughed and shoved his spectacles up his nose. "Ah, well, I never expected to have a baby goddaughter and to enjoy it so very much. But I mustn't grouse about my circumstances; the sooner we get this case solved, the faster I can be back with Lady Cannonberry buying presents and planning a wonderful holiday for my entire household. But let's return to our case. It's too bad that Mrs. McCourt didn't know *how* her husband had found out that Raleigh was allegedly selling fakes."

They discussed the case for the remainder of the ride. Barnes took care to drop tidbits of both the gossip and the facts he'd gotten this morning from Mrs. Jeffries and Mrs. Goodge into the conversation.

"I must say, Constable, you do have a vast network of informants," the inspector said approvingly as they approached Raleigh's door. "You must introduce me to them sometime."

"It's just some of my local sources passing along a few bits and pieces, sir." He banged on the wood.

"Nonetheless, it's come in useful any number of times," the inspector said as the door cracked open and Jerome Raleigh peered out at them.

"May we come in, sir?" Barnes asked politely. He kept his tone just harsh enough for Raleigh to understand he didn't have a choice.

He stepped back and waved them inside. "I don't know why you can't leave me alone," he complained. "I've told you everything I know."

"You didn't mention that Daniel McCourt was getting ready to publicly accuse you of selling fakes," Barnes remarked casually.

Panic flashed across Raleigh's face, but he quickly got himself under control. "I've no idea where you heard such nonsense, but I assure you it isn't true."

"We have it on good authority that it is true," Witherspoon added. "And furthermore, not only was he going to tell Leon Brunel of his suspicions, but he was going to ask another expert, a man from the British Museum, to examine everything you'd authenticated for him to make certain the objects were genuine."

"He wouldn't have done that. He wouldn't risk anyone finding out that some of his pieces weren't as valuable as he'd thought," Raleigh snapped, but then he caught himself. "I mean, no collector will hold himself up to public ridicule if he's been sold a bill of bad goods."

"Was he sold a bill of bad goods?" Barnes took out his notebook.

"No. Alright, I'll admit I exaggerated my abilities as an authenticator, but I do have some knowledge of the business. I am a genuine expert on Chinese ceramics."

"But not on anything else." The inspector was guessing, but he was fairly certain he was on the right track. Jerome Raleigh was beginning to look a bit like a cornered rat. "Is that correct?"

Raleigh looked away. "I may have exaggerated my knowledge a bit. But that wasn't my fault."

"If you're an expert on Chinese ceramics, why did you claim the flap over the Yuan vases was just a mistake?" Barnes asked. "Surely an expert would have known they weren't genuine."

"McCourt wanted those wretched vases so badly he'd have believed a chorus girl if she'd told him the pair was genuine. I never claimed with certainty that they were exactly from that dynasty; I only told him that was my considered opinion and that they were very rare."

"But rarity does enhance their value," the inspector murmured. He wasn't certain he understood precisely what Jerome Raleigh was admitting to, but it certainly didn't sound ethical. "And you led the victim to believe they were very valuable and that the value was derived from both when they were made and their rarity, but neither of those assurances was correct. Mr. McCourt found out what you'd done and was going to expose you. Furthermore, just in the event you managed to evade prosecution, McCourt deliberately chose to expose you at a public social occasion so the gossip would soon be all over London."

"That's not true," Raleigh claimed. "We were going to work something out. I was going to give him his money back. Daniel was desperate for money, and he agreed not to go to the police and accuse me of fraud."

"Is that why you hung around and sneaked into his study after everyone else had left? To offer him money?" Barnes was taking a wild guess.

"That's a lie." He flopped down on the couch and put his head in his hands. "I wasn't sneaking anywhere. Daniel was expecting me. But the moment I told him I didn't have the money yet, that he wasn't getting his precious five thousand pounds, he showed me the door."

Barnes hid his relief behind a stern expression. He'd taken a shot in the dark, and it had hit the target.

"How long were you there after the others had gone?" Witherspoon pressed.

"No more than one or two minutes." Raleigh didn't raise his head. "I waited till everyone had gone before I went into the study, but Daniel didn't even let me sit down. He just stood there and asked where his money was. When I said I didn't have it, he grabbed my arm and marched me to the front door. I kept pleading with him to give me more time.

I told him I could get the money, but he wouldn't listen. He just opened the door and shoved me out."

Barnes sat down on the chair opposite him. "Why didn't you tell us this before?"

"Because he was murdered and I was afraid," he admitted. "But he was still alive when I left, I swear it."

Ruth ducked her head to avoid being seen and then had a quick look across the crowded ballroom. But she was too late. Lady Emma Stafford had spotted her, and with a plate piled high with food from the buffet, she made her way through the crowded tables toward her. Ruth wanted to scream. She'd only come to Horatia Edmondson's luncheon because she'd wanted to see whether she could pick up anything useful. But wouldn't you just know that it was that sharp-eyed old snob who'd seen her first. Ruth plastered a welcoming smile on her face as Lady Stafford's considerable bulk edged chairs out of the way and bumped against the crowded tables.

"Hello there, Lady Cannonberry. That is you, isn't it?" She stopped and squinted.

Ruth knew she had no choice. She stood up. "Yes, how lovely to see you Lady Stafford."

"Excellent, I thought it was you. Can you give me a hand here?" She held out her plate toward Ruth, completely oblivious that the overloaded dish was poised over a small, rabbity looking lady at the next table. "My eyesight is quite good from far away, but as I get closer, I'm never sure."

"Of course, do come sit with me." Ruth hurried forward, grabbing the dish and tilting it up just as a piece of chicken wobbled precariously on the edge. The rabbity woman gave Ruth a wide smile of thanks.

She put the plate on the table and pulled out a chair. She

didn't like Lady Emma Stafford. She'd become acquainted with her on a recent case and found her to be rude, overbearing, and convinced that aristocrats and monarchs ruled by divine right. But Ruth didn't have it in her to be mean to the woman.

Lady Stafford flopped down and scooted her chair closer to the table. She unfolded her serviette and spread it across her lap. Emma Stafford had a florid complexion and jowls so loose they draped over the top ruffle of her elegant green gown. Her hair was white and held up by silver combs in youthful ringlets that belonged on a woman fifty years her junior. "Are you still seeing that policeman person?"

Ruth sat down and picked up the fork she'd dropped. "You mean Inspector Witherspoon?" She smiled broadly. "Indeed I am. We're having Christmas together."

"Humph." Lady Stafford speared a piece of asparagus. "Back in my day, there were certain barriers between people that were simply never crossed."

"Isn't it wonderful that things have started to change!" Ruth exclaimed. She wondered why the woman had wanted to sit with her. The Staffords were one of the most aristocratic families in England, and half the women in the room would have been glad of her company.

Lady Stafford snorted again and attacked the chicken leg that she'd almost lost. "I'm not so certain that all changes are for the better. Some things have become decidedly worse. Just look at the way people behave. No one has any respect for law and order."

Ruth put down her fork. "I'm afraid I don't understand what you mean."

"You know very well what I'm talking about." Lady Stafford glared at her. "Every time one reads a newspaper there are people demanding one thing after another; labor unions and people claiming everyone should have an education and women parading about with ugly signs. It's no wonder we're not all murdered in our beds."

She took a deep breath in order to hold on to her temper. "Ah, I see. But in all honesty, is the world a worse place because women can now control their own property and all children can get some form of an education?" The women's organizations that Ruth supported had long lobbied for the passage of the Married Women's Property Act and the Fee Grant Act.

She said nothing for a moment but simply stared at Ruth, and then she shrugged. "Oh bother, I don't know. To be honest, I don't really believe half the nonsense I say." She smiled. "I like you, Lady Cannonberry, and as I foisted myself upon you, I didn't want you to be bored, so I immediately started being provocative. Forgive me. Though mind you, it's only *half* the things I say that I don't believe."

Ruth regarded her steadily. "I'm amazed that you like me. I should have thought that women like me were anathema to you. Nonetheless, I'm glad you came over to sit with me. May I ask you something?"

"Of course," she replied around a mouthful of chicken.

"Do you know anything about Daniel McCourt? I do like to keep my ears open for gossip about the victim. It sometimes helps my friend, the inspector."

"Sorry, but I'm afraid the only thing I know about the fellow was that he married a Herron heiress." She laughed. "That caused a few tongues to wag, I can tell you that. I know a little about McCourt's cousins, the Brunels. They were the rich branch of the family. Leon Brunel studied at St. Andrews with my nephew. I think he studied medicine—no, no, it was chemistry, or perhaps it was languages. Whatever, I don't really recall." She shrugged. "I

don't expect that's very useful for your inspector, because
frankly, the only thing Paul mentioned when we read about
the murder in the papers was that it was too bad Leon left
school without his degree."

Wiggins had learned from experience that when a household
was disrupted by murder, servants sometimes took advantage of the turmoil and grabbed a few precious moments for
themselves. He grinned as he saw a young maid come out of
the servants' entrance of the McCourt house, but instead of
turning toward the shops as he expected, she went in the
opposite direction. He was after her like a shot, keeping far
enough back so she'd not spot him but close enough so he
wouldn't lose her. He'd no idea whether she was Annie, but
whoever she was, she'd be able to answer some questions.

She went around the corner and vanished from view. He
quickened his pace but didn't run. He didn't want people to
notice and remember him. But when he reached the cross-
roads himself, she really had disappeared. Mystified, he
studied the pavements on both sides of the road but didn't
see hide nor hair of her. There was nothing here but a work-
ingman's pub, a solicitor's office, and a dentist. Where the
devil could she have gone?

"Blast a Spaniard," he muttered. "I knew I shouldn't 'ave
let her get so far ahead." It was unlikely she was inside the
pub, as young housemaids didn't frequent local drinking establishments, but because he had nowhere else to look, he
headed there, pulled open the door, and peeked inside.

It was just after opening time, and the place was almost
empty save for an old man at one end of the bar and the
housemaid at the other. The barman was putting a glass of
gin in front of her. Wiggins watched as she carefully counted
out the coins and paid for her drink.

"I'll 'ave a pint, please," he said as he stepped inside. He went to the bar, taking care to stop a foot away from his quarry. She glanced in his direction, and he gave her a cheeky grin. "And pour another gin for this young lady 'ere, as well."

The barman grabbed a glass from under the counter and stuck it under the keg tap. "You alright with this bloke buyin' you a drink, Annie?" he said to the girl.

"He looks harmless enough." She gave him a smile of her own. "I'm Annie. Why you wantin' to buy me a gin? I don't go with strange men."

Wiggins was rather flattered to be referred to as a "strange man," but he didn't let it go to his head. Instead, he concentrated on his task. "I'm buyin' you a drink because I saw you comin' out of the McCourt house. My name is Albert Jones, and I'm a private inquiry agent. I've been hired to investigate Daniel McCourt's death." It wasn't how he'd originally intended to approach the housemaid, but he'd not expected to track her into a pub, either, and using his limited supply of coins to pay for information seemed a much better idea than pretending to be a lonely, shy footman desperate for company. This girl, with her knowing brown eyes and easy demeanor, would see through that ruse in a heartbeat.

"That'll be eight pence, please," the barman said as he put the beer and the gin in front of them.

Wiggins paid and sidled close to her. She smiled skeptically, as though she didn't believe a word he said. "Will you talk to me?" he asked.

"Sure, as long as you keep on buyin' me gin," she agreed cheerfully. "You look awfully young to be a private inquiry agent. Are you like that Sherlock Holmes fellow? Mrs. Williams, the housekeeper goes mad if the *Strand* is all sold out when she goes to the newsagent's."

Wiggins was a great admirer of both the fictional Mr.
Holmes and his creator, Mr. Arthur Conan Doyle. "I'm not
like 'im, miss. I'm nowhere near as observant. But I do appreciate you talkin' to me. I know I look young, and it
would come across very good for me on my report if you
could tell me as much as you know about what's goin' on at
the McCourt house. My employers want to make sure Mr.
McCourt's killer is brought to justice."

"Shouldn't the police do that?"

"Sometimes they need 'elp, miss," he replied. "And I assure you, if I learn any fact that will lead to the guilty party
bein' arrested, I'll pass it along to the police. Now, what can
you tell me about your household?"

"Like you said, there's been a murder and the household
is in a right old mess. That's the only reason I was able to
slip away today. The mistress has gone to speak to the vicar
about the funeral arrangements, the cook and the housekeeper are plannin' the funeral reception, and the butler's
helped himself to a bottle of Mr. McCourt's best whiskey
and snuck up to the box room for a bit of peace and quiet."
She picked up her glass and drained it. "What do you want
to know?"

Wiggins was suddenly flummoxed, not sure where to
start or what to ask. She solved the problem for him. "I don't
usually hang about in pubs drinkin' durin' the day," she protested. "But Gus here is my great-uncle, and I had to get
away from the house. It was bad enough that when Mr. Mc-
Court was alive he was a mean person, but it's ten times
worse now that he's dead."

"Worse how?"

"No one wants to work there anymore." She reached for
the second glass of gin. "Oh, we all know that none of us
could've been the murderer, as we were all outside when he

was done in, but that don't make any difference. It's still ugly to be in a house where murder was done. You'd think it would be easier, now that he's gone. He was the one that none of us liked."

"Why didn't you like 'im?"

She snorted a laugh. "He was goin' to sack me for chippin' one of his precious plates, and it was his bloody fault that I did it in the first place. He collects all this ruddy stuff from the Orient, plates and swords and heathen statues, and he keeps 'em in his study. He only allows us to clean in there once a week when he's out at his club. I went in this past week at my usual time, and I'd just picked up this plate to give it a good dust when he come thunderin' in, scarin' the life out of me because he's usually at his club until the late afternoon." She took a sip. "He startled me so that I almost dropped the ruddy plate. I thought it'd be fine, as I caught it, but the gold rim had chipped."

"Did 'e realize what'd 'appened?" Wiggins asked.

" 'Course not, he just ignored me and went on over to his armoire. He was carryin' this big, flat case. He put it down and told me to get out. He didn't ask me to leave politely or anythin'; he just shouted at me to get out." She wrinkled her nose at the memory. "I'd not talk to a dog like that, but that's the way he always spoke to us. I knew I'd chipped his stupid plate, but he was in such a foul mood I was scared to say anythin', so I just scarpered off."

Wiggins gazed at her sympathetically. "Workin' there must 'ave been 'ard."

"It was and still is," she declared. "Even with him dead, they ignore anythin' we have to say. They don't think we've got a brain in our heads."

"Why do you say that?"

"The mistress is havin' us clean the house from top to

bottom for the funeral reception, and yesterday they did the crystals from the sconces in the drawin' room. I was carryin' the clean ones back up to the housekeeper, and I dropped one of the small pieces on the stairs. We had a little paraffin fire right before the master was killed," she explained, "and when I bent down to find the crystal I smelled paraffin. Now, the fire was at the bottom of the stairs, not the top, so I ask you, how could the smell of paraffin still be in the carpet?"

"Doesn't it 'ang about for a long time?" he asked.

"Not that long. Like I said, we've been airin' the house for three days now, and that's not all." She picked up her glass and knocked it back. "When I told the housekeeper, she said it must be my imagination and for me not to bother the mistress with such things."

"Did she go 'ave a smell at the carpet herself?" he asked curiously.

"She did not. She just looked at me like I was makin' up tales."

"Has anythin' else 'appened that was odd or out of place?" he probed.

"Can I have another gin?" she asked. "I've got to get back soon."

He caught the barman's eye and pointed to her empty glass. "Go on, then. 'As there been anythin' else you can remember?" he asked.

"On the night that he was murdered, I heard someone walkin' about outside," she said and smiled as her drink was put in front of her. "Thanks, Uncle Gus."

Wiggins pulled another coin out of his pocket and put it on the counter. "Are you sure about that? You couldn't 'ave just been imaginin' it because you were half asleep?"

"That would be hard to do as I was downstairs by the

servants' door and not in my bed," she replied. "I'd gone down to get a drink of water. I don't like goin' downstairs in the middle of the night; for one thing, it's dark and cold, but there's a lamp left at the top of the staircase for us if we need to use the water closet, so I took it and went down to get a drink. I'd started back and was just outside the door when I heard a rustlin' sound and then footsteps."

"Right outside the door?" he pressed.

She frowned in confusion. "That's just it. I was standin' right there and it didn't sound like it was right outside, but it was close."

"You didn't look?"

She drew back, staring at him as if he were an idiot. "'Course not. We'd had murder done in that house. I went back to bed and pulled the covers over me head. I told the housekeeper the next day, and she said it was probably just my imagination."

Phyllis couldn't help herself; she had to find out whether Harriet Adamson was still employed. She crept up the side entrance to the Brunel house and knocked softly on the door. She didn't want to get the girl in trouble, so she'd come up with a plan. As the door opened, she pulled an envelope out of her jacket pocket. But she needn't have bothered, for Harriet stood there. Her eyes widened in surprise. "What are you doin' here?"

"I'm sorry. I was so concerned about you that I wanted to come by and see if you still had a roof over your head," she said.

"How'd you know where I worked?"

Phyllis smiled. "I followed you home yesterday. I wanted to make sure you were alright."

Harriet drew back and then smiled in return. "You're a

really nice person. No one's bothered about me in ages. I've still got my job; as a matter of fact, they seem to have forgotten all about me."

"That's wonderful. I don't want to get you in trouble, so I'd better go." She turned to leave.

"Can you wait for me up on the corner?" Harriet asked, looking over her shoulder. "I just heard the cook tell the mistress we're out of sugar. I'll offer to go and fetch it from the grocer's."

Phyllis wasn't sure that was a good idea, but she didn't want to hurt Harriet's feelings. "Alright, I'll meet you there."

Phyllis went back out to the street and turned in the direction of the shops. She reminded herself that as far as Harriet was concerned, her name was Millicent . . . She stopped in the middle of the pavement, trying hard to remember what surname she'd given herself yesterday. Millicent . . . Millicent . . . Millicent Burns. She sagged in relief as the name came to her.

She got to the corner and waited, promising herself she'd just walk Harriet to the grocer's and then get on with her task. She was determined to figure out how to get shopkeepers and clerks to chat with her.

A few minutes later, Harriet appeared. She was smiling from ear to ear. "It was so nice of you to come and see me, Millicent." She grabbed Phyllis' hand and giggled. "My afternoon out is on Tuesdays. When's yours?" She pulled her toward the grocery shop farther up the road.

"I get Friday afternoons off," she said, feeling terrible that she was lying to this poor girl. The Witherspoon household allowed staff to take whatever afternoon off they wanted within the week. "I'm so glad they didn't sack you."

"I am, too," she said earnestly. "They work us like dogs,

but I expect most households are like that. Do you ever wish you could do somethin' else?"

"I do." She took a deep breath and told the truth. It wasn't as if she'd ever see Harriet again, so what did it matter whether she voiced her dream aloud? "I want to be a typewriter girl."

Harriet gaped at her. "Really? I think that's wonderful. But how do you learn to use such an instrument? I saw one in a shop window on Oxford Street once when I was carryin' Mrs. Brunel's packages. It looked ever so complicated."

"I'm not sure," she admitted honestly. "But there must be a way. I think perhaps you need to go to a special school or somethin' like that. I'm savin' my wages so I'll have a way to pay for it."

"I bet you'll do it," Harriet declared. "You're the bravest person I've ever met. I'd never have had the courage to speak to someone the way you spoke to me. Just havin' someone to talk to helped so much."

Phyllis couldn't believe her ears. She was suddenly overwhelmed by conflicting emotions as guilt over her motive for approaching Harriet warred with pride that someone actually considered her brave. "You'd have done the same," she finally muttered. "I'm not brave. I've just been in the same boat and know how lonely it can make you feel. But that's enough about me. They're bein' nicer to you, right?"

"Only because Cook realized she'd been dead wrong in accusin' me of stealin' her stupid saffron." Harriet laughed. "No one had stolen it at all. It was on the floor in the dry larder up against the flour bin."

"You mean someone had just poured it out of the jar?" Phyllis wanted to be sure she got this right.

"That's what it looks like," Harriet replied. They dodged around a well-dressed man in a bowler. "Saffron is very expensive, so we can make neither heads nor tails about why someone would just dump it on the floor and keep a cheap glass jar. We looked all about the larder, but it wasn't there."

"It was kept in a locked storage cupboard, right?" Phyllis persisted. "That's why they accused you; you had the house-keeper's keys." Every household she'd ever worked in except for the inspector's kept the spices locked up.

"That's right." Harriet slanted her a strange look. "But I didn't steal it. I only had the housekeeper's keys because Cook had lost hers and sent me to borrow the other set."

"Oh, I didn't mean you to think that way," Phyllis protested. "I know you didn't do it. Only someone daft would pour an expensive spice out and keep the jar."

"And I'm not daft." Harriet laughed.

"I'm glad they're treatin' you better," Phyllis said. They were almost at the grocer's.

"Only just." Harriet stopped by the front door. "They're still strict about silly things. Like this mornin', the house-keeper went on and on because she found pine needles and specks of bark on the attic floor landing. None of the ser-vants had tracked it into the house, we're all careful about wiping our feet, but she didn't want to hear that. Because then it would mean that one of the family or a guest had done it."

Everyone was back on time for their afternoon meeting. Mrs. Goodge held Amanda while Betsy put the last of the tea things on the table before slipping into her spot next to Smythe.

"I'll go first," Luty volunteered. "My bit won't take long. Bunch of ya are grinnin' like cowboys on payday, so I can see you've all got plenty to report." She paused, and when no one contradicted her, she continued. "I spent most of the day chasin' up one source after another, and it was about as use-ful as pullin' hens' teeth, but I did hear a couple of things that were interestin'. One, Charles Cochran is as pious as a preacher, and no one I talked to could imagine him killin' anythin', let alone a human being. One of my sources claimed the feller don't even eat meat!"

"He doesn't seem to have a motive, either," Mrs. Jeffries muttered. "Sorry, Luty, I didn't mean to interrupt."

"No offense taken." Luty helped herself to a slice of but-tered brown bread. "I also had a chat with a friend of mine named Carlos Montoya. He collects artifacts from the Middle East and he knows Leon Brunel. He was at the auc-tion house the day McCourt had the ruckus over sellin' them Yuan vases. Now, Carlos, he loves to gossip, and so when he ran into Brunel a few days later, he was all set to pass along that tidbit, but Brunel had already heard about it, and he also told Carlos that he'd stopped usin' Raleigh as an appraiser years ago because he knew he was incompe-tent."

"That's interesting," Ruth said. "I was rather under the impression that both McCourt and Brunel were Raleigh's clients."

"I think we all were," Luty said. "Just goes to show, we shouldn't ever make assumptions. Anyways, that's all I heard."

"I'll go next." Ruth smiled at Luty. "You found out more than I did. Unfortunately, at the Christmas reception I got stuck next to Lady Stafford."

"The one from our last case?" Mrs. Jeffries asked quickly.

"The very same, and she not only sat down at my table; her presence was apparently effective in keeping everyone else far away. We were sitting at a table for six, and I was certain half the ladies at the reception would leap at the chance to make her acquaintance, but I was wrong. The room was crowded, and no one else came near us."

"Cor blimey, you'd 'ave thought one of her own class woulda wanted to sit with 'er. She must be a mean old thing!" Wiggins exclaimed.

Ruth thought for a moment. "She's not so much *mean* as she is overbearing, rude, and opinionated, but that description applies to most of the aristocracy in this country. No, I think people avoid her because there's something pathetic about her, a loneliness that she hides behind a mask of arrogance. It was obvious she didn't want to go home, as she said there was never anyone there but the servants. I felt so sorry for her that I offered her a ride, and I'm glad I did, because I learned a little more about one of our suspects during the drive. She claims that Saxon's uncle, the one that left him the Oriental collection, didn't get the entire collection from his business in the Far East. Lady Stafford says that a good portion of it was picked up cheap at bankruptcy auctions here in England. She also mentioned that Arthur Brunel's grandparents, his mother's family, lost all their money and were forced to sell everything. They had an extensive collection of Oriental ceramics and a number of items from Japan."

"Isn't Arthur the only one in the family that wasn't interested in collectin'?" Mrs. Goodge asked.

"That's what he told the inspector," Mrs. Jeffries confirmed. "And neither Inspector Witherspoon nor Constable Barnes saw anything when they were in his home. In fact, they both said the drawing room was bare of anything except the most basic of furnishings."

"Lady Stafford had never heard of Arthur Brunel taking any interest in collecting. The only fanatic in that family was his half brother, Leon," Ruth added. She told them the rest of what she'd heard that day.

When Ruth had finished, Hatchet looked at Luty. "Was your source sure of his information about Leon Brunel?"

"He seemed to be, why? What'd you hear?" she demanded.

"My source, and it is an impeccable source, told me that a few days before the murder, he saw Leon Brunel and Raleigh having a drink together at Brunel's club."

"Just because they was drinkin' together don't mean that Brunel trusted Raleigh's judgment," Luty argued defensively.

"My informant was sitting close enough to overhear part of their conversation. Brunel was talking to Raleigh about Oriental artifacts, asking him if he'd heard of anything interesting coming in from Hong Kong." He smiled triumphantly.

"That doesn't mean that Luty's information is wrong," Betsy interjected. "Only that you've heard different things."

Mrs. Jeffries gave her a grateful smile. "That's very true. Who would like to go next?"

"I will," Phyllis volunteered. She wanted to get it over with. "I didn't have much luck with the shopkeepers." She smiled hopefully at Betsy. "We'll have to go together sometime so I can watch how you do it. But I made contact with that maid at the Brunel house." She told them the few bits of information she'd heard from Harriet. "I'm sorry," she said when she'd finished. "I know I shouldn't have gone back to see her, but I was so worried about her gettin' tossed into the street."

"We're all glad that she still has her position," Mrs. Jeffries said. "And you did learn a bit." Something tugged at the back of her mind, but again, the idea faded before she could grasp it.

"Let me 'ave my go, then," Wiggins said cheerfully. He told them about his meeting with Annie, taking care not to mention that he'd met her in a pub and then kept buying her drinks. "She's sure she 'eard someone outside the house that night," he finished.

"Which would be useful if she'd heard someone outside on the night before the murder," Mrs. Goodge complained. "But the killer isn't likely to have come back to stomp about the passageway now, is he?"

"I told you, she wasn't sure the person was in the passageway," he corrected. "Look, I know it don't make sense, but that's what she said, and she's got no reason to lie about it."

Again, Mrs. Jeffries felt a nudge in her mind, as if something was right under her nose but she couldn't see it. "All we can do is report what we learn and hope the pieces help us to sort out the puzzle."

"Are you figurin' it out?" Phyllis asked eagerly. "Are the bits comin' together for you?"

"Sometimes I catch a glimmer of an idea but it disappears before I can start moving the pieces together into any sort of reasonable theory," she admitted glumly.

"Not to worry; you'll suss it out," Mrs. Goodge declared. "You always do."

"Maybe my information might 'elp," Smythe offered. He told them about what he'd learned from Blimpey. He took care in the telling, making sure that everyone understood the implications of his information.

"Nicholas Saxon and Glenda Brunel never stopped loving each other," Betsy mused when he'd finished. "How sad. She should never have been forced to marry Leon Brunel."

"Don't be too sympathetic, love," Smythe said. "She

could've refused to marry Brunel, but she didn't. So instead of livin' in poverty with the man she loved, she lived in luxury with a man she didn't love. Strikes me that she's the kind of woman that wants it easy, which means she'd not take kindly to Daniel McCourt blabbin' to 'er husband that she was bein' unfaithful."

"Which means she had a motive to want McCourt dead," Mrs. Goodge said.

"So did Nicholas Saxon," Betsy argued. "Once it was known that a good part of McCourt's collection was either fake or worth less than valued, the entire market for Oriental antiquities would be hurt for the next year or two—isn't that what your source claimed?"

"True," he agreed. "He said that all the other dealers would be put off until the scandal died down."

"So it appears that now we know Nicholas Saxon, Glenda Brunel, and Jerome Raleigh all had a reason to want McCourt dead," Mrs. Jeffries said. "Now we've got to find out which one of them killed him."

CHAPTER 9

Witherspoon leaned back in his comfortable chair and took a quick sip of sherry. "We learned an interesting number of facts today," he said. "But to be truthful, I can't be sure what, if anything, it all might mean. I certainly don't feel any closer to determining who might have murdered Mc-Court."

Mrs. Jeffries felt the same, but she could hardly admit it. Instead, she decided to focus on keeping his confidence high. Witherspoon's faith in his abilities had improved greatly as the years passed and the number of homicides he'd solved increased. But he was still very much prone to bouts of self-doubt. She waited till he looked at her, and then she gave him an indulgent smile. "Now, now, Inspector, I know it's Christmas, but you really mustn't tease me so."

"Whatever do you mean?" He looked genuinely puzzled.

She laughed gaily and took a sip from her own glass before she answered. "You know very well what I'm talking about. This happens every time and with every one of your cases. You work so hard taking statements, following up on leads, and gathering information that you lose sight of what your 'inner mind' is doing. Now, come on, sir. Do tell me about your day."

"Does it really happen with every case?" he asked hopefully. "Truly?"

"Of course it does, sir." She pretended to be exasperated. "You know good and well that while one part of your mind is analyzing statements, looking for inconsistencies, and verifying alibis, the creative, intuitive side of your brain is making connections and seeing patterns of behavior that will undoubtedly lead you to the killer."

He smiled broadly. "Gracious, I certainly hope so, because right now I can't seem to see the forest for the trees, as the saying goes."

Again, an idea flickered into her consciousness and then evaporated, but she kept her encouraging smile firmly in place. "But you will, sir. Now, who did you see today?"

"We had a rather interesting chat with Mrs. McCourt again today." He took another drink. "I don't quite know what to think about her. She definitely had no love for her husband, and as I told you before, we can't find anyone who saw her on the balcony, so she'd have had time to commit the murder before the servants came in from the garden, but on the other hand, she doesn't seem to have a motive."

"The sword that was used to kill him," she began, thinking of her discussion with Dr. Bosworth. "Is it a great, heavy thing?"

"It's long, and I suppose it's fairly hefty," he replied. "Why?"

"Oh, I was just thinking about an article I'd read somewhere that said something to the effect of how difficult it was to kill with a sword unless one actually knew how to wield it properly." She watched his face, hoping he was getting her point. But he continued to stare at her blankly. "And your murderer apparently knew enough to kill the victim with two well-placed thrusts."

"Either that or he or she was simply lucky with the first two strikes," the inspector pointed out. "The police surgeon said that was a possibility. Mrs. McCourt also gave us some information about Jerome Raleigh that cast him in a whole new light." He told her about the remainder of his visit to the widow and then about their second interview with Jerome Raleigh.

While he spoke, Mrs. Jeffries listened carefully as she got up and refilled their glasses. Occasionally, she interrupted his narrative for a point of clarification or to ask a question.

"Five thousand pounds," Mrs. Jeffries mused. "Isn't that the amount of money that Lydia Kent claims McCourt owed her for the sword she sold him?" She knew very well that it was.

"Yes, and the constable and I were going to go back to the Alexandria to have another talk with Miss Kent, but we got called to Chief Inspector Barrows' office, so we'll have to do that tomorrow."

"Why do you need to see her again?" she asked quickly.

"Oh, didn't I tell you? Mrs. McCourt said she'd seen the bill of sale for the Hwando and it was marked 'paid in full.' I want to see if Miss Kent can shed some light on that issue. She claims she only went to the McCourt house on the afternoon of the murder because she had not been paid for the sword."

He'd not mentioned it, and she was suddenly grateful that they had Constable Barnes' kitchen visits every morning. But she didn't fault the inspector; it was impossible to recall every single detail of one's day. "Will she still be in London tomorrow? I thought you said she was meeting friends in Paris."

"She's said she's going to stay until she either gets her sword returned or gets paid for it. But just to be on the safe side, we've got a constable watching her hotel. He'll notify us if she tries to leave. I rather like her. I do hope she's not a murderer." He sighed. "And I suppose you can imagine what the chief inspector wanted."

"Yes, sir, I'm afraid I can."

"They're getting pressure from above," he said softly. "Apparently, someone at the Home Office wants the case solved by Christmas."

"Don't they always, sir."

Mrs. Jeffries reached into the bottom of her wardrobe and pulled out a large wicker basket filled with parcels wrapped in brown paper. These were the Christmas presents she'd bought before the murder case. She put the basket onto the foot of her bed and rummaged through the packages until she found the bottle of Harveys Bristol Cream sherry she'd bought to give to a friend.

She took the bottle and went downstairs. Samson was standing on the table when she walked into the kitchen. He glared at her, and as if to show her who was boss, he flopped his fat rump down and flicked his tail.

"Get down from there you silly boy," she whispered. Samson knew he wasn't allowed on the table, and she was in no mood to put up with his shenanigans. She shoved him as gently as possible toward the edge, taking him by surprise so that he scrambled up, caught himself, and leapt to the floor. He hissed at her and stomped off.

She opened the sherry, poured out a good measure into a glass, and wandered across the quiet room to the window over the sink. She usually only imbibed with the inspector, but tonight, she'd decided it might help her grab that elusive imp of an idea that had plagued her for two days now. At her age, she wasn't worried about succumbing to the "demon rum"; she knew herself too well for that. But there was something she wasn't seeing; something that was obvious and right under her nose, but she was too dense to grasp it properly. She'd come closest to seeing whatever it was earlier this evening when she was with Witherspoon. She hoped the sherry would help open her mind.

She took a sip and stared out into the dark night at the streetlight across the road. From this angle, it looked odd to her, as though it didn't belong there. But that was only because she was used to seeing it from her room upstairs. She closed her eyes and let her mind wander . . . Jerome Raleigh admitted to being in McCourt's study, and he had a motive. McCourt was ruining his career and, worse, was going to prosecute him for fraud. But was it fraud?

She opened her eyes as a hansom cab went past, the clip-clop of the horses and the rattling of the carriage loud in the quiet night. Nicholas Saxon had a double motive for wanting McCourt dead; he was still in love with another man's wife, and if McCourt publicly prosecuted Raleigh, even a genuine collection like Saxon's wouldn't fetch much on the open market after a scandal like that.

And what about Arthur Brunel? Even if the lawsuit had been put to rest, maybe his hatred of his cousin was so great that when he had the chance, he decided to whack at the fellow's neck with a handy sword. Perhaps he'd been pushed over the edge by having to convert his last asset, his home, into rented flats just to keep a roof over his own head. But if that were the case, if his motive were out-and-out hatred because he'd been cheated of his inheritance, then why just murder McCourt? Surely Leon Brunel would be even guiltier, since he was the one who ended up with the bulk of the Brunel estate. She thought of Leon Brunel seeking out Jerome Raleigh and asking his advice. She wondered why he'd done so if he already knew the fellow was incompetent. She sighed and took another sip. Thus far, the sherry wasn't helping. She decided to be more systematic about her task, and mentally, she went through their suspects, looking at the ones who had a motive and the ones who didn't. But when she'd finished, she knew that hadn't enlightened her, either. "Maybe the killer is someone who wasn't even there that day," she muttered glumly. "Maybe it's someone we don't even know about."

Despite the cold, a fog came in off the nearby river. She sipped and watched as it rolled in, floating gently and softening the hard-edged shapes of the stairs and houses along the row. Wispy fingers swirled in front of the streetlamp, obscuring it one moment and then drifting off the next so that she had a clear view. She took another sip and realized her glass was empty. "Well blast a Spaniard," she said to herself as she glared down at her empty glass. "This hasn't helped one bit, and now I'll have to buy Mrs. Rollins another present." She was shaking her head, dismayed at her own foolishness, when her gaze was caught by the lamp again, only this time, someone had stopped right in front of it. He was big and hunched over, his head bent down, forming a silhouette. For a split second it appeared as if the lamp and the person were one, and together they looked like a sword pointing toward heaven. The man was the rounded hilt and the lamppost the blade. Then he straightened, and she could see he'd been lighting his pipe. "I've got swords on my mind," she told herself. It was time to go to bed, but she'd not gone two steps before she stopped, turned, and went back to the window.

The fog had parted, and she could see the lamppost clearly. It looked exactly as it should.

But she'd suddenly seen what her mind had been trying to show her. Ye gods, was it possible? She looked down at the glass she still clutched and wondered whether it was just the liquor that put this idea into her head. But she didn't think so. She took a deep breath, put her empty glass in the sink, and went upstairs, pausing only long enough to grab the sherry bottle.

If she was going to prove she was right, she had a lot of thinking to do.

Despite getting very little sleep, Mrs. Jeffries was the first one up in the morning. She had a pot of tea on the table as Mrs. Goodge came into the kitchen. "You're up early."

"I've got an idea," she blurted out. "But it's so far-fetched that I'm not going to tell anyone yet. There's a number of things we've got to find out today. Let's hurry and get breakfast on the table and pray that no one is late for our morning meeting."

"What about Constable Barnes?" Mrs. Goodge asked. "Do we need to put a flea in his ear about anythin'?" The cook knew it was pointless to try and get the housekeeper to reveal who she thought was the killer until she was good and ready. Sometimes, Mrs. Goodge considered the idea that Mrs. Jeffries had a flair for the dramatic, but, of course, she kept that opinion quiet. She considered herself fortunate and blessed to have found such a good and loving friend in her old age, so she'd never even hint to the housekeeper that she ought to have gone on the stage.

"Goodness, yes, we've a number of tidbits for him," she

replied eagerly. "The inspector said they were going to the Alexandria Hotel to speak with Miss Kent again, and we should get Barnes to ensure he sees Nicholas Saxon again and the Brunels. We'll tell him what we heard about Saxon and Glenda Brunel being lovers."

The others arrived for their meeting only moments after Witherspoon and Barnes left by the front door. As soon as everyone had a cup of tea in hand, Mrs. Jeffries plunged right into the heart of the matter, telling them everything she'd heard from the inspector. She let Mrs. Goodge share the bits and pieces they'd gotten from the constable. "Now that you're all aware of everything, we've got some things we must do."

"That means you've got an idea who the killer is!" Luty clapped her hands together. "I knew you could do it."

"I don't know that I have," she replied. "It's just a notion, and frankly, it rests on the flimsiest of evidence." In the cold light of day, she wasn't quite as certain as she'd been last night.

"You always say that," Wiggins complained. "And even if you get the killer wrong, it comes out right in the end."

"When have I got the killer wrong?" she demanded. "Oh yes, I suppose you're right, there has been a time or two when I've been incorrect about the exact identity. Which is all the more reason to keep it to myself until I'm sure."

"When will you be sure?" Phyllis asked. She didn't feel she'd done her part, and as she didn't much like Christmas, she was quite happy to keep on investigating.

"That depends on what we find out today," Mrs. Jeffries replied. "But before we start our discussion, there's something I forgot to tell you at our last meeting. Dr. Bosworth explained to me that if McCourt hadn't been murdered, he'd have died within months anyway. He had a huge growth in his stomach."

"Does that mean he had cancer?" Luty asked.

"The postmortem didn't report whether or not the growth had been examined in detail; only that it was present," she explained. "But Dr. Bosworth is certain that it was cancer and that McCourt must have been having some rather awful symptoms."

"I wonder if he went to a doctor," Betsy murmured.

"That's one of the things we need to find out today," the housekeeper said. "Dr. Bosworth said the growth was large enough that any reasonably competent physician should have discovered it. We need to find out if McCourt knew how ill he was and, more importantly, if he'd told anyone."

There was a nodding of heads and a murmur of agreement from everyone around the table except Phyllis. "Maybe I'm thick as two short planks, but I can tell from all your faces that there's somethin' about this that I don't understand," she blurted out. "What difference would it have made if he'd told anyone?"

"Because whoever 'e told wouldn't 'ave a reason to murder 'im," Wiggins explained. "All that person 'ad to do was wait 'im out."

"So if we find out that he'd gone to a doctor and told any of our suspects he was dyin', we can cross them off our list," the cook added.

Phyllis looked incredulous. "Just because you know someone is ill doesn't mean you know for certain they're goin' to die. My last mistress waited for ages for her husband to die—he had a bad heart and diabetes—and the old tartar outlived her and the rest of his family."

"Phyllis is right," Mrs. Jeffries said quickly. "Nonetheless, we do need to find this out if we can. I did mention it to Constable Barnes this morning, and he'll make a point of bringing it to the inspector's attention."

"Gerald should already know," Ruth interjected defensively. "He always reads the postmortem report."

"Of course he does. I wasn't implying any dereliction of duty on his part," Mrs. Jeffries said. "But all the report would say was that the growth was present."

"I see what you mean." Ruth gave an understanding nod. "Gerald wouldn't see the implication unless he'd actually spoken with the police surgeon."

"Right, then, Mrs. Jeffries, what do you need us to do? Time is gettin' away from us," Smythe pointed out as he reached under the table and grabbed his wife's hand. The baby was asleep and tucked in her cot, and he suspected that Betsy might be feeling a bit left out. They were reaching the end of the case, he could feel it, and he could see from the expressions on everyone's faces that they felt it, too.

Betsy squeezed his fingers, touched by his concern. They were getting to the final act of this particular play, but she didn't feel cheated at all. Amanda wouldn't be a baby forever, and as soon as she was a little older, Betsy was committed to getting back out and doing her part. Except for her family, nothing in her life was as important to her as working in the cause of justice.

Mrs. Jeffries looked at Luty and Hatchet. "I'd like the two of you to go to the Alexandria Hotel."

"But Lucille might see me," Luty protested.

"That's what I'm counting on," the housekeeper replied. "She's been there for some time now, hasn't she?"

"That's what she said," Luty replied. "She's havin' a new house built in Bayswater, and it ain't finished yet."

"So she might have some idea of who on the staff at the

Alexandria is amenable to bribery," Mrs. Jeffries continued. "Is that possible?"

Luty looked doubtful. "I don't know. I can't see Lucille tryin' to bribe anyone."

"But she'd be in a position to know something about the staff, and that may be all we need."

"What do you want me to find out?" Luty asked bluntly.

"Anything you can about the people who work at the hotel," Mrs. Jeffries said. "Oh dear, I'm not explaining this very well. I've no idea if I'm on the right track or not, but if my theory is correct, the killer had to have had some idea of when Lydia Kent planned on leaving England. Inspector Witherspoon said she told him she was going to Paris the day *before* the tea party. We've got to find out if someone on the staff of the hotel supplied information to one of our suspects about when she originally planned to leave."

Luty stared at her in disbelief. "Nell's bells, you don't want much, do ya? This isn't the same as puttin' a bull's-eye target on one person and jawin' at him until he talks. This is a whole hotel."

"Which is precisely why Lucille Fenwick will come in handy," Hatchet said smoothly. "She's not only a terrible liar; she's a busybody as well. What's wrong, madam? Don't you feel up to the challenge?"

Luty gasped in outrage. "Up to the challenge? You're goin' to end up eatin' them words and then we'll see who's up to a challenge or not."

Hatchet laughed, delighted he'd gotten the reaction he'd wanted. "And providing you can find out what it is Mrs. Jeffries needs to know, I shall happily declare that you were right and I was wrong."

"I've a task at the hotel for you as well," Mrs. Jeffries said to him. "And I'm afraid it might prove more difficult than Luty's."

Luty snickered. "Oh Lord, I hope so."

"I shall ignore that, madam," he said loftily as he turned his attention to Mrs. Jeffries. "What do you need me to do?"

"Get a description of the man who was supposedly hiding behind a potted plant when Daniel McCourt met with Lydia Kent," she replied.

"I will do my best," he promised.

"What about the rest of us? 'Ave we got jobs?" Wiggins asked.

"Oh yes, I've got a task for everyone."

"I wonder why the police surgeon didn't add a note about the growth in the victim's stomach." Witherspoon frowned as he stepped out of the hansom cab and waited while Barnes paid the driver.

"I suspect he didn't think it important," Barnes replied. "After all, if you'd not mentioned it to me and I'd not mentioned it to my wife, she'd not have told me about her Uncle Thomas." The constable was lying through his teeth, counting on the fact that the inspector wouldn't remember what he'd said when he'd read the postmortem report. He'd made up the bit about his wife's uncle to make the point that with a growth like the one described in the report, McCourt hadn't been long for the world.

"But he should have seen the importance and made a special note to me," the inspector insisted as they started up the stone walkway. "That's very pertinent. If Mrs. McCourt knew about her husband's condition, then we can eliminate her from our suspect list. Even if she hated him, she'd hardly take the risk of committing murder when he was practically a dead man anyway. One does hate to complain, but that was very shoddy work."

Wisely, Barnes said nothing, knowing that Witherspoon might grouse a bit but would not make any formal complaints about the matter. He stepped past the inspector and climbed the short flight of stairs to Nicholas Saxon's front door. "Let's hope Mr. Saxon is home this morning." He lifted the knocker and let it drop against the plate.

"Are you certain your informant is right about this?" Witherspoon asked him anxiously. "After all, it could be just gossip."

"My source was sure. He said he saw it with his own eyes," Barnes replied truthfully.

Saxon had a smile on his face as he opened the door, but it disappeared the instant he saw his visitors. "Oh, it's you two. I was expecting someone else."

"May we come in, sir?" Witherspoon said.

Saxon opened the door wider and stepped back so they could enter. "Of course, but do make this as quick as possible."

"Expecting guests, are you, sir?" Barnes commented as they trudged into the drawing room.

Saxon nodded at the settee by the fireplace. "Make yourselves comfortable." He sat down on the love seat opposite. "As a matter of fact, Constable, I've a very busy day, and yes, I am expecting a guest. Now, what brings you gentlemen here?"

"We've some follow-up questions, sir," Witherspoon said. "When we spoke with you previously, you mentioned that you knew Jerome Raleigh and McCourt were somewhat at odds over his incorrect evaluation of a set of Chinese vases."

"I remember what I said, Inspector." Saxon regarded them warily. "What of it?"

"It's come to our attention that it wasn't simply an incorrect evaluation that had upset Mr. McCourt, but that he believed that Raleigh wasn't just an incompetent appraiser, he had knowingly sold him fakes," Barnes said. "Would you be aware of anything about that?"

Saxon said nothing for a long moment and then shrugged. "Why would I? As I told you the last time you were here, Raleigh had never cheated me. I do my own evaluations."

Witherspoon tried another tactic. "As an expert, if you wanted to determine if what you owned was fake or had been wrongly dated and evaluated, who would you go to for that?"

"Either Henry Franks or Edmund Lassitor," he replied. "Franks advises every major auction house in London on Oriental antiquities, and Lassitor is retired but spent years in the Far East and gifted his own collection to the British Museum. Both men live in London." He glanced at the carriage clock on the mantel. "Now, if there's nothing else—"

"Where in London?" Barnes asked quickly.

"I don't have their addresses," he snapped irritably. "You can contact Franks through any of the major auction houses, and I imagine the British Museum can get you Lassitor's address."

"Thank you, sir. We'll do that," Witherspoon said.

Saxon got up and looked at them expectantly. But both policemen kept their seats. "Inspector, Constable, I hate to be rude, but if you're finished with me, I've a lot to do today—"

"We're not finished, sir." This time it was Barnes who interrupted him.

Saxon stood where he was, crossing his arms over his chest and staring at the men with an impatient, annoyed look on his face. "What is it, then?"

"Mr. Saxon, we've had it on good authority that you're, uh, involved in a friendship with Mrs. Brunel." Witherspoon hoped he wasn't blushing as he said this.

"Of course I'm involved in a friendship with Mrs. Brunel. I've known her for years."

"You were engaged to her once, weren't you," Barnes said. It was a comment, not a question.

"You know I was. What's your point?"

"We've heard that your relationship with Mrs. Brunel is rather more than friendship, sir." The constable looked him directly in the eye. "Is this true?"

"Don't be ridiculous," Saxon scoffed. "Mrs. Brunel is the wife of a business acquaintance and a friend, that's all. Now, I don't see what on earth this has to do with McCourt's murder."

"Last week Daniel McCourt followed Glenda Brunel to this house," Barnes said bluntly. "As he is now dead and she's a married woman, you can understand why this might be of interest to the police."

Panic flashed across his face for a brief moment, but Saxon quickly brought himself under control. "Mrs. Brunel did come to see me, that's true," he replied.

"So you admit you're lovers?" Barnes pressed.

"Don't be ridiculous," Saxon scoffed. "If you'd give me a moment to finish, I'll tell you why she was here. She came to ask my advice about a Japanese tea set she'd seen on Bond Street."

"We weren't aware that Mrs. Brunel collected Oriental ceramics," Witherspoon put in.

"She was going to buy it for her husband," he insisted. "It was a very expensive item and she wanted my advice . . ." His voice trailed off as they heard the front door slam, and a second later, Glenda Brunel rushed into the room.

"Oh darling, darling." She dropped her rust-colored cloak on the floor and ran toward him with her arms outstretched. "I knocked but you didn't answer. It's awful, just awful. I told him I wanted a divorce! He was so angry but he knows he can't stop . . ." Her voice trailed off as she saw the horrified expression on Saxon's face. She stopped in her tracks, looking first at Witherspoon and then at Barnes as they rose politely to their feet. "Oh my God," she moaned as the color drained from her face. "I didn't know you were here."

"Then we're all surprised, Mrs. Brunel. We didn't expect to see you, either," Barnes said cheerfully.

Wiggins glanced quickly to his left and right before pushing open the gate to the Crandall property and slipping inside. He closed it carefully, not wanting to make any noise. From the front, the house still looked empty, but he wasn't taking any chances. He stood where he was, surveyed the windows, and was satisfied that he couldn't see any light. It was a dark, overcast day, and if anyone had been home, someone would have lighted a lamp. Cautiously, he moved forward, taking care to be as quiet as possible. Even if the Crandalls were still in Scotland, he didn't want to risk someone from the McCourt house hearing him.

Walking slowly, he examined the wooden fence that separated the two passageways. The fence was a good seven feet tall, sturdy, and painted gray. Between the fence and the walkway was a row of bare rosebushes that had been mulched for the winter with a heavy layer of bark chips and pine needles. When he got to the spot he thought might be directly opposite the servants' door on the McCourt house, he dropped to his knees for a closer look. There was a gap between the ground and fence of at least six inches, and he saw that he'd been right; the door was directly across the way.

He studied the ground beneath the bush and then looked farther up the row. The mulch here had been disturbed. The bark and pine were piled in little heaps under the branches of the bush while the mulch on the other plants was neatly flattened against the earth. Wanting to know how deep it went, he stuck his hand in it and made a face as he continued in all the way to his wrist before hitting solid earth.

Wiggins stood up. He now knew why Mrs. Jeffries had sent him here. He also knew that she'd not been the one to smash the lock on the Crandall gate. He heard voices from next door, and a second later, the servants' door at the Mc-Court house opened. Wiggins froze. He heard footsteps moving up the walkway, and as he was finished here but had another task yet to do, he waited a moment before running lightly toward the Crandall gate.

He peeked out the gate and spotted his quarry. He'd been fairly sure she'd do it again. Because of the murder, the Mc-Court household was in disarray, making it easy for someone who had the craving to take advantage of the situation and slip out for twenty minutes or so.

Wiggins stifled a flash of guilt as he stepped out and hurried after her. Despite her protests at their previous meeting, he'd suspected she couldn't help herself; that the need would take her and she'd go back to the pub. Wiggins had seen the need before and knew it was like a beast that wormed its way into a person's soul, demanding to be fed. As a lad, before the inspector had come, he'd watched the need destroy Euphemia Witherspoon. He'd watched her descend into illness while the other servants had taken horrible advantage of her, feeding her need with whiskey and gin so that she'd not notice they were robbing her blind. He'd never told the others of those dark days at Upper Edmonton Gardens, and he wasn't going to, either. Euphemia Witherspoon had taken him in and been good to him, and that was all anyone needed to know.

He rounded the corner and saw her go into the pub. Sighing heavily, he followed her.

"Good luck, madam," Hatchet said softly as Luty charged toward the front door of the Alexandria Hotel.

"You're goin' to need it more than me," she hissed before turning and giving the doorman a brilliant smile.

Hatchet chuckled and went on, rounding the corner and walking until he reached the mews that ran along the back of the hotel. He glanced around to make sure no one on the busy street was watching him. But this close to Christmas, the shoppers and pedestrians were intent on their own business.

The back entrance to the hotel was easily visible from the mouth of the mews. Pallets, empty barrels with missing slats, and trash bins were scattered along the walls on both sides of the cobblestones. Tall buildings, several of them five or more stories high, blocked what little light there was from the overcast day. Hatchet took his time and surveyed the area thoroughly. Across the main street and kitty-corner to the mews, a narrow road led off at an angle with a pub at the apex. Hatchet laughed to himself. He'd start there.

Inside the Alexandria Hotel, Luty's smile was strained as she tried to get rid of the manager. He'd taken one look at her expensive clothing and the diamonds hanging from her ears and come faster than a bat out of hell to see whether he could be of assistance.

"No, no, that's alright, you don't have to send anyone up to Mrs. Fenwick's room. I'm of a mind just to sit a spell, so if it's all the same to you, I'll just wait and see if she shows up. I don't want to trouble anyone." Luty had decided she'd take matters into her own hands rather than trusting Lucille.

"It's no trouble, ma'am," he exclaimed. He waved at a bellboy. "Hodges, go upstairs and see if Mrs. Fenwick is in her suite."

The boy bobbed his head respectfully before shooting off at a run.

"Sometimes Mrs. Fenwick forgets to leave her key at reception," the manager explained to Luty. "Would you care to wait over there?" He pointed to the circular tuffet. "I'll be happy to send for some refreshment."

Luty knew her plan wouldn't work with him hovering around. But there was one place where she might have some luck. "If it's all the same to you, I'd like to wait in your dining room. A pot of tea would be nice."

"Absolutely, madam, it's right this way," he gushed.

A few minutes later, Luty sat alone at a table. She'd gotten rid of the manager and saw neither hide nor hair of Lucille. She hoped the woman was out shopping and stayed gone for a long time. She surveyed the other diners. It was past ten o'clock, and the breakfast crowd was just about gone. A man in a dark blue suit sat at a table by himself, reading the newspaper, and two well-dressed middle-aged women were sitting near the entrance.

"Here you are, ma'am." The waiter put a serving tray on the table. He unloaded a silver teapot, cream, sugar, and a porcelain cup and saucer. "Shall I pour, ma'am?"

Luty gave him her best smile. He was a nice-looking young man with dark brown hair and blue eyes. "That would be nice, and I'd sure appreciate it." She deliberately exaggerated her American accent.

"Very good, ma'am." He picked up the pot and poured the tea into the cup without so much as a splash.

"Have ya worked here long?"

"Six months, ma'am." He put the pot down.

"Do you like it?"

His eyebrows shot up in surprise. "Well, I don't . . . I've never thought about it . . ."

"Oh, come on, you can tell me," she guffawed. "Ain't no reason you should like your job."

"I get to meet a lot of nice people." He picked up the silver sugar tongs. "Sugar?"

"Two lumps, please." She looked around, making sure that the manager was safely out of sight. "Look, I need some help, and I'm willin' to pay for it."

Alarmed, he gaped at her. "What sort of help, ma'am?"

Luty pulled her hand from under the table, revealing a five pound note. "I just need some information, so if you think you can help a poor old woman, you better start movin' just a little slower, otherwise that fussbudget of a manager of yours will be pokin' his nose in wonderin' what you're doin'."

He stared at her for a moment and then gave her a brilliant smile. "Of course, ma'am. Now, what do you want to know?"

"Do you know if anyone who works here has been askin' questions about one of your guests, a Miss Lydia Kent?"

"I'm not sure what you mean." He looked confused. "What kind of questions?"

Luty decided to take the bull by the horns. "Did anyone git paid to find out when she was leavin'? You know, when she was supposed to check out." She saw his eyes widen in fear and knew she had her man. Nell's bells, today was her lucky day. She couldn't believe she'd struck gold so fast.

"Come on, fess up. I ain't goin' to go tattlin' on you. I just need to know."

"Are you going to tell the police?" he asked anxiously. "They've been here to talk to her, you know. If I'd known the police were going to get involved, I'd never have done it. But he offered me five pounds to find out when she was going, and I needed the money . . ."

"I ain't runnin' to the police." She tapped her finger against the note, which was now on the tabletop. "So tell me what you know, and you'll git another five pounds. Do you know who this feller was?"

"I don't know his name, but I can describe him to you."

"I know it's short notice," Smythe said to Blimpey, "but can you find it out or not?"

Blimpey shook his head. "I can find it out, but it'll take a few days."

"We've not got a few days," Smythe insisted. "The Home Office is puttin' pressure on the inspector to get this case solved. Come on, Blimpey, I'll pay extra." He'd been given his task because Mrs. Jeffries knew he was the only one with the resources to discover what they needed to know.

"I might be able to find out by late tonight," he said. "Will that do ya?"

"That'll be fine." Smythe got up. "I'll be back 'ere at closin' time, and I'll pay you double my normal rate."

"Bloody right ya will." Blimpey grinned broadly. "I'm goin' to 'ave to call in all sorts of markers for this one."

"Mrs. Brunel, I'm glad you're here. We've some questions for you, and this will save us a trip." Witherspoon smiled kindly. He could see she was embarrassed, and he felt a tad awkward as well.

"I'll not have you harassing her." Saxon put his arm around her shoulders in a protective gesture. "She came to ask my advice about buying a gift—"

"Give it a rest, Mr. Saxon," Barnes interrupted. "We all know why she came here, and it wasn't to get your opinion about a ruddy Japanese tea set. Now, we can ask her questions here or we can wait until she goes home. It's her choice."

"I'll answer anything you like." She smiled at Saxon. "Nicholas, it's a bit late to try and protect my reputation. I fear it's already in tatters with these gentlemen."

"I assure you, ma'am, we're not here to pass judgment on anyone," Witherspoon said. "We're merely trying to discover who murdered Daniel McCourt."

"I didn't kill him," she said quickly. "I didn't like him, but he didn't deserve to die the way he did."

"Did Mrs. McCourt ever mention how her husband proposed to her?" Barnes sat back down.

"How he proposed?" Saxon repeated in confusion. "I don't understand the question."

"Neither do I," she added.

"So you didn't know that he was supposed to have asked her to marry him at Christmastime while they were under a sprig of mistletoe?"

CHAPTER 10

"It was jolly decent of Mrs. Brunel to help us," Witherspoon said as he waited for Barnes to pay the hansom driver.

"It was, sir," Barnes agreed. "Mind you, her offering to find out if her husband knew about McCourt's mistletoe proposal was more than a little self-serving, as she did get us to promise we'd not mention her relationship with Mr. Saxon unless we'd no choice in the matter. Little did she know that we'd not have revealed a detail like that unless it was pertinent to finding the killer."

"Apparently, even if she does want to divorce her husband, she doesn't want him to know about her relationship with Saxon. Do you think either of them did it?" he asked. Witherspoon started toward the entrance to the Alexandria Hotel.

"They could have; both of them had a motive. Saxon's got no money, and his only income is selling off his collection.

McCourt threatened to prosecute Raleigh for fraud—an action that could easily have frozen the Oriental antiquities market for a long time. Mrs. Brunel might want to divorce her husband, but if McCourt had told Brunel about the two of them, he can prove adultery on her part, and she'll not even get basic maintenance." Barnes turned and saw the inspector staring straight ahead. He followed his gaze and cringed. Luty Belle and Hatchet were coming out of the hotel. Their heads were close together, and Luty's hands gestured wildly as though she were arguing. She broke off long enough to nod her thanks at the doorman.

Barnes shot forward, hoping his sudden movement would cause one of them to look up and see the inspector.

His ruse worked, for Hatchet glanced their way and, without missing a breath, smiled at the two policemen. "Inspector Witherspoon, Constable Barnes, what a lovely surprise. How very nice to see you both."

"Howdy, Inspector, Constable. I sure didn't expect to see you here!" Luty exclaimed. "What are ya doin' here?"

"We're going to interview a witness who is staying at the hotel," Witherspoon explained.

"My gracious, that sounds excitin'," Luty gushed. "I came to meet a friend of mine who's stayin' here. But we must have got mixed up 'cause I waited and waited and she never showed. But I had me a nice pot of tea, and that warmed me up."

"I told you not to count on seeing the woman." Hatchet chided his employer. He looked at the two policemen. "Mrs. Fenwick has never been reliable." Hatchet deliberately used Lucille's surname. He didn't think the inspector would check their story, but it paid to take precautions. "But come along, madam." He took Luty's elbow. "The inspector is here on official business, and we mustn't keep him." Tugging gently, he pulled her toward the curb. He waved at the driver of the hansom the policemen had just vacated. "Good day, gentlemen," he called. "Give our regards to your household." He paused long enough to tell the driver the address and then shoved Luty inside.

"Good-bye, Mrs. Crookshank, Hatchet," the inspector yelled.

Grinning broadly, Barnes waved a good-bye. "Shall we go in, sir?" he said as the cab pulled away from the curb.

Witherspoon stood staring at the back of the hansom as it disappeared among the traffic. He had a quizzical, puzzled expression on his face.

"Sir? Is everything alright?"

"Oh yes. I was just thinking that it's a small world, isn't it?"

"It is, sir. But it's no surprise that Mrs. Crookshank's friends would stay at an exclusive hotel like the Alexandria, for it's a lovely place that caters to the wealthy, and this time of year a lot of people are in town for the holidays." He wanted to make sure the inspector didn't give their story a second thought. It wouldn't do for him to suspect they'd been there digging for information. "Shall we go and see if Miss Kent is available?"

She was available, but this time, she insisted on seeing them in her suite of rooms. "She's on the fourth floor, so we can take the lift." The bellboy guided them into a metal cage contraption on the far side of the sweeping staircase, clanged the metal gate shut, and slammed the door. Witherspoon's stomach lurched as the lift ascended.

Barnes, on the other hand, was grinning in pleasure. "What will they think of next," he enthused. "Moving staircases. We do live in miraculous times, don't we, Inspector?"

Witherspoon gave him a sickly smile. He felt slightly nauseous. "Yes, we most certainly do."

The lift stopped, and it seemed to Witherspoon that the

simple act of opening up the ruddy thing took ages, but finally, he was able to get out of it. He took a deep, heartfelt
breath, as if a great weight had been lifted off him.

"Miss Kent's room is 408," the bellboy said. He pointed
down the hall. "It's just there, sir."

"Thank you," the inspector muttered. "Where are the
stairs?" he asked quickly. He wasn't getting in that moving
coffin again no matter what.

"At the end of the corridor, sir." He slammed the grate
shut and closed the door.

"You didn't like it, sir?" Barnes asked as they made their
way to room 408. He knocked quietly on the wood.

"No, to be truthful, I hated it. I, er, I'm not fond of small
spaces."

The door opened, and an Oriental man wearing a floor-
length green robe with a high neck collar bowed politely.
"Miss Kent is expecting you," he said as he stepped back and
motioned them inside.

The sitting room furnishings were as elegant and luxuri-
ous as those in the lobby. The floor was carpeted with a blue,
green, and gray rug; the walls were covered in pale green
silk paper imprinted with a fleur-de-lis pattern; and blue
and green velvet curtains hung from the three windows. A
blue sofa and two balloon-back chairs were clustered around
a small, low table on top of which was a silver coffeepot
complete with service and a plate of biscuits.

Lydia Kent sat on the sofa. "Thank you, Wang," she said.
"I'll call if I need you."

"Very good, ma'am," he replied. He bowed politely to
the two men and then disappeared through one of the doors
on the far side of the room.

"Come and have some coffee, gentlemen," she offered.
She gestured at the two chairs, indicating they should sit

down, and then picked up the coffeepot. "I've just had it sent up, and it's a cold day outside."

Witherspoon's stomach lurched, but he nodded agreeably as he and Barnes sat down across from her. The lift ride had been bad enough, and he didn't like coffee, but she was being gracious, so he'd do his best not to be sick all over the carpet.

"Is that gentleman your personal servant?" Barnes asked.

"He is. A woman traveling alone needs protection, and some countries frown on carrying guns, so I have Wang. He's been with me for years. Constable, do you take cream and sugar?"

"Both, ma'am."

She fixed his coffee and then looked at Witherspoon. "Inspector?"

"I'll have the same, Miss Kent," he said. "This is very nice of you. Most of our witnesses don't offer any refreshment."

She put two lumps of sugar and poured a hefty measure of cream into his coffee. "It's my pleasure, Inspector." She handed him his cup and looked at him expectantly. "What brings you here today? More questions?"

"There are always more questions, ma'am," Witherspoon said.

"When we were here before, you mentioned something to the effect that the dealer who sold you the sword had other offers." Barnes frowned, trying to recall her exact words.

"That's correct." She sipped her coffee. "And all three of them were for more money than I paid. But as I said, Constable, I was there with cash in hand, and in Hong Kong, that always beats a paper promise."

"Did the seller happen to mention who else had made offers?" Barnes took a drink. He loved coffee, and this was particularly good.

She looked askance and then gave a slight shrug. "I can't imagine what that has to do with Daniel McCourt's murder, but I suppose you've a reason for asking."

"I do," he assured her, though in truth, he'd no idea why Mrs. Jeffries felt the identity of the other potential buyers might be important. Yet her instincts and ideas hadn't failed them yet.

"I bought the weapon from Park Jin Jae, a well-known antiquities dealer from Pyongyang," she said slowly, as though she were trying to recall the encounter. "Let me see . . . It's been some time since I bought it, but I do remember Mr. Park commenting that he'd received telegrams from a client in Berlin and that a museum in New York had expressed an interest in acquiring it."

"No one from London?" Barnes pressed.

She started to shake her head and then caught herself. "It wasn't exactly from London, but he said that he'd received a visit from Mr. Thomas Mak of Mak and Hartley, who was acting on behalf of a client in England. He said his client was definitely interested in the sword, but he wasn't authorized to make an offer. He'd only just heard the weapon was on the market and had sent a telegram to London. But, of course, by then, I'd already bought it."

Witherspoon glanced at Barnes to make sure he was finished. He wasn't certain why the constable was asking these specific questions, but he knew there must be a very good reason. The constable nodded, leaned back in his chair, and sipped his coffee with apparent pleasure. "We'd like your help in clearing up a matter," the inspector said. "There's a discrepancy between the statement you gave us and Mrs. McCourt's account regarding payment for the sword."

"A discrepancy," she repeated. "I don't understand. I answered all your questions truthfully."

"I'm sure this is just a simple misunderstanding," he replied. "Miss Kent, you said you went to the McCourt home on the day of the murder in order to get your money."

"That's correct." She grimaced. "And unfortunately, I'm now stuck in the position of asking either for the sword to be returned or for Mrs. McCourt to give me five thousand pounds. I imagine the poor widow is quite distraught over her husband's death, but I can't stay in London much longer. My friends are waiting in Paris."

"We've spoken to Mrs. McCourt about the matter, and she insists she saw the bill of sale for the Hwando and it was marked 'paid in full.'"

"Hwando?" She cocked her head to one side and stared at him in confusion. "What on earth are you talking about?"

"The Hwando sword," he explained. "The one that was used to kill him. Mrs. McCourt has a bill of sale."

She smiled slowly. "Inspector, I'm not sure what you're talking about, but I assure you, I didn't sell Daniel McCourt a Hwando. I sold him an extremely rare thirteenth-century sword from the Goryeo dynasty."

Everyone was early for the afternoon meeting, which didn't sit well with the cook. "These scones need to cool for a few more minutes," she complained as she put them on the table. "It's only gone four fifteen! I wasn't expectin' to see any of you back here until half past. What if I'd had a source in the kitchen? Would you have barged right in then?"

"Don't be cross, Mrs. Goodge. It's too cold to 'ang about outside." Wiggins licked his lips as he stared at the plate. "And butter meltin' off them nice, warm scones is a rare treat."

Mollified, the cook laughed. "You can always get round me by complimentin' my bakin'. Go on, then, sit down and

have at it. But if you burn your tongue don't come whinin'
to me."

"They smell wonderful." Phyllis slipped into her chair.
"And I'll admit right off that I didn't have much luck today." She spoke quickly, trying to get all the words out, because once again, she felt like she'd failed them. "I'm so
sorry, but I couldn't do what you asked me. I couldn't find
any sign of my source. I spent hours lingerin' about the area.
I'm so sorry. I know you were countin' on me."

The room went silent as everyone reacted to the panic in
her voice. Luty, who happened to be walking past, stopped
and patted her on the shoulder. "Now, don't be silly, girl.
You've done your fair share." She continued on to her chair.
"Just because you had a bad day don't mean you didn't do
yer best. We all have times when we don't have much luck."

"Don't feel bad, Miss Phyllis." Hatchet swept past and
pulled out his elderly employer's chair. "I wasn't able to accomplish my task, either, and I'm certainly not going to
apologize. We do the best we can, and that's that."

"Sometimes you get lucky, Phyllis." Smythe gave her a
cheeky grin as he flopped down next to his wife and scooped
the baby up into his arms. "And sometimes you don't. I'm
not goin' to find out much if my source doesn't come through
tonight."

"Phyllis, no one expects perfection," Mrs. Jeffries explained
gently. "All we ask is that we do our best, and I know that's
what you've done. Now, let's get the meeting started." She
could tell that Phyllis was overwhelmed by the attention, so
the kindest thing to do was move along. "Smythe, you had the
most difficult task, so would you care to go first?"

Smythe lifted Amanda and kissed her forehead. "My
source said 'e can find out what we need to know, but 'e
couldn't do it as fast as we'd like. I'm goin' to go back out

after supper tonight"—he gave Betsy a quick, apologetic glance—"but even then 'e couldn't guarantee 'e'd be able to give us an answer."

"Let's hope he can come through for us. Come back here afterwards," Mrs. Jeffries instructed. "Mrs. Goodge and I will wait up for you."

"It'll be awfully late," he warned.

"I can wait up, too," Wiggins said.

"You need your rest, lad," the cook interjected. "We don't need as much sleep as you young people. If it's all the same, I'd like to say my bit now. I know I wasn't assigned a task like the rest of you, but I did find out that McCourt went to see a doctor at the end of November, so I think he must have known he was very ill."

"Well done, Mrs. Goodge." Mrs. Jeffries gazed at her with admiration. "How on earth did you learn that?"

"It was easy." She grinned. "An old colleague of mine dropped by today. Doris Atherton, she's the one that used to work for Dorian Kettering," she said, referring to a suspect in one of their previous cases. "Well, she read about the Mc-Court murder, and when she saw his address, she realized the murder was in the inspector's district. She's a sharp one, is Doris, so she stopped in to tell me that McCourt had been to see this doctor on Harley Street. Her cousin is housekeeper to the doctor—that's how she found out. Mind you, she only dropped in because of the coincidence of the whole thing, not because she thought his goin' to the doctor had anythin' to do with the murder."

"But still, even if he knew he was ill, who would he tell?" Betsy said. "I've been thinking about it, and it seems to me his relationship with his wife was so bad he'd not confide in her, and no one else seems to have liked the man, so it's doubtful he had any friends."

"What a sad and pathetic life he had," Ruth said.

"He certainly did," Mrs. Jeffries agreed. "But even the most miserable of people want to talk with someone when they've had bad news. It's only human nature to want to tell someone of a health condition. Everyone needs sympathy."

"Maybe he was one of the few that didn't," Luty said. "But I've never met anyone who didn't love jawin' about their aches and pains till the cows come home. Anyways, if Mrs. Goodge is finished, I'll go next."

"That's all I have."

"I found out that a man bribed a waiter at the Alexandria to find out when Lydia Kent was originally supposed to leave London." She gave Hatchet a quick, triumphant grin. "And I did it without Lucille Fenwick. This waiter didn't know who the man was, and he'd never seen him before, but he was reportedly well dressed, tall, and had thinnin' light brown hair."

"That sounds like a description of Leon Brunel," Ruth said.

Luty nodded vigorously. "That's who I think it was, and that means he thought that Lydia Kent was leavin' the day before the tea party."

"Did you find out anything else?" Mrs. Jeffries asked.

"Nope, that's it, but I think I done pretty danged good." She gave Hatchet a smug smile.

"Alright, madam." Hatchet gave an exasperated sigh. "I'm a man of my word, and you have indeed been worthy of this challenge. I, unfortunately, have not, and running into the inspector and Constable Barnes meant that I couldn't pursue any other avenues of inquiry." He held up his hand as everyone began to speak at once. "Don't worry, madam handled the matter perfectly, and the inspector wasn't the least bit suspicious."

"That's a relief," the housekeeper said. "Who would like to go next?"

"I'll go," Wiggins offered. He told them about his excursion to the passageway next to the McCourt home. "But the fence between the two passageways is a good seven feet tall," he said. "After that, I got right lucky and found a servant from the house, but she didn't 'ave any idea if Mrs. McCourt knew about 'er husband's illness, and when I asked 'er if he'd been sick or anything like that, she said she didn't know that, either. But what she did know was that the sword that killed McCourt 'as been in his study for at least three weeks and maybe even four," he finished.

"But I thought that was the sword McCourt bought from Miss Kent?" Ruth said. "The one he was making such a fuss about at the tea party."

"That's what we all thought," Mrs. Jeffries said. "But then I realized that no one had actually verified that specific detail and that it might be important. Would you like to go next?"

Ruth smiled thinly. "I'm afraid the only thing I found out was something we already know: Leon Brunel is a fanatical collector and has the reputation of doing anything, including some very disreputable things, to obtain what he wants. I had lunch with Lydia Mortmain today, and she told me a very interesting story. She'd heard that last year, Brunel had actually disabled a rival collector's carriage so he couldn't get to an estate sale in Kent. Apparently, some very rare Buddhist statues were on the auction block, and Brunel was determined to get them and succeeded."

"How did he disable a carriage?" Mrs. Goodge asked curiously.

"I'm afraid Lydia didn't have the details. I'm sorry." She smiled at Mrs. Jeffries. "I know that's not what you wanted me to learn, but that was the best I could do. Lydia was the only person I managed to speak to today, and she'd never heard the story about McCourt proposing under the mistletoe. I didn't have time to contact my other sources to see if any of them had heard the tale."

"Don't concern yourself, Ruth." Mrs. Jeffries hid her disappointment behind a smile. One of the pillars supporting her theory was that the story of McCourt's romantic Christmas proposal under a sprig of mistletoe was well known and oft repeated. Thus far, that didn't seem to be the case. "Your task was difficult."

"If you'll wait a moment, I'll tell Mrs. McCourt that you're here," Haines said to Witherspoon. "She's in the drawing room with Mr. Brunel."

"Mr. Leon Brunel?" Barnes clarified. He didn't think she would be having tea with Arthur, but it never hurt to make sure.

"Correct, sir." Haines disappeared down the hall.

"I wonder what Leon Brunel is doing here," the inspector muttered in a low voice.

"McCourt was his cousin. Maybe he's here to help her with the funeral arrangements."

Witherspoon shook his head. "I don't think there's any love lost between Mrs. McCourt and Leon Brunel. As a matter of fact, I got the distinct impression she thoroughly disliked him."

Haines reappeared. "Mrs. McCourt will see you now. Would you care for tea?"

Witherspoon's stomach still hadn't recovered from the coffee. "No, thank you, we're fine. We've just had some refreshment."

"Very good, sir." Haines held the door open and then closed it quietly behind them.

Elena McCourt was sitting by the fireplace and was dressed in a dark sapphire blue day dress. Leon Brunel was in the chair next to her. Witherspoon gave the room a fast but thorough survey. He noted she'd closed the huge sliding doors that separated the drawing room from the study, but the Christmas tree was still in the corner, and garlands of greenery still draped the mantel. There was no sign that this was a house in mourning.

It was Brunel who spoke first. "Really, Inspector, how many times must you disturb poor Mrs. McCourt?"

She put her hand out to silence him. "As many times as it takes to catch my husband's killer, Leon. Please sit down, gentlemen. Mr. Brunel was just leaving."

"I'll be happy to stay if you need me, Elena," he said to her. "After all, I'm now the most senior male member of your family, and it's my duty to ensure you're treated properly. I won't have you bullied by the police."

"These policemen have been very kind thus far." She gave him a strained smile.

"It isn't seemly that you have these men in your home without a family member present," he argued. "A male family member."

"I appreciate the offer, but I'm quite capable of taking care of myself. Now, if you'll excuse us . . ." She let her voice trail off, and for a moment, it appeared as if he was going to stay in his chair, but he finally got to his feet.

"As you wish." He nodded curtly and, ignoring both men, stalked to the door and slammed it shut behind him.

"Mrs. McCourt," the inspector began, but she leapt up, shushing him by putting her index finger across her lips. She tiptoed across the room and put her eye right up to the crack between the two double oak doors. "Good, he's gone," she announced. She went back to her seat. "I'm sorry, Inspector, but he's a dreadful snoop, and I wanted to make certain he'd gone. I'll not have another man sticking his nose into my life and trying to boss me about." She noticed neither man had taken a seat. "Please, both of you, make yourselves comfortable and sit down."

Barnes slid into the chair Brunel had just vacated. "If you don't mind my asking, ma'am, what was he doing here? Offering condolences?"

"Hardly, Constable." She smiled wryly. "He was doing precisely what I expected of him. He wants to establish that he's now head of the family and that I ought to turn all my decisions over to him."

Barnes chuckled. "I have a feeling you set him straight fairly quickly." He hoped this woman wasn't a murderer. He'd taken a liking to her and would hate to watch her hang.

"I most certainly did," she answered. "When he realized I wasn't going to give him control of my money, he then began hinting that he'd like to buy Daniel's collection. Of course that wasn't a surprise; he's coveted the collection for years."

"Would you say your husband's collection was superior to Brunel's?" the inspector asked.

"I don't know what its real worth might be. All I can tell you is that they were both very competitive with each other, and I know that my husband had acquired a substantial number of items that Leon wanted desperately. The two men spent most of their time trying to outfox each other in tracking down rare and valuable objects. It was a stupid and childish competition that had gone on for years."

Witherspoon regarded her curiously. "Would you sell the collection to Mr. Brunel, ma'am? I mean, considering how competitive he was with Mr. McCourt? You wouldn't think it a betrayal of your husband's memory?"

"Not at all," she declared. "Daniel always said that the only person genuinely capable of appreciating it would be his cousin. Besides, I don't want it."

"You know that we've spoken to your husband's solicitor. He said the collection has been valued at over thirty thousand pounds," the inspector pressed.

"That was before we learned that it's possible some of the pieces are fakes," she said bluntly. "And that's exactly what I told Leon. I made it clear I was going to have the entire collection reevaluated, and then if he was still interested, I'd give him first refusal on it. I must say he took it with good grace."

"Ma'am, are you certain you've no idea how your husband came to the conclusion that he'd been defrauded by Jerome Raleigh?" Witherspoon asked.

"I've told you, Inspector, he didn't mention how he'd found out."

"When did he tell you about the fraud?" Barnes asked. "Was it recently?"

She put her palms together and touched her chin with her entwined fingertips as she thought for a moment. "I'm not sure . . . No, wait, I am sure. It was the day he came home from Goodison and Bright with the Yuan dynasty vases. He was utterly furious when he got home. Mrs. Williams and I were doing menus downstairs, but I sat there listening to him slam doors and scream at the housemaids until we finished our business, then I went up to see what was wrong."

"You weren't alarmed enough by his behavior to go up immediately?" Barnes asked curiously.

"No, I was used to it." She smiled bitterly. "He not only had a bad temper, but he couldn't abide being thwarted in any way. It's a trait all the men in the family have; Leon and

Arthur are the same. Of course, with Arthur it's not as no-
ticeable, as he isn't a collector."

"What happened when you went up?" Witherspoon
asked.

"He'd poured himself a whiskey and was venting his rage
kicking the footstool. I got him to calm down enough to tell
me what happened, and then he said he was going to bring
in a real expert to reappraise some of the pieces Raleigh had
advised him to buy."

"Do you know who he brought in?"

"I'm afraid not. The next day I left for my aunt's home in
Buckinghamshire. I was there until she passed away. I know
he'd brought someone here, because he was crowing to me
that the damage wasn't as bad as he'd feared, but he was still
going to make Raleigh's life miserable."

"He said he was going to prosecute?" Witherspoon said.

"He said he wouldn't if Raleigh would pay him back for
the items he'd overvalued. Otherwise, he was going to have
the man put in jail."

"Could Mr. McCourt have actually proved fraud?" Barnes
glanced at the inspector.

"He claimed he could." She smiled wearily. "But I was
only half listening to him. I'd just lost the only remaining
member of my birth family, and though I was very distraught, I knew that her death would free me from Daniel's
tirades."

"How so, ma'am?" the inspector asked.

"As soon as I got my inheritance, I was going to move
into my late aunt's home."

"Did he know you planned on leaving this house?" Witherspoon wondered whether this fact had anything to do with
the murder and then realized he'd no idea what, if anything,
they'd learned thus far was going to be useful. He silently

prayed that Mrs. Jeffries was correct and that his "inner voice" was putting two and two together to make four, because his outer voice certainly wasn't giving him any answers.

"He knew, and he was very upset about my plans. We'd quarreled on a number of occasions, but there wasn't anything he could do to stop me," she replied. "He didn't care if I left; what he cared about was gaining control of my money. He had none of his own, you see. But despite his threats, I wasn't going to stay here."

"What kind of threats?" Barnes asked.

"He said if I left he'd take me to court." She snorted delicately. "Apparently there's some sort of law pertaining to conjugal rights."

Witherspoon glanced at the constable and saw from his expression that he'd also realized the woman had just admitted to a motive. Lady Cannonberry had pointed out to him on many occasions that the law courts were notoriously biased against females when marital cases went before a judge. The judges were male. Blast, why did these things always happen when he was so tired he couldn't think straight?

"Were you concerned about that?" Barnes asked.

"Not really." She smiled. "The courts could order a restoration of conjugal rights, but there was no way to enforce it, and Daniel could only obtain such an order by a long and very expensive court battle. Daniel could be ruthless, but I had something he didn't have."

"What was that, ma'am?" The constable shifted slightly.

"Money to pay a solicitor and court fees. I'm not a monster, Constable. I wasn't going to live in the same house as my husband, but I made no plans to divorce him. I fully intended to pay for the upkeep of this house," she said. "And I was going to give him an allowance."

Witherspoon decided to change tactics. "Mrs. McCourt, you said you saw the bill of sale for the Hwando and it was marked paid in full. Is that correct?"

"That's right. I'll get it for you." She started to rise, but he waved her back to her seat.

"Don't trouble yourself, ma'am," he said, "because we spoke with Miss Kent and she claims she didn't sell him a Hwando. She sold him an ancient and very valuable sword from the Goryeo period."

"Here's your sherry, sir." Mrs. Jeffries handed Witherspoon his glass and sat down opposite him. He looked terrible. His eyes were red, his mouth gaped slightly open, and his hair stood up in small tufts. "You look very tired, sir. Perhaps you should retire as soon as you've eaten your dinner?"

"I'm exhausted. I've had the most peculiar day." He put his head against the back of his chair and closed his eyes for a moment. "On the one hand, we learned quite a bit, but on the other, I've no idea what, if anything, it might mean."

"Perhaps it will help if you talk about it, sir," she encouraged. "Your dinner won't be ready for another half hour."

He nodded mutely and took another sip. "That's an excellent idea. Sometimes discussing it helps me to keep it all straight in my mind." He told her about his day, beginning with the visit to the Saxon house and Mrs. Brunel's unexpected arrival there and ending with his odd conversation with Elena McCourt.

Mrs. Jeffries listened to his recitation, breaking in only occasionally to ask a question or to get him to supply a bit more detail. When he told her about the Goryeo sword, she clamped her lips together to keep from laughing out loud. She was so relieved she'd been right that she wanted to dance a jig, but she forced herself to sit still and pay attention.

"It wasn't the Hwando that he'd bought. It was some ancient thing from the Goryeo period," he explained.

"Gracious, sir, that's a surprise."

"It most certainly was, and I'm not entirely sure what it might mean to the investigation."

"Oh, but I think it must be important," she interrupted. It wasn't just important; it was the crux of the killing. "And I'm certain you'll soon ascertain precisely how it fits into the murder."

"I do hope so," he admitted, his expression glum.

"What did Mrs. McCourt have to say about it?"

"When I asked her, she was sure she'd never seen nor heard of it. Honestly, Mrs. Jeffries, I don't know what to think." He drained his glass.

"You searched the house and the grounds of the communal garden thoroughly on the night of the murder," she commented. "But are you certain the sword wasn't there?"

"I think so." He frowned and pushed his spectacles, which were slipping down, back up to the bridge of his nose. "Miss Kent gave us a good description of the sword, and it's not a thin, rapier-like weapon. It's quite sizable, and she'd given it to McCourt in a large, flat case. We found nothing like that when we searched."

"Did any of the servants at the McCourt home recall seeing Daniel McCourt bring such an object into the house?" she pressed. A vague course of action was forming in her mind; one where Witherspoon would have a reason for questioning the servants.

"I didn't think to ask," he said. "Perhaps I ought to inquire. Miss Kent claims that McCourt took the sword three days before he was murdered."

"That's an excellent idea, sir," she encouraged. There were still one or two missing pieces of the puzzle, but she was fairly certain she was correct. She only hoped she could come up with a way to prove it.

"Are you sure about this information?" Smythe asked. He was back at the Dirty Duck. It was past closing time, and he and Blimpey were alone in the pub.

Exasperated, Blimpey pursed his lips. "Don't be daft. Of course I'm sure, and this is goin' to cost you an arm and a leg. I 'ad to roust one of my sources at the telegraph office out of bed, and 'e was none too pleased."

"But this source is sure of his facts, right?"

"'Course he is! Otherwise I'd not use him. Do ya know how much it costs to get one of them telegraph people in yer stable? Those are bloomin' good jobs, and they know if they get caught passin' on information like this, they'll get the sack. But 'e's sure of his facts. 'E says it was the only message that came in from the Far East for the Kensington district that day, and 'e remembers it well enough."

"Right then, if you're sure, I've got to go. They're waitin' up for me." He stood to leave. "We'll settle up once this case is over. I may need your services again."

"I want yer word you'll not complain about the bill," Blimpey warned. "Like I told ya, it's goin' to be the biggest one I ever gave ya. But my information is golden."

"And that's why you'll not 'ear a peep out of me." Smythe grinned. "I just want us to get this one over and done with so we can enjoy the season."

He left by the back door and hurried over to the hansom he had waiting. He rarely used the inspector's carriage because the two horses, Bow and Arrow, were both getting old and Smythe didn't like taking them out in the cold. "Get me to Upper Edmonton Gardens as quickly as you can," he told the driver as he climbed aboard.

They made good time through the deserted, late-night streets, and Smythe was soon back in the kitchen with a hot cup of tea in front of him.

Wiggins, Mrs. Goodge, Mrs. Jeffries, and even Phyllis had waited up to see whether he'd been successful or not.

"Go on, then. Tell us what you 'eard," Wiggins said.

"Give the man a moment to have his tea," Mrs. Goodge chided the footman. "It's cold out there, and he's half frozen." She patted the big orange cat that was curled in her lap. Samson cuddled closer and butted his big head against the cook's rib cage. Fred, who'd not let the cat get near the table without him being there as well, put his head on Wiggins' leg, and the footman idly scratched him behind the ears.

"My source was able to find out what we needed." Smythe blew on the top of his tea to cool it down. "Brunel did receive a telegram from Hong Kong."

"So he knew Miss Kent was in town and that she had the Goryeo sword with her to sell."

"Yes, but he found out too late. The telegram arrived the day she arrived here, but by the time he got to the Alexandria, she'd already made a deal with McCourt."

"I don't understand." The cook frowned. "What does that sword have to do with McCourt's murder?"

"If my theory is correct, it's the whole reason for the murder," Mrs. Jeffries said. The idea she'd had earlier had proved to be a dead end. The inspector could interview the servants at both the McCourt and the Brunel households until he was blue in the face, and it might not make any difference. He'd learn what they already knew, but those few facts wouldn't be enough to convict a rich man of murder. "Unfortunately, I can't think of any possible way we can prove it."

"What does that mean?" Wiggins demanded. "Are ya sayin' the killer is goin' to get away with it?"

"I'm very much afraid he might," she replied. "Unless the inspector actually finds the sword in his possession, there's absolutely no evidence to convict him that couldn't be interpreted in a dozen different ways by a good lawyer."

"Then the inspector 'ad better find that bloomin' sword," Smythe declared. "Blast a Spaniard, Mrs. Jeffries, we're not givin' up."

"I didn't say that we were," she replied. "But I very much fear that he's taken the sword out of the city and hidden it. We may never find it."

"We've not heard of him goin' out of town," Phyllis said quietly. "And I think one of us would have stumbled across it if he'd gone to the train station or another place like that."

No one said anything as they considered her words.

"I think she's right," Mrs. Goodge said. "We'd have heard if he'd left town."

Mrs. Jeffries considered the idea. "Perhaps," she finally said. "But there's always the chance he managed to slip out without our knowing, and it's of the utmost importance that the inspector find that sword."

"Then let's 'ope it's somewhere in 'is house," Smythe said. "I'm goin' 'ome. We'll be here bright and early tomorrow."

Wiggins walked him to the back door, and their low voices faded as they went down the hall.

Mrs. Goodge stared at Mrs. Jeffries. Her lips were flattened together in a worried frown, and her brow wrinkled in thought. "What's got you so worried?" she asked.

"I don't know that I'm right," the housekeeper replied. "I think I'm right, but then I have moments when the evidence seems flimsy and silly. Everything rests on the characters of the suspect and victim and a specific sequence of events. But if I've gotten even one small part of it wrong, then my whole theory collapses."

CHAPTER 11

Mrs. Jeffries had tossed and turned the entire night but still hadn't come up with a way to point the inspector toward an arrest. She was now certain she was right. It was the only sequence of events that made sense. But convinced as she was, she had grave doubts about how to prove her idea. There simply wasn't enough physical evidence. She went downstairs and made a pot of tea. Mrs. Goodge, yawning and carrying Samson, appeared as she put the mugs on the table.

"You look like you've not slept very much," Mrs. Goodge remarked as she put the cat down.

"I haven't. I'm almost certain I know who committed the murder, but for the life of me, I can't think of a way to get the evidence to make sense enough for an arrest."

"You'll think of somethin'." The cook turned her head and looked down the hall as they heard a soft knock on the back door. "Ah, there's Constable Barnes. Let's see what he has to say. Maybe he'll have an idea."

As always, Barnes listened carefully as Mrs. Jeffries took him step-by-step along the path that led to her current conclusion. "So you see," she finished, "I'm sure I'm right, but I don't think there's enough here for an arrest."

"I'm sorry to say so, Mrs. Jeffries, but I agree," he said glumly. "We can't make an arrest on a theory alone. Mind you, your idea does make a lot of sense. But I can't see how we can prove it."

"But what if you catch him with the Goryeo sword?" the cook asked. "Wouldn't that be evidence?"

Barnes took a sip of tea while he thought. "I suppose it might be enough. We do have Lydia Kent's statement that McCourt had the sword in his possession when he left her hotel room and that it was in a large, flat case. Your source, Annie, claims she saw him bringing such a case into his study, so we can prove he took it into his home."

"And it wasn't there when you searched the house," Mrs. Jeffries pointed out. "So I think that goes a long way toward proving that the motive for the murder was that sword."

Barnes smiled skeptically. "But just because we can't find the ruddy thing doesn't prove that it was the motive. Everyone else who was there that day had a reason to want the man dead, and some of those reasons seem very compelling. Raleigh, Saxon, Arthur Brunel, even Mrs. McCourt, they all stood to gain either emotionally or financially once McCourt was dead."

"Then why is the sword missing?" Mrs. Jeffries argued. "Who else but the killer could have taken it?"

"I'm sure the killer did," he agreed. "But I was just pointing out what a good barrister is likely to do if we ever get Leon Brunel into the dock. And if he did kill McCourt for the sword, I don't think we're likely to find it under the sofa in his drawing room. He'll have hidden it well."

"But he's one of them fanatics, isn't he?" the cook charged. "That's what we've heard about him; that once he's got his hands on somethin', he'll never let it get away from him. And we've not heard of him leavin' town or goin' to the country since the murder."

"He's letting his wife get away," Barnes interrupted. "Yesterday I distinctly heard her say that she could get a divorce."

"You heard her say that? When did that happen?" Mrs. Jeffries asked, her voice sharp.

"While we were at the Saxon home. Didn't the inspector tell you?"

"He did, but all he said was that she'd barged into the room without realizing you and he were there. He said she was dreadfully embarrassed, but he didn't say anything about her mentioning a divorce. Tell me, Constable, what were her exact words when she arrived?" Mrs. Jeffries demanded. "Please, it's very important."

He pictured the scene in his mind. In his years as a policeman, he'd testified in court hundreds of times and developed methods to help him remember things as accurately as possible. "She said, 'I knocked but you didn't answer. It's awful, just awful. I told him I wanted a divorce! He was so angry but he knows he can't stop . . .' Then she saw us standing there and clamped her mouth shut."

"But he knows he can't stop," Mrs. Jeffries repeated. "Oh my gracious, there might be a way. What were you and the inspector going to do this morning?" she asked Barnes.

"McCourt's funeral service isn't until one o'clock, but he didn't say what we'd do this morning." The constable eyed her cautiously. "Why, have you thought of something?"

"I think so," she replied. Her mind worked furiously as one by one the pieces fell into place. Mrs. Jeffries herself had tracked in pine and bark mulch after she'd been trapped in the passageway by the Crandall house, and Harriet had told Phyllis she'd gotten into trouble because that same mulch was on the attic landing. Annie had heard someone walking in the passageway between the houses hours after McCourt was dead, and Smythe had verified that Brunel had known Lydia Kent was in town to sell the sword. A sword he wanted more than life itself. But gracious, what if she was wrong? She thought of Barnes' warning about other suspects with better motives, and she was afraid.

Ye gods, she thought, if I'm wrong, then not only will the killer get a chance to bury the evidence so deep it would never come to light, but the inspector would have the worst kind of black mark on his record. Neither the Home Office nor the newspapers would accept anything less than perfection from Inspector Gerald Witherspoon. All these thoughts whirled through her mind in an instant, but despite the risks, she knew there was no choice. "Can you get the inspector to the Brunel household?"

"I think so," he replied. "What do you want me to do once I get him there?"

"Give me a moment to think." She tapped her finger against the side of her tea mug as she discarded one idea after another. Finally, she looked at the constable. "Once you're there, tell Leon Brunel you've a witness that saw him carrying a large, flat case into his house on the night that Daniel McCourt was murdered."

"He'll deny it, and we don't have such a witness," Barnes pointed out.

"We don't have a witness that saw him." Mrs. Jeffries smiled. "But we do have one that heard him."

"Who?"

"Annie, the housemaid at the McCourts'," the cook said eagerly. "She heard someone walkin' around outside on the night of the murder, and if Mrs. Jeffries' theory is right, that must have been the killer."

"Excellent," Mrs. Jeffries cried. "That's the first thing you ought to do—get the inspector to verify her statement, and while you're there, take him to the Crandall passageway so he can see the pine and bark mulch. You can use that as a pretext to question Brunel again."

"And how will I have heard about either thing these girls said?" Barnes asked in frustration. "I can't keep coming up with mythical sources that tell me bits and pieces we don't hear in the official interviews."

"I got my information from Annie at the Black Horse Pub," Wiggins said as he stepped into the kitchen. "Isn't that the sort of place you'd expect an informer to 'ang about?"

"Annie, don't be alarmed. We're only here to ask you about something that has been brought to our attention," Witherspoon said to the young girl. He and Barnes were in the butler's pantry of the McCourt home. Upstairs, the household was preparing for the victim's funeral, so the two policemen had slipped in unobtrusively. "We'd like to verify a detail with you."

Annie clasped her hands together nervously. "Is this goin' to take long? I don't want to get in trouble, and Mrs. Williams wants me to bring up the linens for the reception. It's not till late this afternoon, but she wants everything ready before Mrs. McCourt leaves for the church."

"It won't take any time at all," Witherspoon said kindly. "On the night that Mr. McCourt was murdered, did you hear anything out of the ordinary after the household had gone to bed?"

Barnes held his breath. If she denied it, they'd be in trouble.

She gave a quick, frightened glance at the closed door of the pantry before looking back at them. "I did. But when I told them, they said it was just my imagination. I'd come down to get a drink of water, you see, and I heard a loud, rustling sound outside, and then I heard footsteps."

Relieved, the constable asked, "Was it right outside the servants' door?"

"It sounded like it was, but then again, it didn't sound close enough," she replied. "It scared me so bad I went right upstairs and put my head under the pillow."

"Let's hope that Mr. and Mrs. Brunel don't object to our speaking to their servants," Witherspoon said as he and Barnes waited in the foyer. The housekeeper had gone to fetch Leon Brunel.

"I don't see why they should, sir. Now that we know someone was in that passageway, we've a perfect right to determine if any of our suspects were seen going in or out of their houses late that night. We've only come here because this home is closest to the McCourt house." This was exactly as he'd planned it with Mrs. Jeffries.

"Do you really think the killer hid the Goryeo sword in the mulch at the Crandall house?" the inspector mused. "I can't see anyone doing murder over a sword, but as you pointed out, it is the only item missing."

"It's a perfect hiding place, sir," Barnes pointed out. "The killer couldn't take the sword with him because there were too many people on the street, so shoving it into the mulch of the house next door was a good solution. Then he or she waited a few hours until everyone was in bed and then sneaked back and retrieved it. I showed you that the lock on the Crandall gate was broken. I think that's how the killer got in and out so easily."

"But there were police constables on duty," Witherspoon protested. "Surely they'd have heard someone."

"There were constables patrolling the road and just one in the communal garden. It wouldn't have been difficult for the murderer to avoid them."

They turned as they heard footsteps pounding down the hallway and Leon Brunel, followed by his wife, appeared. He was dressed in his shirtsleeves with a black tie draped around his neck. Glenda Brunel wore a black mourning dress.

"What is the meaning of this, Inspector?" Brunel snapped. "My housekeeper said you've made the most outlandish request."

"We'd like to speak to your servants," Witherspoon said calmly. "We've no wish to inconvenience you—"

"But it is an inconvenience," he interrupted. "What on earth do you think you can learn from our servants? None of them were anywhere near the McCourt house when he was murdered."

Glenda Brunel said nothing; she simply stared at the two policemen with a strange, cunning expression on her beautiful face.

"This is a murder investigation." Barnes looked him directly in the eye. "And your servants may or may not have information that can help lead to the killer. We won't know until we speak to them."

"What kind of information might that be?" Glenda Brunel stepped around her husband and walked toward them. "I was home that night. Perhaps I can help you."

Leon lunged forward and caught up with her. "This is

none of your concern. Go and finish dressing. We've got to leave for the funeral soon."

She ignored him. "You can ask me anything you were going to ask the servants." She smiled at Witherspoon. "I'll tell the truth."

"Glenda, shut up." Leon tried to grab her arm, but she nimbly leapt to one side and fled down the hall toward the double doors leading to the drawing room.

Alarmed, both policemen went after her, intent on putting themselves between her and her angry husband.

"What do you want to know?" She whirled around and flattened herself against the closed doors, her gaze fastened on her husband's face. "Ask me, ask me. I'll tell you what you want to know. I won't lie to protect him."

"Did your husband leave the house on the night that McCourt was murdered?" Barnes blurted out as he and Witherspoon planted themselves protectively in front of her.

"He did, and when he came home, I saw him carrying a long, flat case up to the attic." She pointed up the stairs. "I'll show you. I'll show you where he put it."

"Good God, woman, what kind of wife are you?" Leon hurled himself in her direction, but Barnes and Witherspoon were ready for him. They caught him by the shoulders and then dragged him back toward the front door by his arms. By this time he was screaming at the top of his lungs, and the housekeeper came charging into the foyer. "Run and get the constable on the corner," Barnes ordered as they tightened their grip on the struggling man. "Use the servants' door," he commanded, because they now had Brunel pinned up against the front door. She turned and fled.

"He hid something up in the attic." Glenda looked at Witherspoon as she spoke.

"Did you see him do it on the night McCourt died?" The inspector gasped the words out. He used his body to pin Brunel to the door, and he could see that Barnes was straining to hold the fellow as well.

"No, but he goes up there every day." She laughed. "He locked the door, but that didn't keep me out."

"Of course it wouldn't, you wretched little sneak!" Brunel yelled. He jerked his left shoulder and almost succeeded in dislodging Barnes. "You're good at sneaking, aren't you? That's all you're good at, you slut."

"There's a sword up there," she continued calmly, as if he hadn't spoken. "It's in a flat case and is very ugly. But he strokes it and fondles it like a lover."

"You stupid cow! You've ruined me!" Leon screamed at his wife. "I've given you everything, and this is how you repay me. I'll kill you. I'll kill you!"

Barnes grimaced. He didn't know how much longer he could hold on, and he wished Mrs. Brunel would shut up, because every time she hurled an insult at her husband, it enraged him so that he doubled his efforts to get away.

Footsteps pounded up the corridor, and two constables suddenly appeared and raced over to the front door to relieve them of their burden. "We've got him now," one of them said as he pulled Brunel's arms behind his back and slapped on the cuffs. "Are you alright, sir?"

"We're fine." Witherspoon could barely gasp out the words, he was so tired.

Brunel suddenly broke away from the constable and hurled himself at his wife. "I'll kill you. I'll kill you!"

"No, you won't." Glenda straightened away from the door. "You're going to hang, and I'm going to have all your money."

* * *

"I wonder if they're there yet," Luty remarked to no one in particular. Ruth, Betsy, Phyllis, Mrs. Jeffries, and Mrs. Goodge sat around the kitchen table and waited. Smythe, Wiggins, and Hatchet had gone to the Brunel house to surreptitiously keep watch. They promised to return immediately if there was an arrest made.

"They had to go to the McCourt house first," Mrs. Jeffries replied. "Then they'll go to Leon and Glenda Brunel's residence."

"And let's hope that you're right," the cook said to the housekeeper. "Otherwise, the inspector is goin' to end up with egg on his face."

"'Course she's right," Luty declared. "And it ain't her fault that everythin' rests on the misery of a wife and the piece of pine mulch in the attic."

Betsy suddenly turned her head toward the back door. "The men are back."

"Brunel was arrested!" Wiggins yelped as they came into the kitchen. "And lucky for the inspector that we was 'angin' about the house, otherwise Brunel might've made a run for it."

"Tell us everythin'," Luty demanded.

The three of them peeled off coats and scarves, caps and gloves, as they crossed to the coat tree before moving to the table. Hatchet popped his elegant black top hat on the sideboard then proceeded to his usual spot.

"I'll get more cups." Betsy leapt up, gave her husband a quick kiss, and hurried to the cupboard.

"Is the babe alright?" he asked.

"She's fine," Betsy said.

"She's havin' a late nap in my room," the cook told him. "Now, you boys sit down and we'll pour you some tea, then you can tell us what happened."

For the next few moments, the kitchen was silent save for

the scraping of chairs and the clink of china as they took their seats and got their tea. Finally, when everyone had settled, Mrs. Jeffries said, "Now, who wants to start?"

"I'll do the honors," Hatchet offered. "As instructed, we went to the Brunel house to keep an eye out should anything untoward develop. Wiggins and I stayed in the front, and Smythe very kindly volunteered to watch the back and servants' entrance on the side."

"We wanted to make sure we 'ad the doors covered just in case 'e tried to scarper off," Smythe clarified.

"Excellent idea. If he attempted such a thing, you could have followed him to see where he went," Ruth added, nodding approvingly.

"Now, as you know, it's a very posh area, and the Brunel home is quite close to the commercial district," Hatchet continued. "That's a pertinent point, as you will see when we get further into our story."

"Oh, git on with it," Luty cried. "We're on pins and needles here."

"If you'll quit interrupting, madam," he scolded, "I'll do just that. Now, as I was saying, we had the doors covered properly, and Wiggins had pointed out the location of the nearest constable. He was stationed just around the corner from the Brunel home by the shops. We'd taken our places, so we had a good view of the premises."

"Where did you hide?" Mrs. Goodge asked.

"We didn't really hide, per se," Hatchet replied. "We walked up and down the street. There were a lot of people going to and fro to the shops, so no one noticed us. Wiggins was on one side of the road, and I was on the other."

"I dodged behind a postbox when the inspector's hansom cab pulled up," Wiggins added cheerfully. "Oh, sorry, Hatchet. Go on with the tellin'."

"We saw the inspector and Constable Barnes go inside, and we waited. A few moments later, Wiggins waved for me to join him. I did, and we could hear raised voices coming from the Brunel house."

"They were yellin' loud enough to wake the dead," Wiggins corrected.

"Yes, yes, that's true, they were very loud," Hatchet said impatiently. "At that point, we decided we'd best get help. We didn't wish to barge in and give ourselves away unless we'd no choice in the matter, so Wiggins dashed off to alert the constable on the corner."

"I ran up and told him I could hear screamin' comin' from the house and I thought maybe a burglar was breakin' in." The footman laughed at his own cleverness. "'E took off like a shot, blowin' 'is whistle so that another constable come runnin', and the two of them flew like the devil toward the house. Just then, the housekeeper come out screamin' that the policemen were inside and they needed 'elp. By this time the inspector and Barnes were scufflin' with Brunel, and from the sounds comin' from inside the house, 'e was puttin' up a real fight."

Ruth gasped. "Is Gerald alright? Is he hurt?"

"And Barnes—is he in one piece?" the cook demanded.

"They're both fine," Hatchet said. "When we heard the noise, we were alarmed as well, and I must say, we'd have probably intervened if the constables hadn't reached the house so quickly. We were very apprehensive until we saw them bringing Brunel out in handcuffs." Hatchet laughed. "Of course, we weren't completely reassured as to the inspector and the constable's safety until Smythe appeared and reported that he'd peeked in the drawing room window and both our policemen were fine."

"They were talkin' to Mrs. Brunel," Smythe explained.

"Mind you, the inspector's hat was off and his hair was mussed up, and the constable's helmet was gone, but they didn't look too much worse for the wear."

"Thank goodness." Ruth sighed in relief. "Sometimes we forget how dangerous catching murderers can be."

Smythe eyed the housekeeper speculatively. "Right, it's your turn now, Mrs. Jeffries. 'Ow did you suss it out?"

"I wasn't sure I was going to figure this one out at all," she admitted with a laugh. "For one thing, so many people had a reason to want McCourt dead. Arthur Brunel hated him for cheating him out of what he considered his proper share of their father's estate, and even though it had happened three years earlier, it was only now that Arthur was forced to turn his home into flats in order to keep a roof over his head."

"And it doesn't take much to spark an old hatred," Betsy murmured.

"Not only that, but McCourt was going to sue Brunel," the housekeeper continued.

"But didn't Mrs. McCourt confirm that her husband didn't have the money to do it?" Phyllis said. "And the solicitor told the inspector he wasn't goin' to do any more work on Brunel's behalf without payment."

"True," Mrs. Jeffries agreed. "And to some extent, that meant Arthur could be eliminated as a suspect. I eliminated Charles Cochran as well. There was no evidence he'd had much to do with McCourt since he'd handled the marriage settlement fifteen years earlier, and they didn't appear to have any sort of personal relationship. Which left Mrs. McCourt, Jerome Raleigh, Nicholas Saxon, or Glenda Brunel."

"All four of them had a motive," the cook declared. "I'm includin' the wife, too. Just because she had money now didn't mean she'd stopped hatin' him. But tell me, what made you think of Leon Brunel? He's the only one who didn't have a reason to want his cousin dead."

"Oh, but he did. Greed. The more we learned of his character, the more I realized there was something almost evil about his need to keep acquiring things," she said. "He'd do anything to get what he wanted . . ."

"Like disabling a carriage so a rival couldn't bid at an estate sale," Ruth added eagerly. "My goodness, Lydia Mortmain wasn't exaggerating; that story is probably true."

"And Brunel wanted the best Oriental antiquities collection in England." Mrs. Jeffries helped herself to more tea. "But his motive didn't become clear until the very end, when I realized that the weapon that killed him hadn't necessarily been the one that Lydia Kent had brought from Hong Kong. Once I had confirmation that the sword she sold him wasn't the Hwando, but something even rarer and more valuable, a thirteenth-century Goryeo dynasty weapon, then the other pieces all made sense."

"What other pieces?" Phyllis asked plaintively. "I'm sorry, but I still don't see how you knew it was him."

"First of all, there was Annie's evidence," she said. "Annie claimed that she chipped the Chinese plate because McCourt startled her when he came in and that he was carrying a big, flat case. Then I kept remembering what Saxon told the inspector. He said that from the way McCourt was behaving at the tea party, he'd thought they were going to see something unusual and rare."

"But the Hwando is valuable, so it could have been that they were goin' to see," Luty pointed out.

"But not particularly rare unless it had been used by one of the great Joseon dynasty kings," Mrs. Jeffries replied. "Saxon made a point of that, and he also made a comment about ancient swords that led me to think that the local antiquities community must have heard there was one on the market."

"What about the fire?" Ruth asked. "Did he deliberately set it?"

"I'm sure he did," she replied. "Once he knew that McCourt had the sword, he only had a few days to come up with a way to get it from him. He had to get everyone out of the house for a few moments so he could steal the sword. He knew that McCourt would never sell it to him. The Christmas tea was a perfect opportunity."

"So 'e set the place on fire?" Wiggins frowned. "'E took an awful risk. What if they'd continued on with the tea?"

"He made sure they wouldn't." She glanced at Phyllis. "Harriet told you that she was frightened she'd get the sack because there had been petty theft in the house."

"That's right, the saffron and some lamp oil from the storage room," she replied. "She was accused of the spice theft because she forgot to give the housekeeper the keys the cook had borrowed."

"But she only had those keys because the cook's had gone missing. I think Leon Brunel had taken them to get at the spice cupboard. The saffron hadn't been stolen; it had been dumped on the floor in the larder," Mrs. Jeffries said. "Here's what I surmise must have happened: Brunel knew he had to get the tea party guests outside so he could not only do the murder but also get the sword. He stole the cook's keys and took the lamp oil and the saffron jar, but he wasn't interested in the spice, so he tossed it out."

"Then why'd he take the jar?" Mrs. Goodge asked.

"He needed something small enough to carry in his pocket," she replied. "He'd been to the McCourt house many times, so he knew there were paraffin lamps downstairs he could use to start the fire, but he needed additional paraffin to spill on the carpet and in the hallway. So he put the lamp oil in the jar and doused the carpet and the rugs with it. He needed the smell to be so bad, the tea would have to be canceled."

"But how could he know that he'd have a chance to start the fire?" Ruth asked. "It began downstairs in the servants' hall. He could have been caught at any moment."

"I don't think he had a choice. He wanted that sword, and this was his only chance. He couldn't steal it once McCourt made it public that he owned it."

"But Lydia Kent would have said that she sold it to McCourt, not Brunel," Mrs. Goodge said.

"But Lydia Kent was supposed to have been gone by then," she reminded them. "Remember, Luty found out that a man matching Brunel's description bribed the waiter at the hotel to find out when she was leaving. If McCourt had paid her properly, she'd have been in Paris by the time the murder was committed and was going straight back to the Far East from there."

"That was Brunel's big mistake," Luty said. "He didn't realize that she stayed in town to git her money."

"That's what I think must have happened," Mrs. Jeffries said. "He got lucky when he did the killing. Everything happened as he'd planned; the servants were busy in the kitchen when he set the fire, and he used the excuse of looking at the vase in the foyer rather than waiting in the morning room with the others. That gave him the chance to get downstairs without being noticed. I think he went down, grabbed the lamp, and started the fire and then got back to the foyer in time for Mrs. McCourt to see him when she came out of the study. Remember, he was the only person that didn't report hearing the McCourts quarreling."

"That's because he wasn't there," Hatchet said thoughtfully. "He was downstairs starting the fire. I still think he took a terrible risk. His plan could have fallen apart at any moment."

"I know, but he was desperate. He couldn't allow the Goryeo sword to become part of the McCourt collection, because he wanted to buy the collection from the widow, and with the sword added, the value would go up enormously," she said. "He was greedy, but he also wanted to get the collection as cheaply as possible."

"He committed the murder when the others went outside," Ruth commented. "But if the odor was so awful, how could Brunel be sure that McCourt wouldn't go outside as well?"

"They were cousins and he knew McCourt's character better than anyone." She smiled wryly. "He knew he'd never go outside with the door and windows open. Brunel left the house when everyone else did. He put his wife in a hansom and then rushed back, slipped into the study, and grabbed the Hwando. Then he committed murder, and while Daniel McCourt was dying, he took the case from the armoire, hung the mistletoe, and, when he was certain his victim was dead, slipped out the servants' door. He shoved the case under the gap in the fence between the McCourt and Crandall houses and then went next door and buried it deep in the mulch. I'm certain he'd already broken the lock on the Crandalls' gate. After that, he got a hansom and went to see his own solicitor. Later that night, when he judged it safe, he came back, retrieved the sword, and went home. What he didn't realize was that he'd dropped pine and bark mulch on the attic floor landing."

"Harriet got in trouble over that!" Phyllis exclaimed. "She'd not swept because no one had been up there in weeks and there was no need. Is that where he hid the sword?"

"Probably. We'll find out when the inspector gets home, but it was when you told us that detail that I remembered I'd tracked the same mulch here that day I hid in the Crandalls' passageway."

"Why did he hang the mistletoe?" Betsy asked. "Why take the time to do that when someone could walk in at any moment?"

"I suspect he did it because he did know that story of how McCourt had proposed to his wife," Mrs. Jeffries guessed, "and he wanted to point the finger at her. Or perhaps he just wanted to muddy the waters. Perhaps if he's confessed, he'll have told the inspector."

The others had gone by the time Witherspoon got home that evening. "This case is finally concluded." He smiled wearily as he handed his bowler to Mrs. Jeffries. "That's why I'm so late. We've made an arrest, and after taking care of everything at the station, I had to go to the Yard and give Chief Inspector Barrows a full report."

"Gracious, sir, who did you arrest?" She hung his hat up and helped him take off his coat.

"Leon Brunel. Let's have a glass of sherry, Mrs. Jeffries. I'm not quite ready for dinner yet."

She clucked sympathetically as she ushered him down the hall and into the drawing room. While he settled into his favorite chair, she poured both of them a glass of Harveys.

"Now, sir, do tell what happened. How on earth did you figure out that Leon Brunel was the killer?" She handed him his drink and sat down.

"Well, it was rather odd, but as you always tell me, my inner voice was apparently working most diligently." He chuckled and took a quick sip. "Constable Barnes had heard that one of the McCourt servants claimed she'd heard someone walking about in the passageway late the night he was murdered. Once we confirmed this fact, it suddenly occurred to me that if we spoke with the servants in all of our suspects' households, one of them might know who had been out and about in the middle of the night."

"How very clever of you, sir!" she exclaimed.

He smiled modestly. "It was simple logic, Mrs. Jeffries, but it did lead to the arrest. The Brunel home is the closest one to the McCourt house, so we went there first and the most peculiar thing happened. When the housekeeper went to get Mr. Brunel's permission for us to speak to the staff, both Brunels came down, and Mrs. Brunel offered to answer our questions. Mr. Brunel became enraged, and within moments, she was accusing him of murder and claiming he'd hidden something in the attic. He tried to attack her, so Constable Barnes and I held him back."

"Are you alright, sir?"

"I'm fine, just a bit sore, and luckily, the housekeeper ran and fetched more constables. We searched the house and found the Goryeo sword in his attic."

"The one that Miss Kent told you about yesterday?"

"Yes, and of course, once we had that, we knew he must have stolen it, because Miss Kent confirmed that she'd given it to McCourt."

"Is that why he did it? To obtain that sword?"

"Oh yes. When we found it, he started ranting and raving that McCourt had no right to it, that it should rightly be his." He broke off and sighed. "It was quite astounding, and frankly, I was happy when the constables led him away. I do believe the fellow is a bit demented. Can you imagine, murdering a relative because you want something for your collection?"

"Did he say why he'd hung up the mistletoe?" she asked.

"He did it to incriminate Mrs. McCourt. Apparently, Mr. McCourt had proposed to her under a sprig of mistletoe." He stopped and stared morosely at his glass. "Honestly, Mrs. Jeffries, I don't understand it at all," he finally murmured.

"You said it yourself, sir," she ventured. "Brunel appears to be slightly mad. Greed can do that to some people. Objects and things become more important than human beings."

"No, no, that's not what I mean." He sighed heavily. "I don't understand why so many of our cases end with a spouse or a sweetheart turning on a loved one."

"You mean Mrs. Brunel?"

He shook his head in disbelief. "You should have seen her. It was bizarre. She stood there with this odd, cunning expression on her face and then threw him to the wolves with great abandon. She actually looked the man straight in the eye and said she'd watch him hang and would get all his money. Thank goodness the other constables had arrived by then, because he was so enraged, I doubt that Barnes and I could have kept him off her. She kept goading him, telling him that her marriage settlement guaranteed that if he died, she'd get it all, and there was sod all—those were her exact words—that he could do about it. I don't condone murder under any circumstances, but she took such obvious pleasure in destroying him. She loathed him, and he was her husband. This isn't the first time I've seen this. It's happened before numerous times. It's enough to put you off the very idea of a decent, loving relationship between a man and a woman."

She wasn't sure how to respond, as he'd gone from delight at catching the killer to depression about the nature of male/female relationships. "Inspector, you must remember that your cases tend to involve the class of people that marry for money or position. It's rare the upper class marries for love. Most ordinary people marry because they do love each other, and they spend their lives taking care of each other."

He looked up, his expression hopeful. "Truly?"

"Of course, sir," she said. "I was married a good many years, and I loved my husband dearly. We did occasionally have words, as all couples do, but we were very devoted to each other." Mrs. Jeffries got up. "But most people don't hate one another, especially at this time of the year. Lady Cannonberry dropped in this afternoon and said she'd like to invite you to breakfast with her tomorrow."

He brightened immediately. "That's a wonderful idea, and now that the case is solved, perhaps we can go shopping tomorrow as well. Yes, yes, I'm sure she'll like that. She knows how I value her opinion. There are two more days before Christmas, and there's no reason we shouldn't celebrate the season properly."

"Of course, sir," she agreed. "Would you care for another sherry or would you like me to serve you dinner now?"

"I'll have dinner now." He glanced at the clock on the mantel. "I feel so much better, Mrs. Jeffries. This dreadful case is over, Christmas is upon us, and I've seen the most enchanting doll that I'm going to buy for my goddaughter tomorrow."